THE COMPLETE CASES OF
KEYHOLE KERRY, VOLUME 1

Fred Davis

FREDERICK C. DAVIS

THE COMPLETE CASES OF

KEYHOLE KERRY™

VOLUME 1

FREDERICK C. DAVIS

INTRODUCTION BY
ED HULSE

ILLUSTRATIONS BY
JOHN FLEMING GOULD

ALTUS

PRESS

BOSTON • 2014

TABLE OF CONTENTS

CRIME FOR A DIME:
FREDERICK C. DAVIS IN *DIME DETECTIVE* I

20,000,000 WITNESSES 1

MURDER MADE EASY 45

CRIMSON BROADCAST 99

MAESTRO OF MURDER 155

CRIME FOR A DIME:
FREDERICK C. DAVIS IN
DIME DETECTIVE

ED HULSE

FREDERICK C. DAVIS was born in St. Joseph, Missouri, in 1902. "My father was a doctor," he explained in 1969 to fellow writer Ron Goulart, "which evidently accounts for my interest in medicine, psychiatry and science in general. His father was a newspaper publisher—a small weekly in Kansas—who is probably the source of whatever talent I may have as a writer."

While still in grammar school Davis became a voracious reader. He particularly doted on nickel weeklies, those pulp-magazine progenitors whose popular heroes included Nick Carter, Frank Merriwell, and Old Sleuth. In his teen years Davis became a mystery fan, devouring the works of Conan Doyle, Gaston Leroux, Mary Roberts Rinehart, and Anna Katherine Green.

The future pulp scribe was still in high school when he sold his first fiction to a story paper called the *Chicago Ledger,* edited by Harry Stephen Keeler. Davis worked for what he later called "appallingly low rates." One 3000-word short story elicited an offer of three dollars, or a tenth of a penny per word. The young author balked and vowed to sell the story elsewhere for better money. Keeler bet him a dinner that no other editor would take it. Davis immediately sent it to Fiction House's *Action Stories,* which purchased the yarn and paid the customary one cent per word. The $30 sale was his first to a pulp magazine, and his fate was sealed.

After graduating high school Fred Davis had taken a job as cub reporter on the *St. Joseph News-Press* for $20 a week. But he continued writing fiction and sold regularly to pulp magazines, even cracking the distinguished Argosy in 1923. Soon he was making more money as a fictioneer than as a newspaperman, so he quit the *News-Press* and moved to New York City, hub of the publishing industry. Brief stints in editorial positions at trade journals followed before Davis enrolled in Dartmouth to continue his education. He left in his sophomore year to get married and resumed writing full time. By 1930 he was a prolific and prosperous pulpster, composing 125,000 words a month and selling nearly all of them.

During his lengthy career as a journeyman pulp author, Frederick C. Davis pounded out Westerns, aviation tales, horror stories, and straight adventure yarns. For a year and a half he wrote monthly book-length novels for the Popular Publications hero pulp *Operator #5*. But he specialized in mysteries, the genre that had appealed to him as a kid reading Nick Carter weeklies. He broke into the legendary *Black Mask* in 1923 but never placed a yarn with the magazine's toughest editor, Joseph T. "Cap" Shaw. Still, he sold to all the major detective titles and to most of the minor ones as well. Popular's *Dime Detective* was among his most reliable markets: beginning in 1933 he sold 73 stories—most of them novelettes, most featuring recurring characters—to editor Ken White. Only T.T. Flynn, with 80 sales, appeared in the magazine more frequently.

Davis' first series featured Beverly Hills-based P.I. Clay "Oke" Oakley, whose firm Secrets Incorporated handled oddball cases. The seven Oakley adventures, penned between 1933 and 1935, made breezy, fun reading, but editor White had a surfeit of hard-boiled dicks and was already asking his regular contributors for sleuths with different occupations. Davis first came up with Carter Cole, a psychiatrist who ran his own clinic and was assisted by nurses who happened to be identical twins (and whose names he could never keep straight). Nine Cole stories adorned the pages of *Dime Detective* over the next two years.

Two months after the last one's publication, Davis was back with a new series. "Murder Made Easy" (May 1937) was the first of eight mysteries built around wisecracking newshawk Guy "Keyhole" Kerry, a hard-charging columnist from the Walter Winchell cloth. Demon reporters were no strangers to the crime pulps; in the mid-Thirties *Black Mask* alone had two of the best: Ted Tinsley's Jerry Tracy and George Harmon Coxe's Flashgun Casey. Unfortunately, Keyhole Kerry never really caught on with *Dime Detective* readers, although Davis created another newspaperman who fared better in the magazine: Bill Brent, who doubled as a lonely-hearts columnist, solved murder cases in 15 *DD* novelettes published between 1941 and 1946.

Like most high-volume producers of pulp fiction, Fred Davis took his craft seriously and was extremely disciplined about it. His workday usually began at nine in the morning and ended at four in the afternoon; his daily output frequently reached 30 double-spaced typewritten pages, or roughly 7500 words. (Of course, this was first-draft copy.) But that was after he had plotted each story, a process which often took as long as the actual composition.

Davis related his process in a 1942 article for *Writer's Digest,* a magazine for aspiring authors:

> You start with six things, as follows:
> First, an idea for a story.
> Second, a plot-pattern in mind.
> That is, having selected a story idea, you decide—or you instinctively feel—what you're going to do with it. You're impelled to shape it toward a certain definite story standard or ideal which you clearly preconceive. If you're writing sheet art for art's sake, the idea makes certain artistic demands of you that the finished story must fulfill. If you're writing a strictly commercial story, you're aware it must have a striking opening, certain novelties of situation, a flow of action involving a dramatic clash which increases in intensity through minor crises to a final climax. In other words, you know, even before you start, exactly what your story should be when you've polished off the tag line.
> Third, a pencil.

Fourth, paper clips.

Fifth, a plentiful supply of scratch sheets. I use five-by-eight pads for reasons that I'll explain later.

Sixth, a brain willing to work.

Now let's buckle down to it. In order to make the procedure as clear as possible we'll use as an example my mystery novel, *Deep Lay the Dead,* scheduled to appear as the Crime Club Selection for October. Accordingly we transport ourselves backward in time to last September. We're about to begin work on the story. So far we have no title, no characters, no plot—nothing more than our stationery ready, an earnest desire to produce a story and an idea on which to base it.

The idea is written on a sheet of scratch, like this:

A murder is committed in a snowbound house.

In variations, it has been used before and it will be used again, because it's a good one. We know what use we're going to make of it. We're going to write a mystery book. It's not going to be a hardboiled-detective whodunit featuring violent shock action, because a storm-bound house doesn't offer much scope for physical action. It's to be a story of suspense and menace growing out of the enforced juxtaposition of the characters, some of them hostile to others, and among them a killer. There will be prowling in the dark, startling discoveries, a series of dramatic situations, always that note of mounting suspense, and finally an exciting exposure and capture of the culprit at the climax. This is our basic story pattern.

The bare idea immediately suggests embellishments. Since a city dwelling is not likely to be snowbound, and since other houses invariably stand nearby even in suburban districts, the house in our story must be a remote and isolated one. All right; it's way out in the country, all alone in a valley. Being familiar with Bucks County, Pennsylvania, where I live on a farm, I plunk it right down here in my own neighborhood. An additional advantage of this setting I know so well is that it's only 80 miles from New York City, and 30 from Philadelphia, so we can easily introduce several cosmopolitan characters as weekend guests. While we're thinking along these lines we're busily making notes.

Storm worst in years. Crews so busy keeping highways open that lone road leading into valley must remain closed, thereby imprisoning all characters for duration of story. No one can get out, help can't get in. Unknown killer always present with ominous possibility that he may strike again.

Another:

Murder solved and culprit captured just as snowplow comes boring down the valley road, bringing help, police, release. Entire story occurs over a weekend.

Davis in this how-to piece provided a veritable blueprint for mystery-story plotting… one that indicated just how much thought went into his yarns, especially the novel-length who-dunits:

> We use scratch pads profligately, a separate page for each note. This is because we're doing two things at once—we're building a plot and at the same time drawing up a working synopsis. Each note being on a separate slip, we can easily shuffle them all into their proper places in the outline later.
>
> As you've already seen, we don't write these notes in any certain order. We scribble them off as fast as new thoughts pop up, without regard to their proper place in the finished story. One minute we may be jotting down a notion for the climax, the next a twist for the opening, the next a point involved in a minor crisis halfway along, and the next a certain trait for one of our characters. Whatever may suggest itself at the moment—even lines of dialogue—we scrawl it on a separate slip and keep working in just this way until the train of associations stop; and then we start again on another track.
>
> We now have, say, a dozen or so notes before us. They concern the house, the storm, the inconveniences forced on the characters, the fact that our story deals with the family living in the house plus an odd and somehow menacing assortment of weekend guests, and so forth. We simply keep adding to them….
>
> Telephone still works, the only connection with the outside world. Phone line is mysteriously cut, thereby completely isolating house. May involve encounter in dark between prowler and hero. Long section of line removed, and hidden somewhere, so that a simple splice will not repair the break. Missing length of wire can't be found—no other wire available.
>
> Our hero has shown himself here for the first time. He's got to be a clever amateur detective. In what ingenious way can he cope with this serious matter of the cut telephone wire? Soon we have it:
>
> By removing all cords from floor lamps (useless anyway while juice is off) and splicing them together to make one long wire, H can repair the break.
>
> The naming of my characters is usually my very last step before the actual writing. Working as we are at present, then, we use initials for convenience and brevity. H stands for the hero. V is the victim. G will stand for the girl when she comes along. Her father may be GF, though actually he will soon appear as Dr—Doctor. Her mother may be GM, but our plot will soon turn her into DrW—the doctor's wife, the girl's stepmother. FS will serve to designate a false suspect, FS2 another,

FS3 a third. Similarly, each character in the story will have his or her own symbol.

All right, H repairs the break in the phone line. An exciting scene immediately suggests itself. H, with one end of his jumper wire already connected inside the house, fights his way through the deep drifts to the nearest telephone pole and climbs in the teeth of an icy gale to complete the circuit. Clinging to the crossbars, he sees a movement in one of the windows of the house. Someone is just barely visible there—aiming a firearm at him! This is an attempt to murder him. Bang! H lets go at the last instant and as the bullet whizzes over him he drops into the drift below, unharmed but plenty scared.

Good stuff—but it stimulates and precipitates still more ideas. Since H isn't the kind to take this lying down, he rushes into the house to grab the killer—but he finds no evidence of the attack. The killer is gone and even the weapon has vanished so mysteriously and so completely that a search fails to uncover it. Point: the gun is still within reach of the killer in some secret place and another attempt to kill the hero will surely be made.

This flurry of ideas has produced four long notes. First, the scene on the telephone pole. Second, H's rush into the house. Third, the futile search for the weapon. Fourth, the highlighted fact that the hidden gun remains available to the murderer.

These in turn stimulate others. All during our plotting process we ask ourselves questions about the substance of our notes. Kipling's six faithful serving men—remember, their names are Who, How, Which, What, Where, and When—are working their heads off for us. We therefore ask ourselves, Why was this murderous attack made on H? Answer: M wishes to prevent news concerning him from reaching the house, for the incoming information will identify and incriminate him and he's desperate to remain under his cloak of secrecy.

There are other questions to be answered. Where is the weapon hidden? What sort of firearm is it? Does M alone know where it is? What is the information that M is so anxious to keep out of the house? Who is H? What brought him here? How is he involved in the mystery? So we go busily on, answering these questions when we can, and when we can't, making a note of them anyway. We'll be coming back to them because they'll have to be answered sooner or later.

And here is the most valuable part of the system—it won't let us overlook any element essential to the story. Our plot pattern is always in mind and our plot material is growing before our eyes, so we can easily see, as we work ahead, exactly what ingredients still must be supplied. If we're unable to supply any given element at once, we don't stew over it long. We simply scribble reminders that these missing links must eventually be found, and shift to some other phase. For example:

Needed: ingenious hiding-place for a rifle.

Needed: innocent-appearing clues to M's identity, which, when H adds them together properly, nails M.

Needed: incident throwing suspicion on FS.

Needed: identity of V and M's motive.

Shuffling back and forth through our growing accumulation of notes, we never lost sight of these necessities and, surprisingly enough, many of them will be filled almost automatically as we work around them.

Any one of these notes, incidentally, may consist of only a few words, or of two or three scratch sheets closely filled and clipped together. The deciding factor is the unity of the thought.

Davis went on in greater detail about his procedure for fleshing out supporting characters and creating dovetailed subplots. Of course, the average pulp-magazine novelette of 15,000 or so words did not require such extensive plotting, so it's likely his Keyhole Kerry stories were produced in a less time-consuming fashion. Many mystery novelettes of the type Ken White bought for *Dime Detective* and *Black Mask* (which was sold to Popular Publications in 1940) hinged on a single idea or gimmick and boasted no more than three suspects.

Although Frederick C. Davis wrote many novels published in hard covers—most of them under Doubleday's Crime Club imprint—he never really graduated from the pulps and kept submitting yarns to rough-paper magazines until the early Fifties. He sold at least a thousand stories to them over a 30-year period, which proves that he learned the knack early on. Davis remains a compulsively readable author, a facile storyteller whose prose style was clean and uncluttered. The best of his pulp work is very good indeed, and in *Dime Detective* he maintained a generally high level of quality. The Keyhole Kerry series may not represent Fred Davis at his finest, but it's extremely entertaining and well worth resurrecting.

20,000,000 WITNESSES

TIME AFTER TIME GUY KERRY, FLASH-NEWS ACE OF THE ETHER WAVES, HAD SCOOPED THE COPS IN STARTING KILLERS ON THE ROAD TO THE DEATH-HOUSE. BUT NOW IT LOOKED LIKE RADIO'S STAR REPORTER WAS CAUGHT ON THE BARBS OF HIS OWN PRIVATE HOMICIDE HOOK-UP, FOR TWENTY MILLION WITNESSES— INCLUDING THE POLICE, THE PRESS AND HIS OWN SECRETARY— HAD HEARD HIS UNMISTAKABLE VOICE RASP OUT CONFESSION TO THE MURDER OF TWO WOMEN, AND EVEN KERRY HIMSELF BEGAN TO WONDER IF THE BLOOD-GUILT MIGHT LIE ON HIS OWN HEAD.

CHAPTER ONE

MURDER ON THE AIR

THE STACCATO dissonance of two rapid-fire type-writers beat the walls of the littered office perched high in the spire of the Universal Broadcasting Company Building. The galvanically nervous young man with prematurely gray hair, and the willowy young woman with turquoise eyes, glanced repeatedly and anxiously at the electric wall clock while they rippled the keys. Their nimble fingers were clicking out words which, within the hour, were due to flash to millions of gossip-hungry ears. Keyhole Kerry, the headline beater of radio, and his secretary, were feverishly pounding out their copy for the most sensational quarter-hour on the ether.

Into this frantic clatter, the zing of the telephone penetrated. At once, Eve Vane swiveled to the instrument, hopeful that it meant another succulent morsel of exclusive inside stuff which Kerry's Gargantuan whisper could spread from coast to coast. Kerry, without glancing up, his shirt sleeves rolled, his collar flying, his tie askew, driven to meet the most relentless of deadlines, intensely continued his mad task of out-winchelling Winchell.

Kerry gloried in every beat. Having zoomed through a cyclonic apprenticeship of newspaper reporting, he now enjoyed the hearty enmity of every legman and city editor in the Fourth Estate because he invariably outdistanced them at their own speedy game. His earnest happiness was marred only by the detail that his broadcasts were sponsored by the cathartic called *De-Luxe-Lax.*

HE ABANDONED the keys, as Miss Vane pivoted toward him. First beholding her in the nude, expertly manipulating an ostrich fan in a night club, Kerry had cannily perceived a rare talent beneath her lovely epidermis. She had vindicated his judg-

ment by becoming a more efficient secretary than many who had never taken their clothes off in public.

With her full lips quivering, her champagne-colored hair in attractive disorder, she hastily delivered the telephone to Kerry, breathlessly saying: "Carola Long. Insists on talking to you. Sounds like she's having hysterics. Whatever it is, I hope it's hot. We need something to step up the voltage of this stuff."

"Thirty-two minutes—"

He broke off because the voice he heard was not that of the girl whose name was widely known as a singer of torch ballads. He heard the angry snarl of a man.

The faintness of the words indicated the man was speaking some distance from the transmitter. Unmistakably, he was uttering a threat: "You little fool! Don't lose your head! Where do you

Kerry continued to broadcast
as the man launched his attack
and the sound of the fight went
out over the microphone to a
public tuned in on murder.

think you'll come out of this? Remember you're in it as deep as I am. You're sending yourself up the river, that's all. You know damned well that just one hint to Kerry is dynamite. Put that phone down!"

Sparks began jumping along Kerry's nerves. He could not identify the man's voice, but he felt dangerous tension at the far end of the line, rapidly mounting to the breaking point. A moment's strained silence yielded to a muffled, scuffling noise. Kerry sensed the man was trying to wrest the telephone away from the girl.

"Miss Long, don't let that mug bluff you."

The singer broke in. Her voice was afire with fury. "Mr. Kerry, get this! It's straight stuff—exclusive. It'll blow the town wide open." An aside, screeched: "Let go of me, you rat!" Then, hysterically, to Kerry: "Listen, I know what I'm talking about. I was on the inside of this dirty blackmailing racket. I want you to give this crook what he deserves—"

TIGHTENING muscles lifted Kerry out of his chair with the receiver crushing his ear. He could hear desperately quick breathing and picture murderous hands clawing a white throat. A metallic click indicated a severed connection. The wire sounds vanished. Kerry gave a lightning glance at the clock, dropped the instrument into his startled secretary's lap.

"Where's she live?" he demanded urgently. "Get her address. Lord knows what's happening there, but she's got something. I want to grab it."

Already, Kerry's personal telephone book was in Eve Vane's capable hands. It contained the numbers of every prominent person in every major city in the country, with special emphasis on New York and Hollywood. The volume was more valuable than many a rare edition, for Kerry's research into this field had left no privacy uninvaded. From it, Eve Vane promptly read the address of Carola Long.

"But wait," she exclaimed, seizing his arm as he started for the door. "It's only a few blocks, but you might get tied up.

You've got a date with the mike in less than half an hour. You've never missed a broadcast yet—"

"And I don't intend to, darling."

Carola Long's interrupted revelation had hinted chicanery worthy of front-page banner headlines. Calls such as hers explained the riddle of how Kerry came by much of his inside information.

He had found it difficult to appear in any public place without being buttonholed by someone longing to spill the works about someone else, but he managed to reach the home of Carola Long without being stopped. He bounded up the brownstone stoop, applied his thumb hopefully to the button inscribed with her name. The end of one minute of unresponsiveness found Kerry trying the door, discovering it unfastened, alertly stepping in.

"Miss Long!" he called.

The air was hushed and full of the odor of new paint. Kerry trod along a freshly decorated hallway and turned into a modernistic living-room. He stopped, galvanized, on the edge of an eggplant rug, suddenly unaware of the surrounding chromium glitter. His widened gaze fixed upon a young woman's huddled form.

It was plainly visible through the tubular steel legs of a center table. She was garbed in luxurious lounging-pajamas. Its scarlet jacket had been thrown wide by her fall. The white satin molded over the young woman's breasts was stained wetly crimson. Her throat bore dull bruises made by crushing thumbs. The lax, waxen face was that of Carola Long.

Keyhole Kerry stifled an instantaneous impulse to snatch up the telephone. His ears searched the house. A huge console radio was playing in the room.

"Radio headliner murdered!" he murmured exultantly. "Made to order!"

The telephone was resting on a table at the side of a maroon sofa. Kerry surmised it was the instrument over which the girl had called him. He covered his fingers with his handkerchief, so as not to efface any latent fingerprints which might have been left on it, then took it up. He switched the radio off, spun a special Universal Broadcasting Company number. He directed crisply: "Put me on!"

THE EXPENSIVE arrangements made for Kerry, by *De-Luxe-Lax*, enabled him to break into any program at any hour of the day or night for the purpose of flashing his latest scoop to the populace while it was still piping hot. Because the expectancy of catching Kerry at any moment kept millions listening continually to the nation-wide network, other sponsors had found it highly profitable not to protest his intrusion. Since he could and did use any telephone as a microphone, he was able to launch himself upon the ether with amazing dispatch.

"Attention, Mr. and Mrs. United States! This is Keyhole Kerry, your headline beater, bringing you a sensational flash. You, as well as the local police, will be startled to hear that in this room from which I am speaking, not five minutes ago, the famous radio thrush, Miss Carola Long, was brutally murdered.

"Murdered, I repeat, Mr. and Mrs. John Public, not five minutes ago. The dead woman is lying not five feet from me. I am bringing you details which are absolutely unknown at this moment.

"Carola Long, of course, is—or was, until her very recent demise—the warbler of torch songs who has so often entertained you over this network. In addition, she had been filling a lucrative engagement at the Club Eden. She was a most alluring young woman, constantly in the company of fashionable men about town. She often chanted, as you know, concerning a broken heart. Hers is now shattered by two bullets.

"Those two shots, ladies and gentlemen, were fired by a man involved in a blackmailing intrigue. A few moments ago, Miss Long telephoned me, intending to expose that man's racket. He was desperate to stop her. It seems clear that he murdered her in order to silence her. He evidently escaped from this house a few seconds before I entered. In case he is now near a radio and listening to this flash, I have a message for him. Here it is, Mr. Murderer. In due time I will reveal your name on the air!"

This was a bluff which Kerry was temperamentally unable to forego.

He abandoned the telephone, glanced at his strap-watch. In nine minutes, his regularly scheduled program was due to begin. He ardently hoped he might glean further inside information to embellish his copy before he must rush back to the studio. He leaned over the dead singer, gaze flicking from detail to detail. Almost at once he made a discovery.

IN THE thrown-back jacket of Carola Long, just under the right arm, he found a small, ragged puncture. Kerry guessed it was the hole made by a third bullet which had missed the girl's body but pierced her clothing. He glanced up, hoping to find a scar somewhere on the maroon walls, but they were unblemished. Their fresh shine told him that this room had also been redecorated. Taking no time for a more thorough search, he looked down again, at the little automatic which lay beside the corpse.

The .25-caliber Mauser smelled pungently of burned powder. Again covering his hands with his handkerchief, Kerry removed its clip. He counted seven cartridges remaining. Assuming it had contained its capacity of ten, Kerry judged this to indicate that a third shot had been fired. He replaced the clip in the gun, the gun on the floor, and straightened. A glitter turned him to the center table.

Silver reflections gleamed up from a new cigarette case. It bore a monogram, *CL*. It rested on ruffled tissue paper in a satin-lined box imprinted with the name of a famous Fifth Avenue jeweler. It was, Kerry deduced at once, a gift to the singer. Certainly the case had been presented to her only this evening. It was a definite indication that an admirer had been present. Perhaps, Kerry thought, that admirer had turned into a killer.

Risking dire legal consequences for removing evidence, Kerry closed the case into its box and slipped the box into his inner pocket.

With another urgent glance at his strap-watch, he stepped into the small room adjoining at the rear. It was a bar, newly and whimsically decorated. The walls depicted a crowd of celebrated radio performers in caricature. Kerry recognized Rudy Vallée's drooping eyes, Eddie Cantor's banjo stare, Fred Allen's acidulous grimace, Paul Whiteman's sleek forelock—a score of other public personalities.

Kerry jerked to a stop at a sound. It was the gentle thud of a closing door. Instantly, Kerry spun, intent on locating the source of the noise. It was from somewhere downstairs.

A short flight carried him to a level below that of the street. A hallway, also gleaming with fresh paint, gave into two bedrooms and a bath, and ended in the rear at a door connecting with a court. Kerry opened the door, looked out, saw nothing but fenced darkness and a checkerboard of lighted windows with the U.B.C. spire rising beyond. He turned back, stepping into a bedroom which was evidently that of the dead singer.

He noted only one unusual detail—a nail file lying on the floor in the corner, beside a table at the head of the bed on which a telephone sat. Its mate was lying on a dressing-table. Kerry began a quick investigation of the drawers. He found a plentitude of enchanting silk things, blue and pink, a wealth of stockings, many expensive feminine oddments—and, tucked far back in a corner, four bankbooks.

The large amounts entered in them brought a note of envious astonishment from Kerry's puckered lips. He began a rapid calculation of the most recent deposits. Then a shrill whine lifted his eyes. It was the lowering screech of a siren in the street. It meant that the police were responding to Kerry's murder-broadcast. With prowl-cars being curbed in front of the house, Kerry again risked legal punishment by tucking the passbooks into his pocket. Then, grinning delightedly, he ran up the steps, and turned hurriedly to the entrance.

The big man who strode briskly in, glowering, was Police Commissioner Endicott. His prompt appearance told Kerry he had been at the nearest precinct station, or, as was his habit, cruising in a squad-car at the moment of Kerry's startling flash. Kerry made a move toward the dead girl, but his smile faded under the commissioner's stare.

"Kerry, you're under arrest!" Endicott exploded.

Two plainclothesmen marched to Kerry's side, firmly took his arms. Their eyes gleamed grimly. A third detective straddled in front of Kerry with a police positive leveled. Kerry gave another quick glance at his strap-watch, saw coldly that only a few minutes remained until he was due to hit the mike.

"What the devil is this?" He asked quickly.

"You ought to know, Kerry," Endicott growled at him. "It's murder. And we've got you cold for it—got you cold, with millions of witnesses to prove it."

CHAPTER TWO

RADIO MAN-HUNT

KERRY'S GRIN finally came back as he made an impatient gesture. "Skip that stuff," he said. "My program goes on the air in four minutes. I've never missed a spot yet, and I don't intend to. You can't hold me up with this crude horseplay. I'll see you at the studio."

He started toward the door, but managed to make only one step. The two detectives tightened their hands crushingly on his arms. The gun of the third jerked ominously. Paling, Kerry gazed at the commissioner. Endicott had entered the living-room, was staring at the red splotch on the top of Carola Long's pajamas.

"You think I'm kidding? Listen, Kerry. You've been making

headquarters seem like a home for the feeble-minded with this damned inside stuff of yours. I've been trying to find out which of my men has been leaking to you. Every time you have broadcast, I've had every word taken down in shorthand. I have a record of what was said here, between you and that young woman. Why, a good part of this country heard you shoot her!"

Kerry swallowed hard. "Come off—come off," he begged. "I tell you I'm due in the studio. You're not talking sense. Do you think I'd kill a woman, and then broadcast it? She was dead when I came in here. You couldn't have heard any shots. You couldn't have heard my flash."

Endicott's frown deepened. "You didn't know it was going out over the air, Kerry, naturally—but it did. Anybody who heard it can be used as a witness against you. Millions of 'em, I said, and it's true." The commissioner turned to a florid man whom Kerry knew as Inspector Tarrant. "Call his bluff. Read it to him."

Tarrant drew a stenographic notebook from his pocket, flipped it open, began translating lines of shorthand scribbles.

"Station WUBC. Time, nine thirty-nine P.M. Program of dance music faded. The voice known as that of Keyhole Kerry spoke as follows: " 'Attention, Mr. and Mrs. United States. This is Keyhole Kerry, your headline beater, bringing you another news flash. I have just obtained exclusive inside information on a blackmail racket which is operating in New York City. Many prominent citizens have been victimized and forced to pay fortunes in blood money. They have been snared by a high-class badger game. A young woman—' "

"Wait a minute!" Kerry broke in. "Where'd you get that stuff? I didn't broadcast that. I don't know anything about it. I spilled the dope about—"

"Hold it, Kerry," Commissioner Endicott interrupted. "I heard it come out of the radio—exactly those words. Do I have to tell you again that millions of people heard exactly the same thing? Go ahead, Tarrant. There's not much of it, Kerry, but it's plenty. And this is one story the newspapers are going to beat you to—your own trip to the chair."

A glance at Kerry's watch goaded him, but he could not tear himself away from the rumble of the inspector's sardonic voice.

" 'A young woman, famed as a radio singer, the police will be interested to learn, is the perpetrator of this intrigue. She lures men into compromising situations—' Interruption. A girl's voice speaking: 'You can't do that to me, Kerry! I'll tell the whole world that you're the blackmailer—and I'll make 'em believe it! Listen, everybody. Keyhole Kerry is a human bloodsucker who—' "

"At that point," Endicott told the astounded Kerry, "there was a noise like that of a telephone being replaced in its cradle. But you did it with such haste, trying to fight the woman off, that something went wrong. The connection wasn't broken. The next words weren't so loud, but they were clear enough. Go ahead, Tarrant."

Tarrant obliged with dour satisfaction. "Kerry's voice: 'Get away!' The woman's voice: 'Don't point that gun at me!' Kerry's voice: 'You asked for it.'"

"Then we heard two quick shots and a woman's scream," Endicott added.

"The control man faded the dance band right back in. I had that call traced plenty fast. We closed in on you before you got out of the house, because you didn't know the whole thing had been overheard, and you took time to do a bit of cleaning up. The telephone's O.K. now, for instance. Probably, you've wiped off all fingerprints, but I couldn't hope for a more conclusive case."

Kerry's nerves were snapping. "You've all had a nightmare!" he blurted. "Nothing like that happened, and you know it. You want my scalp, and this is your way of discrediting me. You know damned well you can't make any murder charge stick, but this talk about blackmail will wreck me. Damned if I'll let you get away with it! I'm due to go on the air in two minutes and—"

"And you won't be there," the commissioner interposed. "I've suspected you for some time, Kerry. What a set-up for blackmail! You used that girl. The trick was to have her compromise some man, then threaten to broadcast it if he didn't pay plenty. Tonight, for some reason, she turned on you. You put that flash on the air to scare the wits out of her. She called the play, and you let her have it. Well, how about spilling it, Kerry—so the newspapers can print it first this time!"

CONSTERNATION momentarily silenced Kerry. A glance at his strap-watch electrified him. Looking up, he saw two reporters shouldering in from the street. He realized his own arrest was a flash of stop-press importance, and was rashly determined that his arch-rivals in the city-rooms must not beat him to it. He turned a crafty gaze upon the commissioner, as he stepped toward the dead girl.

"All right," he muttered. "I didn't know the damned line was still open. What good is my word against twenty million witnesses? Let me have a drink and I'll give you the low-down."

He stepped briskly into the little bar-room. Instantly, he whirled, slamming the door shut, driving a bolt into its socket. He heard an enraged howl break from Endicott. Fast footfalls warned him that detectives were bounding down the stairs, intent on rushing out into the court. While celebrities watched him from the walls, Kerry pushed a basement window wide open. His springy jump carried him out into darkness.

Kerry's soles slapped against cement. He bounded across the court, pulled himself atop a wall. Shadows were blurring on the pane of the rear entrance of the Long apartment when he dropped over. He scurried to another door, found it locked. One thrust of his heel smashed the pane. He reached in, twisted the inner knob. Kerry loped along a hall, out a door, across a street, through a parking space, into the foyer of the Universal Broadcasting Building.

His feverish command sent the elevator cab flying upward. His watch was already indicating the zero moment of his broadcast. He sprinted along a corridor, flung himself through a door lettered *Studio X*. Inside it he found Eve Vane distractedly walking the floor, a sound-effect man pecking at a typewriter, the announcer crooning blandishments concerning *De-Luxe-Lax* into the microphone.

EVE STIFLED a moan of despair, mingled with elation, as Kerry bolted the entrance. He knew that Milton Raney, the full-dressed man at the mike, would finish the commercial in about thirty seconds, when Kerry must follow at once. While Raney, pale and perspiring, read on dulcetly, Kerry slipped his copy from Eve's trembling hand and tugged her into a sound-proof telephone booth in the corner which was specially provided for last-minute flashes. She sobbed as the door closed them in.

"Guy, you fool—why did you do it?"

"Good Lord!" he exclaimed. "You mean you heard it, too? Some girl calling me a human bloodsucker, then two shots? Then it's true—it went from coast to coast! Eve, you know damned well I didn't do it and that I'm no blackmailer. I've been framed—"

"Plenty of people will jump at the chance to swear you blackmailed them, just to get you off the air, Guy," the girl wailed. "There'll be a line of newspapermen two blocks long, waiting to take the witness stand and perjure you into the electric chair. It *did* sound like your voice. It was faint and distorted, but everybody knows your—"

"Framed by the man who killed Carola Long, of course," Kerry broke in insistently. "I'm not in the death-house yet. Listen to me." He slipped from his pocket the box containing the initialed cigarette case. "Find out who bought that for her. Ten to one, it was Lewis Gaylord—she's been seen everywhere with him lately." He produced the four bankbooks. "Total those, then check up on that young woman's income. Looks to me like there's plenty more there than she's earned."

In the studio, Raney was making frantic signals, beckoning Kerry to the mike. Kerry gestured: "Coming!"

"I've already talked with Timothy Branton," Eve Vane said. "He phoned right after you finished killing that girl in front of the whole country. I made him promise to help you. You're going to need a lawyer. You're going to need fifty of 'em."

"Mrs. Kerry's little boy is going to have to get me out of this, and nobody else," Kerry retorted. "Listen, will you? Locate Gaylord. If you can't find him, get hold of his secretary. Check his movements tonight. Then—"

THE FRANTIC Raney was having something similar to an epileptic fit at the microphone. Kerry bounded from the booth. As Raney sank into a chair, exhausted with anxiety, Kerry perched on the opposite side of the desk, his copy in hand but unopened. He began scribbling a note as he launched into the machine-gun delivery of his impromptu flash.

"Good evening again, Mr. and Mrs. John Public! This is Keyhole Kerry, once more romping out of your loudspeaker with the latest sensational development in the Carola Long murder case. Your correspondent wishes to announce, ladies and gentlemen, that he is a fugitive from justice. Only a few moments ago, I was placed under arrest for the murder of the famous torch singer. I hope it is needless for me to add that I am innocent."

The note Kerry passed to Raney read: *If you unlock that door I'll break your fat neck.* The sound-effect man kept rattling the typewriter to create a busy-background noise. Kerry glanced around to see that Eve Vane was still inside the telephone booth, putting through a call. Already, he knew, she was carrying out his instructions. Kerry rushed on without a break.

"All of you probably believe you heard me fire the shots that killed Miss Long. I did not fire them. The noises you heard could not have been shots at all, for I was in the apartment at the time and heard no reports. Neither could the voice you heard have been mine. It must have been a clever impersonation.

Many people have a genius for voice mimicry, and my voice is generally familiar. It is, in fact, at this very moment, leading the police toward me with the purpose of capturing me!"

Eve Vane had slipped from the booth. She dropped a scrawled slip of paper under Kerry's eyes and hurried back. Her message read:

> Your special-control man says that after you asked for the air from the Long place the rest came in over the same wire without any hitch. You wouldn't fool me, would you?

Kerry's mental teeth promptly fastened upon that information.

"The actual murderer of Carola Long was still in her apartment while I was there! It is certain that he had already contrived a plot to fasten the guilt of the murder upon me. He managed this by quickly disconnecting the living-room telephone, which I made use of, and speaking, himself, over another instrument in the front downstairs bedroom." Kerry's eyes lighted. "He manipulated the connections by using a nail file as a screwdriver. A simple matter, ladies and gentlemen. As for the shots, he might have produced the reports simply by twice slapping a pillow with the back of a hairbrush close to the transmitter!"

Suddenly a dull, pounding sound came from the entrance of the studio. The powerful hammering produced bigger beads of perspiration upon Milton Raney's brow. Eve Vane, again issuing from the phone booth, went white as she paused to listen. To Kerry it was news to be spread from coast to coast as fast as possible.

"The police, headed by Commissioner Endicott, himself, are now searching for me in the Universal Broadcasting Company studios! They believe they're within easy reach of me, but they're mistaken. I don't intend to surrender to them. In fact, I'm determined to remain a fugitive as long as possible. I must do this in order to vindicate myself and keep my promise to you to name the murderer. My first step toward identifying the killer will be to give you a partial description of him—now."

Fists were pounding dully on the entrance. The muffled voice of Commissioner Endicott carried through: "Open up, Kerry! We know you're in there!"

Eve Vane, a terrified light in her turquoise eyes, left a second message on the desk, again hurried back to the booth. Kerry read—

Can't locate Gaylord. His sect'y out on a date—expected back soon. Both addresses below.

Kerry slipped the page into his pocket, went grimly on.

"The murderer is a man to whom his voice is of more than ordinary importance," his tones went over the air. "He has trained it for a purpose. He speaks normally on a low note but can change his tone convincingly and with great facility. He is shrewd, capable of quick thinking in a crisis. Likewise, he is daring, avaricious and dangerous. His motive for implicating me in murder was to muzzle me in order to keep his blackmailing operations covered. Keep your dials turned to this station in order to learn more about him as soon as Keyhole Kerry gets it!"

While the subdued clamor at the door continued, Kerry launched into his prepared copy. The sound-effect man industriously clicked the typewriter. Milton Raney's Adam's apple popped in and out of his wing collar. Eve Vane talked earnestly in the soundproof booth. Kerry glanced around the studio as he spoke, remembering he was more than forty floors above the street and that the policed door was the only way out. Soon Eve delivered another slip, which read—

Manager of jewelry firm very evasive. Remembers nothing. Says must see case first. Even so refuses to talk except to cops. Lots of men have got into hot water with their wives because their jewelers didn't stay mum. Will give him the works tomorrow.

THE RED second hand of the big electric clock signaled that Kerry's allotted time was expiring. With a long, silent breath he abandoned the mike. Milton Raney began insinuating himself into millions of ears with a new paean to *De-Luxe-Lax*. The entrance was still thudding under the impacts of official fists. Kerry drew Eve Vane back into the booth, closed the door.

"Listen," he said tersely. "Nobody's going to keep me off the air, if I can help it. Not even being accused of murder is going to make me break a perfect record of never having missed a broadcast. I hate to think of deceiving my devoted public, but I'm damned if I'll fry for 'em. I've an idea. This bird who broadcasts on the *Parade of Events* program—the one who imitates everybody's voice from President Roosevelt's to Shirley Temple's—the 'Man of a Thousand Voices'—"

· "Earl Franken," Eve Vane answered him. "I almost had him in to read your stuff for you tonight."

"Maybe he couldn't have come," Kerry answered, a spark in his mind flaring into fire. "Maybe he was busy murdering a young woman. I've noticed him and Carola Long together several times, acting strange. But that's why I want him—to read my stuff in case I'm unavoidably detained. Get hold of him, Eve. I want to see him in about an hour at wherever he lives—"

"Hotel Montblanc," the girl said, "Once I went to a cocktail party he gave there. Lousy liquor. You listen to me, Guy. You're sunk. You're cornered. The dogs of the law are yapping at your heels. What're we going to do?"

"Let 'em in," Kerry directed.

The dismayed girl made a gesture of tragic resignation. "I'll let 'em in," she agreed, pushing out the booth. "Then I'll go out and hunt up a nice second-hand fan." She saw Milton Raney turning from the mike, the control man in the monitor-room signaling the program was cut. She paused, with her fingers on the bolt, glanced back. Amazed, she saw that Guy Kerry had vanished.

EVE STEPPED back in cool defiance as the entrance opened. The red-faced Inspector Tarrant led the charge. Commissioner Endicott tramped to an angry stop, staring around. Two detectives with hands itching for Kerry, looked dumbfounded. The men strode in farther, peering all about, opening the empty booth, muttering maledictions.

Endicott angrily leveled a forefinger at Eve Vane and growled: "Well, where is he?"

"That just shows how smart you are," she answered archly. "You've been wasting a lot of valuable time, that's what you've been doing. Why, he hasn't been here at all. At the last minute he switched over to some other studio. If you want me to tell you exactly where he is, I'm happy to say I don't know!"

Endicott's face purpled. "Get out of here!" he ordered his men. "Watch the elevators in the foyer. I want that man, and I want him in a hurry. Move!"

They moved with dispatch out into the corridor. Eve looked benignly inscrutable, while they hurried away. She signaled Raney and the sound-effect man to be gone. They complied, mystified. Once the monitor booth was empty, Eve stood against the door. She addressed the emptiness: "All clear, Houdini."

A panel in the wall slid aside. It was one of four in the studio which could be manipulated to make the room acoustically hard or soft. Guy Kerry, grateful that the panels looked like solid wall when closed, squeezed his thin frame out of the shallow space, drawing a deep breath. Smiling elatedly, he opened the door a crack, warily gazed out.

"Track fast," he said. "Get all the dope you can, darling, and join me at Franken's rooms. Don't let yourself be shadowed. Once I'm grabbed, I'll never have a chance of clearing myself. And tell the boys at the control board to watch for some quick flashes."

"Would you like me to arrange so you can broadcast your own finish from the electric chair?" Eve Vane asked bitterly.

Kerry bounded across the corridor. He dodged into another studio, larger and empty. A rear door gave him entrance to a labyrinth of narrow hallways and iron stairs interconnecting the big broadcasting theatres, to which the sight-seeing public were not admitted. He rapidly gravitated into a hallway far below street level. Minutes later he emerged cautiously from a freight entrance to mingle with the sidewalk crowd.

He found a telephone booth in a small eatery on a nearby side-street. He dialed his special number. His "Give me the air!" brought a gasp over the wire, then, "Take it away!" Again, he knew, the ether was his. Resolved not to allow any competitor to beat him to the news of his own predicament, he addressed himself to a startled nation.

"It's Keyhole Kerry, your headline racer, back again, Mr. and Mrs. United States! I am still a fugitive from justice. I have just eluded the police and escaped from the Universal Broadcasting Company Building. At any moment I may be captured, but, as long as I'm a public enemy at large, hang onto this wavelength to get the hottest news-breaks first!"

Then Kerry skirmished along the gloomy street in darkest obscurity.

CHAPTER THREE

KILOCYCLE CHASE

A JITTERY cleaning woman turned her pass-key in the door of Room 1521 in the Hotel Montblanc. Guy Kerry held it open, put a promised ten-dollar bill into her palsied hand. He had entered the hotel through the kitchen and reached this elevation by way of the service stairs. As the conscience-stricken maid fluttered away, he stepped into the room of Earl Franken, known as the 'Man of a Thousand Voices.'

Immediately, Kerry paused, gazing at an unusual device sitting on a table. He recognized it as a stenographic recorder. It was connected with an amplifier, the amplifier in turn to a microphone. A blank aluminum disk gleamed on the turntable. Others, each in a paper envelope, were stacked at one side. Kerry fingered through them, lips tightening with excitement. He found on the labels many familiar names. He paused with a record in his hand inscribed *Keyhole Kerry.*

Kerry felt the sting of suspicion. He turned to a phono-radio standing against the opposite wall, clicked it on. When the tubes were hot, he started the record playing. The voice that issued into the room was his own. Rasp, speed, breathlessness and all, it was Kerry announcing a break in a celebrated case—a record which had evidently been caught from the ether months ago.

The sound of a step in the hall darted Kerry's hand to the switch. The reproducer went silent, as a key clicked in the lock. A chubby man with gray temples stepped in, stopped, startled. Kerry warily shut the door behind him.

"I unlocked your door with a saw-buck," he answered Earl Franken's unspoken question. "You were expecting me, weren't you? I want you to help me and keep it strictly under your hat. My next regular broadcast is scheduled for tomorrow night at ten o'clock. I may not be able to make it. Will you do it for me? Can you imitate my voice well enough to fool the whole country?"

"I don't imitate," Franken said with dignity. "I re-create."

"Go ahead, then—re-create me," Kerry urged. "Let's hear me."

Franken shrank in his chest, lifted his chin, drew the tendons in his neck tight, proclaimed: "Attention, Mr. and Mrs. United States! This is Keyhole Kerry, the tattle-tale of radio, bringing you the latest gossip. In Sixteen-twenty, the *Mayflower* landed at Plymouth Rock. Four score and seven years ago our forefathers brought forth on this continent a new nation—" He reverted to his natural tone. "How's that?"

Kerry's jaw had fallen. "It's good," he said. "It's perfect. It's incredible." The fire of suspicion had returned to his eyes. "You look here, Franken. Nobody could have pulled off that frame tonight any better than you. Where were you between nine-thirty and nine-forty-five?"

Franken colored. "Rehearsing," he answered. "I can prove it. *You* look here, Kerry. I don't intend to get dragged into this mess." His tone began to quaver. "Do you want to wreck everything for me—the only big thing that's ever happened to me? The only real happiness—"

A clatter of the doorknob stopped the race of Franken's words. Kerry's eyes had sharpened. He stood scrutinizing the pallid face of the 'Man of a Thousand Voices.' The strange surge of panic that had seized Franklin whetted Kerry's suspicion. He gazed at the pile of records on the table, then at the aluminum disk on the turntable of the phonograph. Shrewdly choosing not to press the point, Kerry stepped to the door.

He retreated before Eve Vane's anxious advance.

SHE SAID: "Guy, you crazy newshound, you listen to me. Don't you dare to put any more flashes on the air. Commissioner Endicott has a general alarm out for you. The next time you do that, they'll trace the call so fast you won't even be able to get out of the booth."

"If I make 'em quick enough—"

"You said yourself that once you're caught you'll never stand a chance of clearing yourself. What about your broadcast tomorrow night, when you're due to be on the network for fifteen minutes? You can't hide behind panels every time. You'll either have to break your record of never missing a broadcast, which'll give lots of people lots of pleasure, or—"

"If I can't make it, Franken will."

"Let me talk to you, Kerry." Kerry looked at the brisk man who had followed Eve into the room. He was heavily built, with deep-set, sagacious eyes. "Miss Vane has retained me as your attorney." Timothy Branton was, Kerry knew, the lawyer for scores of radio performers in matters of contract. "I think it's unwise for you to try to keep playing hare and hounds with the police. It's detrimental. You'd better give yourself up."

"Not until they catch me," Kerry protested.

Branton's brows lowered. "Sit down and listen," he said. "Yours is no easy case. I think we can prove Miss Long was the come-on in a fancy badger game. Singing on the radio and in night clubs, she had glamour, besides natural allure, and probably used it as bait. She went after big fish—big goldfish." Branton chuckled, but no one else did. "Your secretary has checked up on Miss Long's earnings—"

"In the past six months, Guy, that young woman banked a hundred thousand more than her salaries can account for," Eve put in.

"Certainly!" Kerry agreed explosively. "She told me herself on the phone—"

"But, proving she was an extortionist, is of no help to you, Kerry," Branton broke in. "Quite the opposite. The prosecution will link you into it. I've never believed it for a moment, but this isn't the first time I've heard it hinted that you're using your radio program as the basis of a blackmailing racket. Apparently the guilty man has been using your name to back up his threats. All that will come out at the trial—your alleged connection. It will be your word against others' who will incriminate you, believing they're telling the truth. There's only one move—"

"What's that?"

"A plea of self-defense."

"Rats!" Kerry snapped. "You want me to get on the stand and swear I'm a sissy? Self-defense against a woman! Anyway, it's no good. Endicott's shorthand notes will blow that all to hell and gone. According to that stuff, I pulled the gun on her. Besides, there are no powder-marks on her blouse. That shows the gun was fired at a distance. Branton, I'll use you once I'm put into a cell, but, until then, I'm going at this case my own way."

"But how?" Eve Vane protested. "What've you got to work on? I haven't been able to get hold of Gaylord. Marie Blaine, his secretary, is back home now, if you want to see her, but what good will that do? Even if I get the jeweler to open up, the cigarette case may not mean anything. In the meantime, you've got ten thousand police at your heels—"

The telephone rang. Earl Franken automatically reached for it, but Eve Vane's graceful arm outdistanced his. "I'm expecting a call," she murmured. She followed with a series of monosyllables, while Kerry moved nervously about the room. He saw color fade from Eve's face, alarm spring into her eyes. Breaking the connection, she gave a quick glance at Franken. Her gaze caused him to blanch. Both turned tightly to Kerry. His fist was pounding his palm.

"Well? Well? Is it something I can put on the air?"

The girl sprang up. "Don't you dare try it!" She restrained herself with a visible effort. "You can judge for yourself what it's worth. After you skipped out of the studio I began digging into Carola Long's past. I'd heard she'd been in vaudeville years ago. It's true. She was not so young as she was made up to be. I just heard from Smythe, the theatrical agent. He had to hunt it up in the files. She used to be in a double-ventriloquist act with her husband. He's—"

Kerry was reaching for the telephone. "That's a flash!" he exclaimed. "Give it to me!"

"Her husband Is Earl Franken."

KERRY'S hand paused. Eve Vane's closed over his wrist. They both gazed intently at Franken. Now, his round face was pasty. He made a gesture of hopelessness, but could not speak. Kerry's reach for the telephone resumed. Vehemently, Eve restrained it.

"You can't do that," she said quietly. "Endicott would trace it. It would implicate Mr. Franken for harboring a fugitive."

"That might not be serious—if added to a murder charge," Kerry said grimly.

"I had nothing to do with it!" Franken sputtered. "I was married to her—yes. We were divorced long ago. I didn't see her—didn't even hear from her for years. It's not so strange we should be brought together in the same field, is it? The stage was in her blood and mine, too. There isn't any more vaudeville. Naturally, we both went into radio—the biggest thing in the amusement field. We let each other strictly alone—"

"Alimony?" Kerry asked shrewdly.

Franken's face became as vividly red as it had been lividly white. "There's no use of my trying to lie about it. It's all a matter of record. I paid Carola heavy alimony. It was granted when I was making big money. I've kept paying her all this while. She was full of cupidity, after every cent. I've been in arrears. She'd already started court action to recover. But, if you think I killed her—if you think that's why—you're wrong." Franken's voice had strained upward. "I had nothing to do with it!"

"Then, why are you so terrified by all this coming out?" Kerry asked sharply.

"Because now there's someone else. I'm not going to tell you her name. I *would* commit murder rather than have her dragged into it. She's only a kid, sweet, unsophisticated and real—everything Carola never was. She told me once she'd never marry a man who'd been married to another woman, and she meant it. That's why I never told her. I'd rather die than lose her." Again Franken's voice quavered. "I know what you're thinking, but it's not true! I told you, Kerry, I was in the studio, rehearsing, when it happened!"

The room was tensely silent. Eve Vane gazed at Franken compassionately. Kerry's mind was full of flying sparks. He was gazing again at the recorder and at the metal disks on the table. He turned, trod across the room, paced back. Abruptly, he stabbed a forefinger at Franken.

"All right! If you're innocent, you must be as eager as I am to nail the murderer in order to remove suspicion from yourself. How about that? Will you help me?"

"Cer—certainly," Franken stammered.

"Then, whenever it's not absolutely necessary for you to be at the studio, stay right here," Kerry went on grimly. "I'll phone you. It might be at any time of the day or night. I'll want you to do something special. If you don't come through, strictly according to orders, I'll spread this news from coast to coast. Understand that?"

"Y—yes."

Kerry grimly signaled Eve Vane and Timothy Branton from the room. Franken stared after them haggardly. The closing door effaced him. In the corridor, Kerry drew the girl and attorney close.

ALERT against observation, he said: "Carola Long was threatening to wreck him. He's panicky now. An emotional explosion like that might easily drive him to murder. A moment ago, a bombshell exploded in my brain. Until now, I've thought only that my flash was faked on the air. But maybe the first call was an impersonation, too. Maybe the message you took, Eve, didn't really come from Carola Long."

"Please put it into words of one syllable, Guy," Eve pleaded. "I'm going to pieces!"

"Look!" Kerry urged. "Suppose Carola Long was already dead when that first call came in? Suppose the murder had been planned ahead of time? Suppose Franken did it, and baited me into her apartment as part of his scheme? He says he has an alibi—check that up, Eve—but maybe he had rigged up an electric phonograph to the telephone line. Hooked up so that a few seconds after I lifted the receiver in the living-room, that wire was automatically cut off and a record began playing—one he'd already prepared, imitating my voice and Carola Long's. The thing could have been planted outside the house—under the stoop, for instance. Then, all he had to do later was slip out of the studio a few minutes, pull the wires loose and carry the thing back with him. There's motive, means, opportunity—"

"Great Scott!" Branton exclaimed. "Why in Heaven's name didn't you corner him with that on the spot. Your own life is at stake, man!"

"I haven't forgotten it, but that's conjecture, not proof," Kerry answered. "I don't dare make a false move. I've got to clinch this thing before I can get clear. My next logical step is to eliminate other possibilities—make it inevitable. Stay on the job, Eve. I'm off on Lewis Gaylord's trail."

"I'll keep in touch with her, Kerry," Branton promised. "All this is valuable to our case."

KERRY gestured his secretary and the attorney toward the guest elevators. He angled into an el to the service stairs. Descending the flights warily, he passed through a basement, dodged without explanation past a watchman at the freight desk, turned along the dark side-street. Possibilities entangled themselves in his mind as he sought a telephone.

He did not dial his special number this time. He called the home of Lewis Gaylord. The distant bell purred repeatedly. The lack of response furrowed Kerry's forehead. He removed from his pocket the slip which Eve Vane had passed him during his besieged broadcast. He noted the address of Marie Blaine, Gaylord's secretary. Stepping out of the lunch counter, he signaled a taxi.

It zigzagged him into the Murray Hill section. As his cab swung around the last corner, Kerry saw another just starting up from the curb directly in front of the address he sought. A man was climbing to the entrance of the brownstone house. The glow from the pane revealed him to be garbed in a tuxedo. His jauntily tilted black hat shaded his face, but Kerry recognized his distinctive profile as he pushed the door open. It was Lewis Gaylord.

Kerry watched Gaylord vanish. He pushed a banknote at his driver, paused, gazing speculatively at the entrance. Gaylord he knew was a private detective with well-appointed offices near Broadway. A man of smooth manner and self-cultivated charm, he had of late been Carola Long's frequent companion. Only a few days ago, in fact, Kerry had whispered this romantic item into the ears of the nation. Now, scenting further news, he quietly mounted the stoop.

The door was locked. Kerry pushed a button at random. A deluded occupant, somewhere in the house, obliging, tripped the electric bolt for him. Sidling in, Kerry heard soft footfalls mounting the stairs. He followed even more softly, listening. He heard the footsteps pause on the third landing. A soundless pause was followed by the quick closing of a door.

On the third level, Kerry gazed at the door numbered *12*. That, Eve's note had told him, was the apartment of Marie Blaine. He stepped to it, listened, heard nothing. He applied his knuckles. The sound produced no answer. Impatiently, Kerry took the knob, thrust the door open. He stopped short just over the sill, gazing shocked at the limp form on the bed.

One of the girl's bare legs was dangling, as if she had been flung back. Her pink-silk nightgown was drawn up to her knees, her robe flowing open. Her jaw was agape, her eyes staring sightlessly at the ceiling. Just above the line of her brown hair was a ghastly crushed hollow. The implement which had broken the girl's skull lay on the floor beside her—a brass Statue of Liberty.

Kerry gazed alertly around the silent room. Light was shafting out of the open door of the bath. The only other door, except the entrance, was closed. Kerry figured it gave upon a closet. He strode directly to it, took the knob, pulled it wide.

"Come on out, Gaylord," he said.

THE MIDDLE-AGED man stared hotly. His right hand slipped ominously toward his left shoulder as he stepped from the closet. Kerry's steadfast eyes did not waver from Gaylord's. Alter a galvanic moment he said: "Well?"

"I advise you to get out of here, Kerry," Gaylord said in an edged tone. "Forget all this."

"Some private detectives have been known to be not above blackmail," Kerry observed. "In fact, with some of them it's their main line. You've never seemed to lack money, Gaylord— fine car, expensive clothes. All the most exclusive hot-spots know you. Naturally, one's secretary learns things. A girl who kept her mouth shut about extortion might begin talking about murder."

Gaylord stepped forward with a clubbed fist. "Cut that out, Kerry! When I reached home a short while ago, my Jap boy told me Miss Blaine had called. He said she insisted I come right over to see her. I called her back, but there wasn't any answer. I decided to come, and did. I found her exactly like that, only a moment ago. I don't know a damned thing about it, but I do admit my being here is dynamite."

"Is this the first time you came here tonight, Gaylord?" Kerry inquired quietly. "I know you've been out all evening, because my secretary tried to reach you and couldn't. Perhaps you felt, after your first visit, that the river would be safer—an unexplained disappearance rather than a mur—"

"Skip that, Kerry!" Gaylord snapped viciously. "There's a good reason why I'm not calling the police about you right now. I want to keep clear of this. It would wreck me. Once I get into the headlines on the wrong end of a killing my agency is sunk. I'd be able to clear myself, but the effect would ruin me. Listen, Kerry. If you put anything on the air connecting me with this, I'll hit you with everything I've got. I'll work night and day to clinch the case against you. I promise you, you'll never see the outside of a cell. But give me a chance to side-step this and I'll do my utmost to clear you."

Kerry's lips tightened. "A bargain?" he asked. "No go, Gaylord. You couldn't possibly put me in a hotter spot than I'm in already. I have nothing to lose, you have everything. Remember, you'll be questioned not only about this killing, but about the murder of Carola Long. For instance, Endicott will ask you if you were with her tonight, just before—"

"I was not!" Gaylord's denial tore from his thinned lips. "I'm warning you again, Kerry. Implicate me, and I'll see you in the chair."

He strode from the room. Kerry saw him glance around warily, heard him lightly running down the stairs. Kerry stepped into the hall, closed the door. Eyes narrowed thoughtfully, he emerged into the dark street to find Gaylord out of sight. He hurried to a cheap restaurant in the shadow of the elevated. He shouldered into a telephone booth, dialed his special number.

Kerry reasoned rapidly that his wisest move was to allow Gaylord to believe he was bluffed. Naming Gaylord now would result in the private detective's arrest, remove him from the field of action, rob Kerry of any subsequent flashes concerning him. Allowing Gaylord to remain at large, unsuspected, might enable Kerry to force him into a damning move. What was far more important, if this happened, it would give Kerry another sensational news-beat. He decided on the gamble, as his signal came through, "The air's yours!"

His twang lightninged from coast to coast. "This is Keyhole Kerry, your fugitive newshound, Mr. and Mrs. Public! Again I bring you the first news of a startling murder. At an address which the police may find opposite her name in the telephone directory, Miss Marie Blaine lies dead—killed. Your correspondent believes that her murder is somehow connected with the death of Miss Carola Long. Since I am suspected of the latter crime, and since my undercover moves tonight make it impossible for me to establish an alibi, the local gendarmes will promptly suspect me of both homicides. May I say again, ladies and gentlemen, I am innocent. Now, in order to escape the police, who are closing down upon me even at this moment, allow me to bid you a hasty good-night!"

A minute and a half later two prowl-cars screamed to the front of the little restaurant. When four patrolmen charged at the empty telephone booth with drawn guns, Keyhole Kerry was huddled in the corner of a subway car, hidden behind a newspaper, intently reading the details concerning his own arrest and escape.

CHAPTER FOUR

TRIAL BY AIR

AT NINE-TWENTY next evening, Earl Franken's taut nerves hopped him out of his chair in response to a quick knock on the door of his hotel room. The disreputable-looking man who sidled in was Keyhole Kerry. A day's dark beard gave contrast to his ruffled white hair. He was unpressed, looked hungry, had the haunted light of the hunted in his eyes. He seized Franken's arm.

"Call Eve at my office," he directed tersely. "Tell her to have Smitty ring back from some public phone right away. Snap it up!"

As the distressed Franken complied, Kerry thoughtfully stared at newspapers rumpled on the floor. He knew every line in them. All day he had been hiding in a cheap rooming-house on the East Side, snitching extras from neighbors' doorsteps, absorbing every printed detail concerning the two murders. Paramount in importance was the fact that no clue had come to light to hint even remotely Kerry's innocence.

The police had learned that the gun that had killed Carola Long was registered in her name. They had found all fingerprints effaced at the scenes of both murders. They had questioned Gaylord in connection with Marie Blaine's death. He had professed complete ignorance of the crime and been released. Commissioner Endicott was quoted as saying that a private detective's secretary was extremely likely as a spy for a radio gossiper. The intimation was that Kerry had eradicated her too abundant knowledge of his blackmailing operations. Endicott publicly added that if Kerry dared attempt his regular broadcast this evening he was certain to be apprehended.

"Damned if I'll let him scare me out of it!" Kerry exploded. Franken, having completed the call, looked up blinking. "See here, Franken. Can you imitate—that is, re-create—Commissioner Endicott's voice?"

"Certainly. I've got a record of it somewhere. Listen." Franken swelled his chest, lowered his chin, pronounced boomingly: "The campaign of the police department to encourage safe driving is undertaken in the cause of saving human lives—"

THE TELEPHONE zinged. Kerry exclaimed, "Swell! Exactly like him!" The receiver buzzed with the voice of Smitty. Smitty, once had been a copy boy on the *Herald*, before he became Kerry's legman, had never boasted a fuller name.

"Get hold of a good mike, Smitty," Kerry rattled orders at him. "I want a hundred feet of cord connected with it. You and Eve bring it to Carola Long's place in fifteen minutes. Tell her I know damned well I can't keep crawling into holes much longer. I'm going to shoot the works on my broadcast tonight. I'm going on the air, from Long's apartment."

"Listen, chief!" Smitty broke in breathlessly. "That's what she's afraid of. Talking for fifteen minutes will give the cops the chance they're waiting for to grab you. But she found out something, chief. You know who bought that cigarette case for Miss Long? Lewis Gaylord!"

"Thanks, Smitty!" Kerry answered. "Get busy!" He broke the connection, consulted the slip Eve had given him at the studio, called Gaylord's home number. The private detective's suave tone answered. Kerry greeted him with: "Nice work, my friend. Now, listen. I've got evidence tying you right into Long's murder. I can prove were there. We'd better talk this over. Be at Long's place in fifteen minutes. If you don't show up, I'll spill it from coast to coast."

He disconnected before Gaylord could answer. He spoke quickly to Franken, uttering crisp directions. Franken swallowed hard, took up the instrument, called for the number of the Long apartment. Kerry, leaning close, heard a man's voice respond—that, he surmised, of a detective on duty.

It was Franken's lips that moved, but Commissioner Endicott's voice that said: "The commissioner calling. You're relieved of your detail. Every man in the place is to report back. I want to look it over myself, alone. Leave the front door unfastened. Be out of there in five minutes. That's all."

As Franken relinquished the instrument, Kerry said fervently: "I pray to God Endicott wasn't there!" He maneuvered Franken from the room. Together, they followed Kerry's secret circuit to the street via service stairs and basement. They ducked into a taxi. Kerry clipped out the Long address. A few minutes later, his order curbed the car near the murdered woman's door.

PRESENTLY a detective, whom Kerry knew by sight, emerged from the house. He walked away. No other appeared. Assuming he was the last to follow the falsified orders, Kerry left the taxi with Franken. He entered the Long door, paused, listened to silence. "Watch," he directed Franken. Leaving Franken at the entrance, he began a quick circuit of the apartment.

He hurried first into the dead woman's bedroom. He scanned the walls, ceiling, floor. Inspecting the telephone, he found that this instrument was the first connected with the main line, that the other in the living-room upstairs was an extension. He went up. The room where Carola Long had died showed evidences of the police search. Kerry continued his own, again examining the walls, the ceiling, the floor. A call from the entrance stopped him.

Eve Vane and Smitty hurried in. The simian-nosed boy was carrying a microphone wound with flexible cord.

"We've been across town and back six times, throwing off a dick!" he exclaimed.

Kerry took the instrument, looked up to see Eve impaling him with a censorious, turquoise gaze. He glanced at his strap-watch, began unwinding the cord.

"I should have stuck to my fans and bubbles," she said. "Don't you realize you can never get out of this now? You've invited the cops to close in on you the same way they stormed Two-Gun

Crowley. I suppose you'll be happily broadcasting while the bullets fly."

Timothy Branton had appeared in the doorway. He had entered the house with Eve and Smitty. He seconded the girl.

"You're making matters worse," he declared. "If you'd remained in the hands of the police, this second murder could never have been connected with you. These stunts are prejudicing your case."

Kerry took Smitty's jackknife, began using it as a screwdriver to open the telephone box. "This is my only chance. In a few minutes, I'm going on the air. Maybe I can prove something—I don't know yet. There's only half of it so far. I'm going to try myself before the American public before I get heaved into a cell—but don't talk to me now!"

He tightened the tips of the microphone cord under the terminals of the telephone line. Lifting the receiver, he called his special number. Listening, he spoke through the microphone. "Kerry calling. I've hooked a mike onto the wire. Is it working?" The answer came, "O.K." Kerry continued: "Catch the commercial from Raney in the studio, then switch to me. I'll synchronize with the radio here." He left the connection open, carried the mike with him, switched on the radio.

"Stand by that box with your knife, Smitty," Kerry directed the shaggy-headed lad. "When I signal, disconnect one of the mike leads, so that only the telephone will be left working. At the second signal, hitch the mike back on. Got it?"

Smitty nodded that he had it.

At that moment, Earl Franken appeared in the door. Franken announced nervously: "Gaylord's coming in." From behind him came a rattling knob.

Kerry directed Franken, "make sure all doors and windows are fastened!" and waited for Gaylord to appear. He extended his hand to Eve Vane as Franken trotted away, asked for "The case." The girl removed it from her purse, put it on his palm.

Gaylord, stepping into sight, stopped short with his eyes upon it.

"You forgot this little detail last night, didn't you?" Kerry said levelly. "You came bringing gifts and stayed to murder. You lied to me in Marie Blaine's place, Gaylord. You said you weren't here last night, but you were!"

Fierce light filled Gaylord's eyes. "The rest of what I said to you, Kerry, still goes," he threatened. "I'll see you get the chair, if you spill any of this. I can account for that case—for everything. If you'll listen, and promise to keep it under your hat, I'll tell you."

THE RADIO had begun playing. Again the program was dance music, which Kerry's broadcast was scheduled to follow. Kerry's wrist-watch told him only a few minutes remained until the *De-Luxe-Lax* quarter-hour was due to hit the air.

"I promise nothing," he answered Gaylord grimly. "If you can vindicate yourself, you'd better do a good job of it, and do it fast. This may be Keyhole Kerry's last broadcast, and I'm going to make the most of it. Well?"

Gaylord stepped forward belligerently, while the others in the room watched intently. "I admit I was here last night," he declared. "It started while Carola and I were having dinner. We came here to have it out. We did. I feel like a hell of a mug for telling you about it, but this is straight. The whole trouble was that Carola had fallen in love with me."

"That's no motive for murder," Kerry observed wryly.

"Let me talk, Kerry," Gaylord protested. "I saw a lot of Carola. I'd begun to suspect her. She had too much money. I thought she was playing me for a sucker. I openly accused her of black-mail. I told her I was damned if I'd let her hook me—was through with her. She almost went into hysterics. But she admitted it."

"Check," Kerry said jubilantly.

"She admitted she started out with the idea of bleeding me,

but now she couldn't do it. She said she loved me. She wasn't going to let that stand between us. She was going to get out of it. To prove she meant it, she called somebody on the telephone. I didn't catch the number. She didn't ask for any name. Whoever was on the other end of the line, she told him she was never going to work with him again."

Kerry was listening to Gaylord with one ear, to the radio with the other. The dance program was drawing to a close.

"She hung up and begged me to forget the whole thing. I repeated that I was through with her. A private detective of my standing can't take the chance of marrying a crook, and anyway I wasn't in love with her. I simply left. I'd given her that cigarette case earlier in the evening because it was her birthday. That's all I know. Isn't it logical to suppose the man she called came in here and settled with her?"

"If there is such a man," Kerry said.

Gaylord colored.

AT THAT moment the radio announced: "This is Station WUBC." Bewildered, Kerry glanced around. Smitty was hunched at the telephone box, the knife poised. Gaylord, Franken, Branton and Eve were watching Kerry. He became almost unaware of their presence as he listened to the radio. He turned the volume control very low, intent on Milton Raney's whisper.

Raney was expressing a high estimation of *De-Luxe-Lax*. The commercial ended with, "Now, ladies and gentlemen, your celebrated newshawk, Keyhole Kerry, bringing you his latest flashes!"

Promptly, Kerry's rattling delivery began. "Attention, Mr. and Mrs. United States.'" He heard his own voice in the radio loudspeaker, which told him his microphone was functioning. Snapping off the radio switch, he began searching the walls. "Sometime during this broadcast, ladies and gentlemen, your correspondent is certain to be seized by the police. Until such time, listen carefully. I am speaking to you from the room in which Carola Long was murdered. It is my purpose to present evidence to prove that I am not guilty of killing her."

Smitty was watching Kerry hypnotically. Eve Vane's face was whitely bewildered. The three men were silent.

"This is the first opportunity I have had to check this evidence, Mr. and Mrs. Public," Kerry went on. "Follow me closely. Carola Long was hit by two bullets, but *three* shots were fired from the gun that killed her. The third bullet passed through the jacket of her lounging-pajamas, under her right arm. Obviously, it had to strike something in the room in which she was murdered. Bear that clearly in mind, ladies and gentlemen, because I am at this moment hunting for the scar which the bullet must have made somewhere in this apartment."

Kerry's auditors looked around, light springing into their eyes, as he continued: "I was arrested as a result of voices, allegedly those of Miss Long and myself, which went out over the air from a telephone. The sound of shots was also heard. There is a telephone in this living-room, another in the bedroom downstairs. I have already searched the bedroom. There is no sign of a bullet mark in it. That is absolute proof the murder was not committed there. In fact, Miss Long's body was found where I am now standing. It is logical to conclude, then, that she was killed here. But, ladies and gentlemen, *neither is there any bullet mark in this room.*"

KERRY'S signal galvanized Eve Vane. At once she began a rapid inspection of the furniture. Her gestures pressed the same duty upon Franken, Gaylord and Branton.

"No bullet mark is in this room, where the murder is supposed to have occurred," Kerry went on. "It did not hit the walls, the floor or the ceiling. It did not lodge in any of the furniture." The three men and the girl, searching on, were wagging their heads negatively. "Therefore, ladies and gentlemen, Carola Long was not killed where her body was found, but in some other part of the apartment. I am searching now for the mark that must have been made by the third bullet."

Kerry stepped into the whimsically decorated bar, trailing the cord behind him. Eve and the three men watched through the door, while Smitty craned to keep Kerry in sight.

"It's possible that the third bullet flew out the window—possible, but not likely," his rasp went on. "It might have passed through an open door. I hope to learn what actually happened to it. I am now in the little hall adjoining the living-room. I am searching the walls. They are painted with caricatures of well-known radio performers, which makes the search difficult. Keep listening, ladies and gentlemen. The arrival of the police may interrupt the hunt, but— There!"

Kerry swerved behind the bar. His fingers passed over a face painted beside the mirror. It was that of Eddy Cantor, eyes popping. One of those wide eyes was marred by broken plaster. In the big black iris Kerry found something embedded. Quickly, he removed his pencil and probed at it. It would not yield. Eve Vane and the three men watched him in silent fascination as he caught up a corkscrew from the bar.

"I have found the bullet, ladies and gentlemen!" Kerry announced exultantly. "It is in the wall, near the bar. It could not possibly have reached this spot by flying through the door from the living-room. That means Carola Long was murdered near this spot. Then her body was transferred to a position near the telephone in the next room. Why? Because that was necessary to the murderer's plan to broadcast the faked dialogue. Now, stand by for an experiment which will prove that a trick was played upon the American public and the police!"

Kerry's gesture cleared the doorway. He stared at Smitty. "I am now talking through a microphone. I am perhaps twenty-five feet from the telephone in the next room. The line is open. The question is, could my voice have been heard, speaking in this bar, where the crime was committed?"

Kerry signaled. Smitty detached the microphone. Kerry's voice lifted.

"I am shouting, ladies and gentlemen! Can you hear me?

Only the telephone is connected now. I believe you will find my voice very faint. The murder could not have been committed this far from the telephone." At his signal, Smitty reconnected the mike. "This, Mr. and Mrs. Public, proves beyond all doubt that you did not actually hear the murder committed. What you heard was a falsification of my voice and Miss Long's coming from the telephone downstairs, where the murderer was speaking!"

Kerry was breathlessly digging the point of the corkscrew into the wall. Flakes of plaster fell from Eddie Cantor's eye. The dull lead of the embedded bullet appeared more clearly. During a moment of silence, a heavy pounding sound echoed from the front of the house.

"The police are at the door, ladies and gentlemen. They are demanding that it be opened in the name of the law. I'm afraid I do not feel in an obliging mood. They will have to break it down to get me. I am still digging the bullet out of the wall. It is conclusive proof. Why? Because this wall, like the rest of the apartment, was redecorated only a few days ago. This shows the scar cannot be an old one—that the bullet was fired at the time of the murder. Ballistics experts will have no trouble establishing that it was fired from the murder weapon."

A misshapen pellet rolled into Kerry's palm. Delightedly, he bent close to examine it. He glanced at his strap-watch, saw that he still had minutes to go. Suddenly, the dial disappeared before his eyes.

"The lights have gone out! The electricity in nearby apartments is still functioning, as I can see out the window—"

Suddenly a rush hit Kerry. He flattened against the wall. A heavy blow clicked his teeth—a sound that echoed from border to border. Kerry could see nothing of the man who had attacked him. He staggered back. He mouthed through bleeding lips: "Someone is attempting to get the bullet away from me!"

FAST breath panted in the darkness. Still Kerry was blind.

His fist was closed on the bullet. One of the three men, he knew, had assaulted him.

Kerry struck back desperately, delighted with the knowledge that the sound of the fight must be flashing across the entire nation. His fists pelted a face. He jumped upon a writhing figure.

Kerry's man sagged down.

"You heard the sounds of an attack upon me, ladies and gentlemen," he sped on. "It was a desperate attempt to get hold of the bullet. Losing it would have blown up my only chance of clearing myself. The guilty man is now cornered.

"I am now keeping my promise. The name of the man is Timothy Branton!"

Kerry's mind was speeding. He saw that the attorney was out cold. He caught Earl Franken's arm. "Listen, ladies and gentlemen!" he boomed. "Branton may talk!" He whispered into Franken's ear: "Imitate Branton's voice. I'll cue you, as we go along." Then, into the microphone: "Branton knows he hasn't a chance now. There are witnesses to his attempt to destroy evidence. Branton, you murdered Miss Long!"

Kerry whispered in Franken's ear. The voice that issued from his lips was Timothy Branton's broken, strained.

"You were working a blackmail game with Carola Long," Kerry said. "You, well acquainted with prominent persons. Threatening suit as a lawyer. Using my name to force payment. You fill the description I broadcast last night—you, a lawyer, whose voice before a jury is an instrument vital to his success."

Franken said for Branton, cued by Kerry: "It's no use. I knew she was—falling in love with Gaylord. I was afraid she'd turn on me. That's why I hired Gaylord's secretary to tell me everything that went on between them. Marie Blaine could have turned the police upon me. That's why I—last night— Oh, God—"

Kerry jumped up. In the hallway, a door was splintering down. Heavy footfalls beat closer.

"You have just heard the voice of Timothy Branton, confessing murder, ladies and gentlemen!" he rushed into the ether. "I trust Commissioner Endicott, as it is his habit to do with my broadcasts, has had a stenographic record made of it! Keyhole Kerry signing off!"

KERRY paced back and forth in Commissioner Endicott's outer office in police headquarters. Eve Vane watched his every move, tearfully. Kerry listened to Endicott's rumbling voice in the next room. He turned for the telephone, as the connecting door opened.

Kerry glimpsed Branton sitting slumped in a chair beside the commissioner's desk. Endicott tramped in, eyeing Kerry. He had a typewritten sheet in his hand which bore the signature of Branton.

"At first he repudiated what he said on the air, Kerry. Claimed he didn't remember saying it," Endicott announced. "Maybe he was only half conscious, but that's what made the truth come out. I opened him up. Every detail checks with what you made him say into the mike."

Kerry had the telephone at his lips.

"Flash, ladies and gentlemen! Keyhole Kerry is the first to announce that Timothy Branton has made a confession!"

MURDER MADE EASY

WHEN THE ACE CRIME-
COMMENTATOR OF THE
ETHER WAVES STARTED
MRS. BEVERLY REYBURN
OFF ON HER PHONY SLAY-
RIDE JUST FOR A RED-
HOT NEWS FLASH, IT HAD
ALL THE EARMARKS OF
PURE GENIUS. BUT THEN
A SIMON-PURE KILLER
MUSCLED IN ON THE
STAGE-SET TO DEPOSIT
A CORPSE THAT WAS FAR
FROM COUNTERFEIT, AND
GIVE KERRY A SCOOP
THAT WAS TOO HOT TO
HANDLE—A GILT-EDGED
MURDER RAP PINNED ON
HIMSELF!

CHAPTER ONE

DEATH ON ORDER

KEYHOLE KERRY hunched from the taxi, dodged across the sidewalk, warily paused in the gloomy stone archway to make sure the gardened court of the Embassy Arms was momentarily deserted. His abrasive voice was familiar to millions of radio listeners as that of the most sensational flash-news broadcaster ever to pervade the ether. He gloried in the acclaim he had won, but tonight this prematurely white-headed young man was unwontedly shunning public notice.

With electrically nervous strides, Kerry followed a dimly lighted walk to a shadowed entrance. The move took him out of sight of the street, deep into the landscaped area enclosed by the rearing walls of the exclusive apartment hotel. The door he approached connected with a series of private suites remote from the central foyer, in which the Embassy Arms customarily housed notables of retiring inclination. It opened abruptly before Kerry reached it, causing him to duck his head and shade his face with his hat-brim in his anxiety to avoid recognition.

A woman flung herself out of it. She stumbled directly into Kerry. She caught at his shoulder, gasping, sobbing, laughing with delirious mirthlessness. She was racked with distress, clamping a purse under one arm, clutching her swagger-coat closely around her wabbling body. Alarmed, Kerry supported her, catching only a brief glimpse of her white, tear-streaked cheeks. Before he could ask her a single solicitous question, she suddenly thrust from him, tottered along the walk. Kerry, concernedly retaining the obscurity of the dimness, watched her pause, compose herself with a desperate effort, then vanish outward through the arch.

Kerry's almost maniacal curiosity urged him to follow, but he did not. Possessing an insensate hunger for personal news, filled with an unquenchable zeal for telling the world, and telling it before any other agency of news dissemination had a chance, he sensed a choice tidbit of gossip in the unknown woman's anguish. But, tonight, he was engaged upon a specially important mission. Time pressed. His strap-watch said that, in thirty-five minutes, he must meet the most relentless

of deadlines with his latest barrage of exclusive inside chatter. Always feverishly intent upon his mad task of out-winchelling Winchell, cherishing his record of never having missed a broadcast, he let the woman go, hurried on to the dark entrance.

It yielded into a richly hushed hallway which led Kerry to another door lettered *M*. This he opened with a key which he tucked out of a vest pocket, still alert against observation. He entered darkness, pulled on a pair of pigskin gloves, then snapped a wall-switch. An aureate glow revealed a luxurious living-room

He hurled the mike as Kerry
barged in the window.

and a bedroom, both subtly scented with the hint of a feminine presence. Kerry immediately set about a series of strange tasks.

HE TOOK up a number of letters and telegrams which had been slipped over the sill. He transferred these to the desk, cut them open, spread out most of them without bothering to read them. The others he crumpled and carried to the fireplace. Igniting a paper match, he set the wad aflame on the hearth. While it blazed, he stepped through the connecting door and attacked the bed.

He stripped off its taffeta spread, pulled the sheets loose, punched the pillows violently with his fists. He heaved into the disarray, rolled, kicked. Rising, he drew a pack of rare imported cigarettes from the same pocket that had held the key. He lighted one, dragged on it several times, dropped it to the rug and let it remain, smoldering fragrantly. Next, he flung the closet wide, pulled a light traveling-case from its place among others on a shelf. He opened the case on a chair, jerked evening gowns and négligées from their hangers, spilled them into it. He added pastel lingerie snatched from commode drawers which he left open. Having wrought havoc, he returned to the orderly living-room.

There he tugged up his left sleeve to the elbow. From the same pocket that had produced the key and the cigarettes, he took a new razor blade. He peeled it, poised its gleaming edge over his forearm, steeled himself with a grimace, sliced. Blood welled out of the cut. Taking care that the crimson drops fell upon the ivory satin cover of a period chair, he rewrapped the blade, returned it to his person. When the chair was liberally sprinkled, he kicked it over, then stooped so that a larger scarlet blot soon stained the white-fur throw-rug. Finally, he brought a patented adhesive bandage from that same abundant pocket, bound it over the self-inflicted wound to stop the flow. He looked about with elated satisfaction.

Rearranging himself, but leaving the rooms in startling disorder, he gazed narrowly into the hallway to make sure no one was there. He sidled out, leaving the door lettered *M* unlocked. Striding obscurely through the court, he glimpsed the warning of his wrist-watch that the rest of his arrangements must be effected quickly, if he was to reach the studio in time for his widely awaited program of gossip. Accordingly, he sought the nearest drug store, shouldered into a telephone booth, dialed his special number.

An answer came from one of two men who were constantly on duty in the Universal Broadcasting Company tower, at the behest of Kerry's sponsor, to receive his calls at all hours of the day and night. Eagerly he directed: "Put me on."

KERRY preferred not to remember that his sponsor was the manufacturer of a cathartic called *De-Luxe-Lax*. But this alleviator of the national ailment paid him a staggering stipend, under a holeproof contract restricting his hair-raising performances to the air-waves, and it expensively provided him with an extraordinary arrangement enabling him to break into any program at any time with a hot flash. Because of this privileged dispensation, he could call from any telephone, using it as a mike, and almost immediately hit the ether. Other sponsors had found it highly advantageous not to protest his intrusions, for the expectancy of catching Kerry with a breathtaking scoop kept millions listening continually to the nation-wide network.

In response to his signal, Kerry knew, the wavelengths were being cleared for him. A program of dance music, which Kerry's was scheduled to follow was fading from numberless loudspeakers. The line brought him his cue, "Take it away!" Kerry impatiently waited five seconds more, then began machine-gunning words into the transmitter in his characteristic slate-pencil rasp that made Fred Allen's twang seem melodious by comparison.

"Attention, Mr. and Mrs. United States! This is Keyhole Kerry, your headline-beater, romping out of your radio with his latest spine-tingling flash. You have heard many times, exclusively from this news-buster, intriguing items concerning Mrs. Beverly Reyburn, who is the talk and the toast of all Europe, and the intimate companion of a certain reigning monarch. I bring you now an even more startling revelation about this glamorous widow, the favorite of a royal bachelor. You, and the metropolitan police, as well as all diplomatic circles the world over, will be amazed to learn that I have just received a confidential report saying the captivating Mrs. Reyburn became, only a few minutes ago, the victim of violence—perhaps of murder!"

Kerry delightedly imagined millions of gasps arising simultaneously from coast to coast, epithets exploding in the headquarters office of Police Commissioner Endicott, despairing moans of defeat being emitted by the city editors and newspaper reporters to whom his name was anathema.

"Mrs. Reyburn's fate is, at the moment, a baffling puzzle," Kerry zestfully rushed on with a speed that made Floyd Gibbons seem comparatively tongue-tied, "but my report has it that the local gendarmes will find much to concern them in her secluded suite at the Embassy Arms. If Mrs. Reyburn has been killed, her death is certain to have international repercussions. Every news agency in the world will immediately begin chasing this stop-press break, but let me remind you that Keyhole Kerry brings you the hottest news first. Keep your dials tuned to the station to which you are now listening, for I promise to make further exclusive revelations within a few minutes. This is your scoop specialist signing off, ladies and gentlemen, until my regular program hits the air exactly on the hour."

It lacked six minutes of the hour when Kerry exultantly bounded from the booth. He flagged a taxi, urgently ordered the driver to become color-blind to all traffic lights, perched tensely and grinned. He knew his cryptic announcement was launching an immediate police investigation. He was sure that, while he zigzagged across Manhattan, wild-eyed newspapermen were converging upon the Embassy Arms. Content to let them scramble for the morsel he had publicly thrown them, he dove from the cab with no second to spare.

A nonstop elevator whisked him into the heights of the

Universal Broadcasting spire. He pushed into Studio X to find his chubby, tuxedoed announcer, Milton Raney, already crooning dignified blandishments, concerning *De-Luxe-Lax,* into the microphone. A sound-effects man was diligently tapping a typewriter and ringing a telephone bell at frequent intervals, to simulate the feverish activity of a news headquarters. Just inside the door a willowy, champagne blonde was having a case of jitters.

EVE VANE'S turquoise eyes lighted with dizzy relief at sight of Kerry. He had discovered her remarkable talents as a secretary while watching her weave through a blue-spotted dance in a night club, clothed only in purest epidermis. Appearing sublimely nude in public had never occasioned her nearly the panic that quaked her supple figure each time Kerry was due to whisper his confidences from ocean to ocean. With trembling hand, she passed him the copy she had prepared.

Eve agitatedly followed Kerry to the microphone on the desk. Raney was completing his guileful praise of the sponsor's product. While the typewriter and the bell continued their mute accompaniment, the most listened-to voice on the air crackled into its staccato monologue.

"Greetings again, Mr. and Mrs. United States! Your headline-racer of the kilocycles, Keyhole Kerry, is here to keep his promise to reveal further details of the startling case involving Mrs. Beverly Reyburn. The police, quickly acting on your correspondent's tip, have had just enough time to arrive on the scene. If they have taken advantage of the radio in Mrs. Reyburn's apartment, they will learn now what happened there less than an hour ago. To you and you, and to them, I announce definitely that this is murder."

Eve Vane was listening entranced. Milton Raney was transfixed attention. In millions of homes, Kerry realized, millions of other ears were bent as intently upon his very word. Ignoring his prepared copy, he rushed on.

"This is definitely murder, ladies and gentlemen, but Mrs.

Reyburn may, or may not, be the victim. She had been so self-effacing since returning to this country a week ago, that even your radio oracle, who alone has kept you informed of her movements, is not sure of her position in the case. This is a point which I will clear up very soon. There is no doubt, however, that tonight Mrs. Reyburn's rooms were disrupted by a violent quarrel. The heated altercation took place between a woman, who was already there, and a man, who forced himself in on her. It resulted in a struggle which caused the woman's death. The man, desperate to forestall the discovery of his crime, then undertook the grisly task of disposing of her dead body."

Kerry pictured the homicide squad, having sped to the apartment, listening amazed to the conclusions he was drawing from evidence which they were only just discovering.

"I do not know how the murderer was able to remove the woman's corpse from the rooms without being observed, but it has vanished," he continued breathlessly. "I cannot say where he secretly transported it, or how he contrived to conceal it, but I believe it highly unlikely that the body will ever be found. The identity of the murderer is unknown to me, but I suggest to the police that they search for a foreigner who was madly in love with Mrs. Reyburn and insanely jealous of her faithful relationship with her devoted royal lover."

Kerry's secretary was watching him with enraptured admiration, yet her turquoise eyes were worried. Afire with the excitement of his own account, he swept on.

"This news-buster, Mr. and Mrs. America, was the first to reveal Mrs. Reyburn's regal romance. Until my initial flash, disclosing her to be the bachelor king's intimate companion, nothing was shown of her outside the highest diplomatic circles abroad. Since then, she has become the most glamorous woman in the world. Her recent return to this country, incognito, was news that I announced exclusively. Immediately she arrived in New York, she was sought out by countless interviewers, but she succeeded so well in secluding herself that no information concerning her could be unearthed—except by Keyhole Kerry."

Eve Vane's nod declared this to be a proud fact.

"I told the world that she is an American citizen, the widow of a retired army officer, a woman of great charm, culture and intelligence," went on Kerry rapidly. "Respecting her request, which she made of me by telephone as soon as she landed here, I did not make her address public until tonight. The Embassy Arms, upon her insistence, also closely guarded the fact that she was a guest. Now, however, the secret can no longer be kept. Tonight's murder must turn the spotlight upon her. Keyhole Kerry, ladies and gentlemen, promises to inform you of the developments in this sensational case as fast as they break."

CHAPTER TWO

BLOODY BOOMERANG

KERRY SAW Eve Vane vacate her chair with a dancer's nimble bound. While he turned to his copy, to rattle out gossip concerning prominent persons for whose privacy he had no respect whatever, he watched her anxiously attempting to close the door against two dogged-looking men who were pushing in from the corridor. They had vanquished the immaculately uniformed attendants, who always stood guard outside, but Eve's adamant admonitions effected a compromise just over the sill. A moment later, hands trembling, she slipped the tersest possible note under Kerry's eyes.

It read—*Cops.*

Kerry tensely continued his grating, headlong delivery, opening wide his dossier of inside stuff. The spinning red second hand of the huge electric clock warned him he was nearing the end of his allotted period. "The latest angle on the startling case of Mrs. Reyburn is that the police have come to question me," he announced as a parting shot. "They will learn nothing from me, Mr. and Mrs. United States, any sooner than you. Keep your dials tuned to this wavelength for further exclusive flashes.

This is your scoop-specialist going off the air until more white-hot news brings him back—at any moment!"

Kerry relinquished the mike at the last second. Immediately, Raney began his closing paean to *De-Luxe-Lax*. With Eve's anxious eyes upon him, Kerry turned to the two men from headquarters. His warning gesture kept them silent until the monitor in the double-paned booth signaled that the program was off the air.

The bigger of them then asserted gruffly: "Commissioner Endicott wants to see you pronto, Kerry, over at the Embassy Arms."

"I strained a point, when I announced that as news," Kerry retorted. "Endicott's always too damned eager to collar me, instead of nailing the crook. It won't do any more good this time, than usual, because everything I know goes out over the air as soon as I get it. Besides, I've a strong hunch this case is destined for the unsolved file. Let's go."

Eve Vane had already slipped into her coat, was perching a haughty hat on her winey head. She caught Kerry's arm as he marched towards the elevators with the two plainsclothesmen. "How you dug up that Reyburn stuff is beyond me, Guy Kerry, but I hope you're not pulling a terrific boner," she told him with fond concern. "One mistake about a woman as prominent as Reyburn being involved in murder will finish you off very neatly. If ever your head falls, every newspaperman within miles will carry it through the streets in a torchlight procession. Then, what'll I do? Buy a new fan and take all my clothes off in public, that's what."

Kerry chuckled. Descending, with the detectives eyeing him truculently, he strove to keep a grave face, but Eve sensed the glee effervescing within him. Her eyes suspected him all the way into the rear of the waiting police sedan. With the two headquarters men seated in front, he permitted himself a blissful grin.

Eve put a censorious hand upon his arm to ask quietly:

"Besides being a lunatic about anything that smells like news, what the hell's the matter with you?"

Kerry placed one arm snugly across her shoulders, brought his lips to her ear, kissed it, whispered in a tone so low the plainclothesmen could not hear: "I was never happier in my life. This Reyburn stuff was exclusive from the very first. It's going to keep on being strictly exclusive until it fades. Darling, I can't keep it from you any longer. I not only gave birth to Mrs. Beverly Reyburn and created a fascinating life for her—I murdered her."

"What?" Eve gasped.

It bubbled out of Kerry. "Honey, there's no such woman. She's purely a figment of my imagination. I made her up. I pulled her, and everything about her, out of this delicious New York monoxide. That's why she's all mine. Nobody else can get anything about her, because she exists only in here." He tapped his forehead, squirming with sheer elation. "Oh, God," he gasped, "It's priceless."

"Guy, you crazy fool, who—who else knows about this—this brainstorm?" Eve managed.

"Nobody," he exulted through her champagne hair. "Not another soul, except you now, darling. I didn't tell you sooner, because you were my credulity test. I thought if a born skeptic like you believed it, everybody else certainly would. And you did. Think of it, Eve. Newspapers howling out extras about a murder when there isn't anybody who could have been killed. The cops sniffing around after a murderer when there isn't one. It's the sweetest thing that ever happened. I did it because nothing sensational enough has been breaking. Now, look— fireworks, with Keyhole Kerry holding the fuse. Lord, how marvelous!"

EVE VANE'S eyes were full of wild alarm. This, she well knew, was pure Kerry. His creed was to get the news first, no matter how, and, if the world failed to supply him with electrifying flashes, he manufactured them. He developed this dangerous genius because his existence depended upon his nerve-wrecking necessity of consistently scooping the entire universe. At the moment, he was transported to the seventh heaven of a newshawk's delight, but Eve, her consternation rapidly reaching the bursting point, could only stare appalled.

"Everything, darling, about Mrs. Reyburn, is faked," Kerry quietly chortled. "I rented the suite at the Embassy Arms in her name. I ordered lots of you-just-know-she-wears-'ems sent there. I wrote her love letters, and sent her amorous telegrams, all signed with fictitious names. Tonight, I framed all the signs of murder that the cops are mulling over now. It'll keep 'em guessing so long, and it'll be played up in the headlines so much, I'll get a thousand swell flashes out of it. It's a masterpiece. Eve, honey, don't you think it's wonderful?"

"It's so wonderful and so crazy, I could make a grand flash, myself, by murdering you," she choked. "Guy, don't you realize what you've done? Suppose it comes out? If you aren't sent to Sing Sing for the rest of your life, you'll be lucky, and even then it'll be the end of Keyhole Kerry. There'll be lots of deliriously happy city editors in this country, once the truth prevails. Why, Guy, you—you're on your way to be grilled right now." In sheer dismay, she flung her arms around him.

Wary that the two detectives should not overhear, he reassured ecstatically: "But I worked it so it can't be connected with me, honey. I arranged everything by remote control. I rented the apartment over the phone, had the bags sent by taxi, ordered the clothes through a shopping service and paid for them by messenger, in cash. Nobody's seen me near the place. There isn't any tie-up. I was never sitting prettier in my life. Don't worry, Eve—just stand by and enjoy the show."

"What I'll watch will turn out to be your funeral," Eve returned in despair. "When I realize that I let myself fall in love with a lunatic like you, I suspect I'm not quite bright."

The police sedan was swerving into the car entrance of the Embassy Arms. Alighting, with Eve's cold hand clutching his,

Kerry noted that patrolmen were stationed in the archways, restraining a curious crowd on the sidewalks while others were patrolling the court, that excited guests were grouped in speculative conversation, that the atmosphere was explosively charged. The two detectives promptly escorted Kerry and his secretary to the entrance through which he had so unobtrusively come and gone, earlier in the evening. The way opened before them with ominous dispatch.

Reporters were clogging the hallway. They eyed Kerry poisonously. He repaid them with an exuberant grin. Uniformed men were posted at the door lettered *M,* and at another directly opposite. Behind the first door, tense activity bustled, voices spoke authoritatively. The gruff tone dominating the room was, Kerry knew, that of Police Commissioner Endicott. Immediately, word of his arrival was passed in, and Kerry was dourly invited to enter.

Just inside, he froze. The homicide squad was engaged in the delicate routine of photographing the scene, developing fingerprints, hunting clues, but this Kerry scarcely saw. He instantly became totally unaware of the massive hulk of the commissioner at his side. With his expression distinguishing him as the most dumbfounded man in the suite, he gazed, transfixed.

A woman's figure huddled on the floor.

She was bunched partly on the fur throw-rug which Kerry had stained with his own blood. Under her twisted neck, another dark blot shone wetly. Her head, adorned with a hat that looked Russian, was wrenched over her hunched left shoulder so that Kerry could not see her face. She was voluptuously plump, tailored in a black suit, utterly inert. A dainty automatic, with mother-of-pearl butt-plates, lay glittering near her crimson-nailed fingers—fingers that were obviously lifeless.

CHAPTER THREE

KEYHOLE KERRY—KILLER

FOR **A** long moment, the female corpse was a nightmare image in Kerry's rounded eyes. With the reality of her dead presence forcing itself upon him, he dazedly looked about. A rubber-gloved detective was gathering together the fake love messages which Kerry had signed with a variety of romantic male names. Another detective was gingerly collecting the charred flakes in the fireplace. A third one was tweezering the stub of the imported cigarette into a test-tube. Everything here was, beyond all doubt, the murder scene Kerry had staged— except for the astounding detail of the dead woman.

A console radio in the corner was reproducing a variety program spotted to follow Kerry's own. The police had, he surmised, started it going immediately upon their arrival. Through it, they had certainly heard the exclusive revelations which Kerry now fervently wished he had never made.

A dapperly tuxedoed man at Commissioner Endicott's other arm suddenly broke into distressed speech. Kerry recognized him as Lucius Milbank, manager of the Embassy Arms. Usually, Milbank, whose duties included the welcoming of world notables, was charmingly suave, but now his round face was hotly beaded, his perfectly kept hands were fluttering frantic gestures. Endicott had been pointedly questioning him, when Kerry's entrance interrupted.

"Yes, I assigned this suite to her," blurted Milbank. "Yes, my guests are my responsibility. But I never saw Mrs. Reyburn. None of my employees has ever seen her. Desk clerks, bellboys, maids—no, none of them. She kept to herself more than Garbo. The mistress of a king—why not? It is perfectly understandable. That's why I tell you I cannot identify this dead woman as Mrs. Reyburn—I cannot."

"All right, all right," Endicott growled. "Go into that other suite across the hall, and stay there. I'm coming back to you."

Milbank shrugged despair, turned to comply. His blue gaze flickered reprovingly at Kerry. "Good God," he moaned. "When you announced Mrs. Reyburn was coming to New York, I was so anxious to have her as my guest. Why did I ever write to you to invite her to stop here? Look what has happened—murder."

"Not suicide?" Kerry asked huskily.

"Murder," Commissioner Endicott affirmed it, staring banefully at Kerry. As Milbank shouldered out, with the reporters clamoring around him, the commissioner impaled Kerry with a sober forefinger. "You know I have a stenographic record made of every word you broadcast. You're going to explain tonight's performance, mistakes and all, 'The woman's corpse has vanished,' you said. Well, has it? What made you think it had? 'I believe it's highly unlikely the body will ever be found.' Does it look like it's been secretly transported and concealed anywhere, as you announced? Either you know less about this than you claim, Kerry—in which case I'm delighted to see that you're slipping—or you know more about it than you pretend and are up to something you'll damn well regret."

"Take your choice," Kerry retorted noncommittally.

"Where did you get your stuff about this killing?" Endicott persisted. "How could you know so much about what happened here? Whoever tipped you off has guilty knowledge and a hell of a lot of it. I want that person's name and address, right here and now, Kerry. Come out with it."

Kerry's swallowing mechanism stalled. "You're wasting your time. I never reveal my sources," he challenged. He was intensely gratified now that he had never violated this principle. Though he worked at fever heat, he always double-checked the authenticity of each item before broadcasting it. As important to him as getting the news first was getting it right. From the beginning, he had protected his informants with consistent loyalty, though at times he had been placed under alarming official pressure. Tonight, he felt coldly, he was facing the supreme test of his adherence to his code, with failure certain to mean his complete collapse.

"Where," Commissioner Endicott demanded powerfully, "did you get your inside information?"

It was a question which every newspaper publisher in the country would have liked answered. Kerry's swift technique made their fastest extras seem dusty stuff, by the time the still-wet editions reached the streets. His instantaneous flashes gave the *Parade of Time* program the stale flavor of last year's almanac. Other news commentators sounded like white-bearded porch gossips compared with Kerry. All his frustrated rivals, baffled by his method, sought the secret that made him unbeatable.

KERRY was not, as the uninitiated believed, the mastermind of a far-reaching and insidious espionage system. Though his personal payroll did maintain a few spies at tactical points, the truth was that most of Kerry's scoops were thrust upon him. He was telephoned at all weird hours of the night by persons eager for the national publicity he could give them. He was constantly being buttonholed, on the streets and on his nocturnal rounds of the city's hot-spots, by those who were proud to demonstrate that they were wise guys in the know. The local banditti, respecting him for making an enviable clean-up, in what seemed to them a new racket, supplied him with some of his choicest flashes. Kerry's own investigations were constant and intense, but, besides his personal discoveries, he was literally showered with priceless inside information. This fact, however, he sagaciously never divulged.

He now evaded the commissioner's demand with, "You should know, from past experience, that you can't bully me. I've already told the whole nation everything I've learned, except where I learned it. I'm keeping that strictly to myself. What's more, Commissioner, if you try third-degreeing me, I'll broadcast it, blow by blow."

"I'll handle that point later," Endicott bridled. "There's a murdered woman. I want to know exactly who she is. Take a good look at her. Tell me whether she is, or is not, Mrs. Beverly Reyburn. Tell me, I said, Kerry. If you hold out on me until you can spill it to your radio audience first, it'll be the sorriest mistake you ever made."

The commissioner's edged threat chilled Kerry. He stepped toward the plump, dead body. The homicide squad, having photographically registered its exact position and surroundings, were removing the little automatic and rolling the stained fur rug. Kerry moved deliberately, listening while two of the detectives reported to Endicott.

"There're three bullets in her," the first said. "Here're five cartridges left in the clip. Of course there's no way of telling whether the clip was full before the shooting started, but, if it was, that leaves two bullets unaccounted for. I've just checked the serial number with headquarters, by telephone. The gun's not registered in New York."

"There's no purse, Commissioner," the second said. "There she is, dressed as though she'd just come in from the street—hat on, and all—but her purse isn't here. That's funny—no purse."

Kerry stooped over the lifeless figure. He had to kneel and almost touch his chin to the rug in order to see her waxen face. It was full-cheeked, vividly made up. The lips were sensuous and petulant, the eyes closed, the natural line of the brows strong yet arrogant. These were features which Keyhole Kerry had never before seen. He had not the remotest notion as to whose this corpse might be. But, realizing that the revelation of her identity would give him a stop-program flash, Mrs. Reyburn or no Mrs. Reyburn, he kept his position, thinking fast.

The woman's left hand was curled under her stubborn chin. The sharp bend of her wrist was partly covered by her coat, but on it Kerry caught the glitter of a diamond-set wrist-watch. Its black-cord band, he noted quickly, was frayed. Immediately, he decided upon a stratagem which meant risking dire consequences for removing evidence. He hunched nearer the dead face, pretending to desire a closer scrutiny, covertly insinuating his fingers into the black circle. His pull snapped the worn cord. Having deftly transferred the watch to his vest pocket, he straightened.

Endicott, glowering at him in a way that apprehensively speeded his pulse, inquired: "Is that Mrs. Reyburn, or isn't it?"

"I can't say," Kerry answered with complete truthfulness. "You see, I've never seen Mrs. Reyburn."

The commissioner's scowl darkened. He began, with menacing finger, "If you're trying to put one over on me, Kerry—"but the hallway door opened. A detective entered, gingerly holding a wadded bit of linen by one corner. It was a lady's dainty handkerchief discolored with blood. Immediately, another member of the homicide squad gaped an envelope to receive it.

"Step across the hall, Kerry, and wait there," Endicott gestured commandingly, before the plainsclothesman could report. "You're not out of this yet, by a long shot. In fact, I hope you never come out of it. And you can depend on one thing. Whatever breaks come in this case, the bad boy of the wavelengths is going to get the news—last."

That filled Kerry with sharper misgivings than any other phase of his perilous predicament but, edging to the door, he opened his ears to promising information.

"Found this handkerchief," the detective who had just entered reported to the commissioner. "It was outside the entrance off the edge of the walk. No monogram, but it might belong to the dead woman—might help identify her."

KERRY caught those last words, as the door was thrust shut behind him. While hostile reporters eyed him through a haze of cigarette smoke, he remembered his encounter in the court with the hysterical woman who had immediately vanished into the street. The bloody handkerchief had been found at the spot where she had collided with Kerry. He surmised that she, and not the murder victim, had lost it. Mystified, he stepped into the rooms opposite Suite M.

Lucius Milbank was agitatedly pacing. He stopped stiffly, stared at Kerry, dabbed silk at his beaded forehead, paced again. The second man in the room was heavy-set, with eagle-sharp eyes under a bulging brow. He was, Kerry knew, Christy Leach, ace reporter for the *Intelligencer.*

Leach's calculating gaze expressed more than enmity for Kerry. Because Kerry had served a cyclonic apprenticeship in the *Intelligencer's* city-room, Leach, like all other members of the staff, considered Kerry had become a traitor to the Fourth Estate. However, it was, a new, enigmatic quality in his scrutiny that now brought Kerry apprehension. Kerry turned thoughtfully from him, at a tug on his arm by Eve Vane, who had been nervously waiting here since his entrance into the murder room.

"Guy, are you sure you've told me everything—*everything?*" she asked him, her voice wretchedly husky.

Had he, she meant, omitted to confess that he had filled out the crime picture by actually supplying it with a human corpse? Kerry was too nettled to protest the implication.

"I'm in one sweet spot," he told her. "I announced to the entire United States that the victim had vanished, but she most certainly is present. How I'm ever going to justify that piece of misinformation is beyond me at the moment, but, somehow, I've got to do it or I'm sunk. Endicott's boycotting me. What's worse, he might hold me for questioning at headquarters long enough to give every sheet in town the chance to crow over scooping the scalp specialist. Eve, we've got to beat the world with finding out who that dead woman is. I have something—"

"If they throw you into prison, it'll be just dandy with you, so long as you can broadcast the event," Eve wailed. "Oh, Guy, darling—"

"Sorry to interrupt." It was Christy Leach, making an ominous advance. "Kerry, you're tops as a news man. Well, I have news

for you. You won't want to put it on the air, though—not this."
Leach's level gaze was threatening. "Here it is. For weeks now,
Kerry, I've been shadowing you, watching every single move
you've made, day and night." He repeated it significantly:
"Every—single—move."

Eve Vane gasped. An icy dart shot into Kerry's heart, but he
took it without wincing. Instead, he contrived an innocent smile.
"In that case," he observed, "you haven't had your accustomed
sleep."

Leach continued in a low tone which the distressed Lucius
Milbank could not overhear. "I followed you to this place tonight,
Kerry. I saw you go into those rooms across the hall. I saw you
come out. I'd already watched you make other visits on other
nights. I can testify as an eyewitness that your actions have been
damned suspicious. Couple that with your exclusive radio flashes
tonight, and it gets big. I haven't spilled this to Endicott. I felt,
perhaps, you'd rather he didn't know about it."

Kerry was maintaining a calm exterior, with the greatest of
difficulty. "That's very thoughtful of you, I'm sure," he remarked.
"Considering I flatly deny the whole thing."

Leach smiled with sardonic tolerance. "I haven't spilled it to
Endicott," he continued evenly, "because my business also is
news. I, too, my friend, like scoops. So, instead, just a little while
ago, I phoned the complete story to the chief, citing times and
places. It's being shaped up now for an eight-column head. It'll
be in large, black type, and going out over the wires, pretty
damned quick—as soon as I say the word. The chief is waiting
for me to call him back. He wants me to tell him you don't want
him to print it."

Eve Vane's face had gone deathly white. Sparks were jumping
along Kerry's nerves.

"Special orders from the chief gave me the job of trailing
you, Kerry," Leach went on. "He doesn't like the day you're
making his high-priced columnists read like selections from
the *Britannica*. He's curious about just where you find your

inside information. Frankly, his feelings on the subject of Keyhole Kerry are so violent he's ready to buy up the entire *De-Luxe-Lax* Company, in order to bounce you off the air. That won't be necessary, as matters stand. He has a far better idea."

Leach's chief was a man of enormous power and incredible wealth, the fearless publisher of the greatest string of dailies in the country.

"He authorized me, a moment ago, to make you a business proposition," the reporter added. "Briefly, it's to break your radio contract, then sign a new one with him for an exclusive piece every day, for which you will be paid twice the money you're now getting. Sounds very inviting, doesn't it, Kerry? Of course, we'd never publish a story about a member of our own staff, incriminating him in murder, if we believed him innocent. But, about the chief's deadliest competitor—that's different."

Kerry's fists clenched. "Leach, you're a rat," he said. "I don't belong in an antiquated news organization where I'd probably have to wait a whole hour before my stuff found its way out of the pressroom. You can't buy me, and you can't bluff me. Just press the point, if you'd like to supply me with a new exclusive flash on the air, because I'll be delighted to inform the forty-eight states that I've just broken your neck."

LEACH, a saturnine smile on his face, made a move that galvanized Kerry. He reached for the telephone. Instantly, Kerry stepped forward, gripped his arm, in a crackling tone informed him: "This one's mine. The one in the next room is yours." His heave against Leach stumbled the reporter across the sill of the connecting door. His second jounce spilled Leach blasphemously over a chair. While Leach sprawled, Kerry snatched up the instrument from the bedside table, wrenched back, ripped the cord from the box. Before the reporter could find himself, he was bounding from the room. He slapped the door shut, twisted the bolt.

"Guy, does he mean it?" Eve Vane exclaimed, aghast.

"We'll soon know," he assured her breathlessly. He took up

the desk telephone, while Lucius Milbank inarticulately gestured at him.

Leach began knuckling the panel, howling, "Damn you, open that damn door."

Kerry remembered that, in these air-conditioned suites, the windows could not be opened, and found grim satisfaction in the fact that Leach was, therefore, a prisoner. Eve bit her luscious lips, as Kerry demanded his special number from the hotel operator. Immediately, he directed: "Put me on."

Five seconds after he was signaled, "It's all yours," his voice went off like a string of firecrackers.

"Attention, Mr. and Mrs. America. Keyhole Kerry, your headline racer, is again first under the wire. Flash. Attempts are being made, at this moment, by a certain New York newspaper, to implicate your correspondent in the amazing Reyburn murder case. I pledge you that I will explode this vindictive piece of shady journalism, ladies and gentlemen, and I assure you my connection with the Reyburn affair is solely that of the newsbuster who always gives you the hottest breaks first." Here, realizing that this statement would forever destroy his huge audience's faith in him, if an inkling of the truth should be established, he drew a deep breath.

"Flash," he barked again. "The New York police, who are at this moment investigating the scene of the crime, are completely baffled as to the identity of the murdered woman who lies not twenty feet from this spot, but again your radio oracle is able to impart to them a vital piece of information. The fate of the celebrated Mrs. Beverly Reyburn is still a dark mystery, Mr. and Mrs. America, but it is an absolute certainty the slain body found in her rooms is *not* hers."

Kerry had been itching with fiery impatience to shoot that startling revelation into multitudinous tingling ears. In his exuberance, he could think of nothing but the whirlwind of sensational speculation he was stirring up. No longer aware of the wrathful pounding on the connecting door, or of Lucius Milbank's suffering, he resumed.

"The name of the murder victim is still unknown. I am hot on the trail of that salient detail. Keep your radios tuned to Keyhole Kerry's waveband, so that you and you and you will be the first to hear the dead woman's identity revealed. Your news-clairvoyant of the kilocycles is now signing off, to come back soon with white-hot information that will make tomorrow morning's headlines look like last summer's circus posters."

Kerry was almost jumping up and down, when he swung around to the jittery Eve Vane. He maneuvered her into the far corner, back turned to Lucius Milbank's miserable stare.

Cautiously sliding his hand into the pocket which concealed the watch he had purloined from the corpse, he whispered: "We've got to learn who that female cadaver is. The Missing Persons Bureau must be checking up now. The cops will start tracing the labels on her clothes right away. They may identify her pretty fast, but we've got to do it faster. That's a flash I absolutely must have first, Eve. Here, take this watch and for God's sake keep it dark. Use long distance to connect with somebody in the plant that made it, and insist—"

Kerry got no further than that before the hallway door exploded. Its violent opening caught him with the wrist-watch scarcely out of its hiding-place. He had no opportunity to pass it to Eve, could only slide it deeper. His hand closed hotly on it, as he turned to confront the belligerent Commissioner Endicott. Kerry did not need to be told that the commissioner had heard his latest flash over the radio still playing in the death room.

Endicott was seething with choler. "I warned you," he thundered. "I warned you, but you held out on me. No more of that. You're coming to headquarters. You're going to talk plenty. When I get through with you, you won't know the difference between a microphone and a brass spittoon." His huge hand clawed crushingly on Kerry's arm. "We start right now."

CHAPTER FOUR

ORDEAL BY HEADLINES

THE HAGGARD, blue-jowled, exhausted young man, who dragged into the littered, file-crowded office high in the Universal Broadcasting spire, was not the aboundingly elated Keyhole Kerry of the earlier hours of that same night. He had been severely used. He wavered to his desk chair, sagged into it with a profound sigh, gazed ruefully at the almost equally worn Eve Vane.

She had been waiting in Kerry's lofty retreat, since returning to it immediately after Endicott had blustered him into a waiting police machine. Her lips were swollen with toothmarks, her turquoise eyes were teary, her handkerchief was twisted to shreds. A sob broke from her throat, as she surveyed the forlorn figure in the chair.

"I can't stand it," she wailed abruptly. "I can't stand any more of this. I'm going back to a peaceful, respectable life with my bubbles and fans. Tell me the worst, Guy. What did they get out of you?"

"Nothing, thank God," Kerry answered. "They didn't dare manhandle me because they knew I'd tell the whole world about it, down to the last whack of the rubber pipe, if they did. But they shouted me into this condition. I took it, because admitting the truth would have been worse. They're not finished with me yet. They'll crack down again, if they can catch me off guard. But, praise Heaven, they didn't search me."

Kerry wearily pulled from his pocket the jeweled wrist-watch which had weighed on his person heavily all during his grilling. He put it into Eve's unsteady hand, directing: "That belongs to the dead woman. Headquarters hasn't learned who she is yet, or it would be out by now. It's our only chance to beat the papers. Get busy on long distance, Eve."

Her cold fingers, their nails bitten short, moved to the telephone.

"Get the factory that made the watch. If nobody answers, try to reach one of its executives at home. Maybe we won't be able to connect until the plant opens, but don't give up. That's a valuable, guaranteed timepiece. Even if the guarantee has expired, there'll be a record of the serial number." Kerry was prying open the white-gold case with his penknife. "That'll tell to what store it was shipped. The store will have a record of to whom it was sold. I hope that woman bought it herself. If it was a gift, it'll mean more digging, and we'll have to dig fast."

Eve was already talking. Kerry sat in troubled thought until, waiting for the connections to go through, she looked up to ask: "But how could it have happened, Guy? Where did the body come from? You strewed a lot of fake clues about, and a real murdered woman pops up right in the middle of 'em. How is it possible?"

"It's possible, on only one assumption," Kerry answered, beginning to revive. "Somebody took advantage of the stage I had all set. Somebody, with murder in his heart, deliberately put that corpse there, in an attempt to shield himself. Either that person had been planning a long time to kill that woman, and seized upon my set-up as a chance to do it, or the thing broke at precisely the right time to provide the way out of a *crime passionel.*"

"You mean you're in this awful mess through sheer accident?"

"If this is coincidence," Kerry philosophized morbidly, "the answer is that every hour of every life, and every death as well, is influenced, if not absolutely determined, by circumstances in a constant state of ferment, which inevitably gets mixed up. We can't get away from the fact that it happened. I salve my repentant soul with the thought that the murder would have been committed anyway, even if I hadn't all unwittingly made it easier. I provided the setting, without dreaming how it might be used, because I felt sure nobody else knew it was there. But no, it wasn't by any means pure accident. The guilty person had to know, ahead of time, exactly what I was up to—had to know I was fabricating Mrs. Reyburn."

"That wouldn't be a hard conclusion to reach by anyone who'd been watching you," Eve pointed out with marked disapproval, still waiting at the phone. "This isn't the first time you've brewed your own news. Plenty of your rivals suspect it, if they're not perfectly certain of it. Guy, darling, I don't care about cracking any case, no matter how many beats it might give you. But I don't want anybody ever to find out what you've done."

"If the truth comes out, Kerry is no more. We can't let it." He sat up. "Leach, he had me spotted. He had the chance. He's out to get me. What better way of finishing me off—" Kerry steadied himself, gazing alertly into his secretary's lighted eyes. "Wait a minute. Jumping at conclusions is dangerous. I'm going after Leach, but there are other angles." His voice faded into pointed meditation.

EVE ANNOUNCED from the telephone, a moment later: "The watch factory doesn't answer. The operator's trying to connect with the manager's home." She held the wire tenaciously as Kerry thought aloud.

"Just when I was going into the Embassy Arms to plant the fake clues, a hysterical woman bumped into me," he muttered. "She couldn't have come from the Reyburn suite. She must have come from another in the same part of the hotel. She dropped a bloody handkerchief. It seems to connect her with the murder. Maybe the murder had already been committed then, but she couldn't have had anything to do with putting the body in the Reyburn apartment. A third person was involved, and did that. That woman must know something. We've got to find her."

"That's a flash," Eve exclaimed.

"Not yet," Kerry cautioned. "I'm still determined to get the breaks in this case first, but I'm damned if I'll give Endicott a chance to crowd me out. He'll do it, if I air the hysterical woman too soon. He can use a whole army of cops to hunt for her and get the papers to help him. Then, when they find her, they'll leave me in the dark. Announcing her now would be giving them a chance to beat me. I got scarcely a glance at her, Eve—I don't know where she went or anything else about her—but we've got to locate that hysterical woman."

Now Kerry was galvanically charged. Eve remarked that he already had one potentially hysterical female on his hands, but he didn't hear. He jumped up, the old zealous gleam in his eye.

"Nobody else even knows she exists— she's all mine. She's better than learning who the dead woman is, because she's alive and can talk. If she's connected with the murder, at all, she's dynamite that can blow it wide open. I'll put her on the air, and get her to tell the inside story to the whole country. It'll lick the police, all the papers, every—"

"And, incidentally, if she knows you were framing a fake murder, it'll be a neat way of Kerry's committing suicide," Eve reminded him wretchedly.

As the ominous possibility dawned on Kerry, banishing his elated grin, the office door swung wide. Smitty ran in. Smitty was a tousle-headed, simian-nosed, freckle-bespattered young-ster of indeterminate age who tirelessly served as Kerry's leg-man. Once a copy boy in the city-room of the *Herald,* he had collected succulent morsels of gossip which that dignified publication had not deigned to print, and had deliberately served them piping hot to the avowed foe of the reporters from whom he had picked them up. Soon he had employed himself to Kerry as field scout, with huge ears unfurled for all varieties of scandal. If Smitty had any fuller name, no one had ever thought to inquire about it, but, unmindful that he was largely ignored, he had a way of popping up suddenly with something startling. This time it was a copy of a special edition of the *Intelligencer,* the front page of which was blazoned with glaring billboard headlines.

Smitty blurted, spreading the paper so Kerry could not miss a single giant letter: "It just hit the street. It's selling like wild-cakes." He meant either hot-cakes or wildfire, but neither Kerry nor Eve at that moment cared which. "Boss, you'd better, head for the tall timber," he warned.

The newspaper read—

KERRY SEEN IN REYBURN SUITE
AT TIME OF MURDER

EYEWITNESS REVEALS RADIO STAR'S SUSPICIOUS CONNECTION WITH CRIME HE FLASHED TO NATION.

Police Commissioner Endicott will be enlightened by reading the following detailed eyewitness account of the mysterious movements of Guy "Keyhole" Kerry—

"Leach meant it," Kerry gasped. "He's made his threat good. They're determined to yank me off the air, even if they have to send me to the chair to do it. Leach kept his stuff dark until it could hit me hardest. That means Endicott's just getting it. He probably has a fleet of prowl-cars closing in on me now. If he collars me this time, he'll never let me go. Smitty, you dropped an excellent hint. The tall timber is my destination."

Smitty mouthed, "Gosh, boss!" Eve stood rooted, her telephone forgotten, her eyes turquoise despair. Kerry's heels beat to the door.

"Stay here on call, Smitty. Eve, follow up that watch for everything it's worth. I'll phone you later. If I don't ring by nine o'clock it'll be because I'm behind the bars—permanently." He paused tightly on the sill. "What gripes me most is that I let Leach publicly slit my throat instead of doing it myself."

With Eve wailing, with Smitty gulping, with ten thousand policemen presenting the threat of an abrupt termination of his flight, Kerry bolted.

CHAPTER FIVE

A CORPSE TO CHRISTEN

K **ERRY FOUND** vast comfort this morning in the fact that his face was not one millionth as familiar to the world at large as his voice. His grimy beard, plus the deep lines graven by his hours of eluding police scrutiny, and a pair of pawnshop eyeglasses, afforded him an effective disguise. Perched on the rearmost stool of a greasy Third Avenue eatery, he intently scanned the latest edition of the *Intelligencer.*

Keyhole Kerry's name led all the rest. Six-inch type condemned him. The statement under Christy Leach's byline was appallingly complete. It left no doubt that Leach had actually observed Kerry's every suspicious movement, upon which he had not hesitated to put the most damaging construction. The circumstantial evidence was so overwhelmingly incriminating that Kerry was almost ready to confess to the murder over the air in order to be the first to announce his doom.

He studied the sparse facts in the murder case, dismissing, with a glance, the paragraph saying that attempts to elicit a comment from the *ateliér* of the fanciful Mrs. Reyburn's royal lover had been of no avail. The identity of the victim was still unestablished. No one of her description had been reported missing in New York. Her clothing disclosed that she had traveled frequently, for her suit bore a Chicago label, her hat one from Philadelphia, her shoes the imprint of a Washington retailer and her gloves the stamp of a Bermuda shop—all of which made tracing her exceedingly difficult. Her name might have been discovered more easily, it was pointed out, but for the strange absence of that essential item in a woman's street attire—her purse.

The three bullets removed from the body, police tests proved, had been fired from the small automatic found by her dead hand. It was a dead-end clue. The investigators were puzzled by the bloodstains. Analysis had revealed three different types. The victim's was not the same as that on the lady's handkerchief found in the court, and both of these differed from that on the chair and the fur rug. Kerry, knowing that an experiment, once he was captured, could definitely show that the third blood-type was his own, shuddered with apprehension.

He found no hint anywhere of a hysterical woman having fled the murder scene. His search of the entire paper disclosed no item which might be she. He returned to the matter of the missing purse. He speculated upon it. Presently, he inserted himself into the telephone booth, dialed his office number. When Eve Vane answered, he began impatiently: "Have you—"

"Not yet, but almost," she reported wearily. "A few minutes ago, I connected with the watch factory. Their record says they sold the watch to Blackwell's, a jeweler in Chicago. I've just had Blackwell on the wire. In his little book, that serial number is entered opposite the name of Clyde Smythe. *He's* not the dead woman, Guy. He must have given her that watch as a present. At the moment, he's neither at his home nor at his brokerage office. As soon as I reach him, we'll have it."

"Keep after that man," Kerry urged fervently. "Make him talk. In the meantime, I'm going to stick my neck out by following down another lead—the missing purse. It means something important. The victim must have had her purse with her, when she went into the hotel. What became of it? Did the murderer carry it away? Why would he have done that? I can't think of a good reason. The most logical answer is that the woman simply put it down somewhere. Therefore, she wasn't killed in Suite M."

"I can't gasp, because I thought we already knew that," Eve returned.

"But, listen," Kerry insisted. "She went into the hotel with her purse—into some other suite in that same part of the building. She put the purse down. It's reasonable to infer she was killed in the same apartment. The murderer then carried her body from it into Suite M. The bag remained on the scene of the crime. By this time, the guilty person has probably had a hundred chances to get rid of it, but maybe he hasn't done it, and, even if he has, maybe there's some trace of it left. What's more important, there must be some mark of the crime there—perhaps bloodstains. I'm going to look for the room where that murder happened."

"Very good, Guy," Eve commented hopelessly. "I'll see you in jail."

KERRY sidled from the booth, strode from the restaurant. Four long blocks of blowing his nose, in order to mask his face with his handkerchief, brought him to the huge Embassy Arms. He circled it, ventured through the car arch. His nervous purposefullness carried him unchallenged through the entrance leading to the Reyburn rooms. Poised to break into a sprint, he saw with profound relief that the hallway was empty. He trod along it, ears sharp.

Movements rustled inside M. The radio was playing. Kerry surmised several headquarters men were posted inside. He went on, noting six other lettered doors. A stairway at the rear led upward, making even more suites possible as the scene of the murder. Desirous of a chance to observe comings and goings, Kerry sought shelter. Gratification filled him when he found that the rooms, opposite M, had been left unlocked in the confusion. About to slip in, he caught a muted voice.

"O.K., chief," it said.

Kerry electrically tightened. The words had not been spoken inside the door he was about to open. They had come from across the hall. Kerry stepped to M, heard the same sounds. Then it came again: "O.K., chief." At once, Kerry shifted alertly to the next door. He heard a telephone being cradled. With new heat seeping along his nerves, he paused, then, abruptly, rapped at the door lettered N.

At once, he bounded across the hall. One second later, he

was standing tightly behind the door directly opposite M, gazing through a thread-thin crack at the entrance of the suite directly behind it. He saw the knob turn. A face looked out. It was Christy Leach's. Leach's aquiline eyes fearfully examined the emptiness. He drew back. His latch clicked. Now, Kerry's nerves were red-hot wires.

He spun to the desk telephone. Of the hotel operator, he demanded connection with Lucius Milbank. The girl informed him that Mr. Milbank had not yet come to his office. "Then connect me with his apartment," Kerry insisted.

Immediately, he heard the purr of a bell. Milbank's voice followed quickly. "Yes? Yes?"

Kerry spoke quietly, stating his name. "Don't worry about more unfavorable publicity. I'm going to be out of here soon. You don't want any big headlines shouting that Kerry was arrested in the Embassy Arms, and I certainly don't either, so keep this under your hat and answer questions. Just how much access has Christy Leach to Suite N, and how long has he had it?"

Milbank's hard breathing soughed over the line. "Leach? Suite N? There's no connection. Suite N was assigned about ten days ago to a Mr. Frank Fisher. I was informed of it particularly because he brought in only one suitcase, and was asked to pay in advance. He did. I was told, too, he'd demanded that suite and no other. What's this mean, Kerry? Is there something suspicious about him?"

"Maybe," Kerry evaded. "Listen, Milbank. I want a list of every guest in every apartment in this section of the building. You want to get this thing out of the papers as fast as I do, so it'll be to your advantage to give me that dope. I'll call back later."

Kerry broke the connection, eased back to the door. Again he noted that the room in which he had heard Leach speak was closest of all to the spot where the unknown female corpse had been found. He crossed to N, lips tight. He knocked, heard quick strides answering.

Again, the face of Christy Leach appeared. Leach stiffened, eyes narrowing.

Kerry promptly put his foot over the sill, said wryly: "Good morning, Mr. Fisher."

LEACH started out. Kerry pushed him back. Leach retreated before Kerry's dogged advance. Closing the door behind him, Kerry took in details. Ash-trays were overflowing. A bed in the next room was rumpled. A pair of gaudy pajamas draped a chair. The closet in the bedroom was standing wide, disclosing only one suit hanging. It was obvious that the occupant of this suite had established only the slightest temporary residence. Leach was beginning to smile shakily.

"Have you had any woman visitors, Mr. Fisher?" Kerry asked incisively.

"Don't get smart," Leach defied him.

"This isn't very smart," Kerry countered. "You shouldn't have come back here after last night. You should have faded, because the hotel doesn't know who you really are. Now, the whole world's going to find out, by radio. Mind if I look around?"

"Go as far as you like," Leach assented sardonically, "but it won't be far. You haven't forgotten, have you, Kerry, that the cops are looking for you? The *Intelligencer's* going to break a big story by turning you in."

"Touch that telephone, and I'll beat you to a pulp," Kerry threatened, his eyes glinting. "At least I'll try it. I might not succeed, in which case, when I do my talking to Endicott, I'll enlighten him about your having this place. It's the handiest possible for transferring a dead body into M. That'll interest the commissioner, don't you think?"

"I don't scare easily, Kerry."

Kerry was warily moving about the room, tight-muscled to balk Leach's reach for the telephone if it should come. He looked for spots on the rug, which might be washed-out blood-stains, but he found none. The bullet-pierced woman, he reasoned, might have bled onto something which Leach could have since removed. He looked into the drawers of the desk and the dresser, found stationery and a clean shirt, no purse. Hoping less to find evidence than to taunt Leach, he prolonged the search.

The tightening silence ended when Kerry observed: "That's exactly what happened, of course, Leach. The woman was carried into M, from the room where she was killed, between the time I made my first flash about Mrs. Reyburn, and the time the police arrived. You've already told the whole populace you saw me come and go. You were watching in here, while I was in M. Opportunity is a very important factor in building up a murder charge. You had it."

Leach's big shoulders were pugnaciously hunching. "You can't cover yourself by trying to incriminate me, Kerry. I told you I started shadowing you two weeks ago. You slipped in and out of here so often I knew you were up to something. My chief ordered me to rent this apartment so I could find out what you were doing. This Reyburn stuff of yours was getting under his skin. My job was to keep you spotted and to try to get the inside track on her away from you. That explains it, and you can't make anything else of it."

"One essential of this murder is that the murderer had to know exactly what you found out," Kerry pointed out grimly. He stepped to the door. "Call down the hounds of the law on me now, if you choose to, my friend. When I tell my story, backing it up with plenty of details you don't know about yet, you'll be in a worse spot than your favorite enemy. If you think that's a bluff, just pass your tip on to the commissioner." He opened the way, fixing Leach with a condemning stare while Leach's bulging brow beetled furiously. "How did you get rid of the purse?" he asked abruptly.

Leach started.

KERRY, having asked the pointed question, solely for the sake of its effect, elatedly slid out. Swift strides carried him into the nearest drug store. Wedged into a telephone booth, he flamed with impatience to blast Leach with his damning discovery, but he realized that publicizing it now would rob him of the hotter breaks that were sure to follow. Shrewdly, instead of calling his special number for the flash, he dialed Eve.

"Have you—" he began.

"Got it," she exclaimed. "Yes, just now I connected with Smythe in Chicago. I promised to keep his name out of it, and he talked. Two years ago, he gave the watch to a woman answering the corpse's description. He hasn't seen her in the last eighteen months. He spoke of her in a strange way that made me think he regretted having had an affair with her. Her name, darling, is Rhoda Donnell."

"God, I want to flash that," Kerry burst out. "But I can't—not yet."

"Rhoda Donnell, Smythe told me, comes of a moneyed Chicago family, but she's always been on the loose," Eve went on. "When she's in New York she takes an apartment alone. I got her address simply by calling information. It's on West Fifty-Fifth. The number—"

Kerry registered it, but, at that moment, a sound from the next booth warned caution upon him. He heard someone enter the cubicle, but did not hear the dial spin. Warily, he lowered his tone. "We're going there right away, to look it over," he told Eve. "Make sure no cops are on your trail, and wait for me outside. I'm on my way." Then, nerves tingling, he folded the door. Easing out, he peered into the adjacent hut.

"Leach, you rat," he rasped. "Come out of there."

Leach's finger was holed into the disk. He sneered at Kerry through the pane. "I'm pretty damned good at shadowing you," his voice came out. "So you've got a new break, have you, Kerry? Well, I'll take my chances with the cops just to keep you from following it up." He twirled off a number.

With alarm raging in him, Kerry slammed at Leach with a violence that jarred the reporter back. He grabbed an arm, heaved to drag Leach from the phone. Leach twisted, angrily fastened his hands upon Kerry's forearms. His right clamped hard over Kerry's self-inflicted cut. Kerry howled: "Ow-oo!" He attempted to pull away, but Leach's grip grew even tighter. A fierce, amber gleam sprang into the reporter's eyes. Suddenly, he spun, stretching Kerry's arm, catching it under his, yanking the sleeve upward.

He saw the bloody bandage.

Kerry was unaware that the encounter was dismaying the pharmacists and the counterman. Numbly, he staggered, as Leach jumped back into the booth. The reporter rattled the door shut, braced it there with both feet. Kerry knew instantly that nothing short of homicide could prevent Leach's smearing the damning fact of the wound into headlines.

Leach was barking, "Give me the chief," when Kerry dove into the next cubicle. Kerry whirled his special number off the dial. The answer had scarcely come before he demanded: "Give it to me, quick." He heard Leach's voice rushing, before "Take it away," came.

"Special attention, Mr. and Mrs. United States. Keyhole Kerry will not be scooped. I can bring you now the most amazing of all the flashes you have yet heard in the startling Reyburn murder case. It concerns the bloodstains found on the chair and the small rug where the dead woman's body was discovered. The commissioner of police will be delightfully surprised to learn that the particular type of those stains matches my own blood exactly." Frantically, he added the inevitable conclusion: "More than that, ladies and gentlemen, I faithfully confess to you and you and you—hereby making radio history, since this is the first time anyone has deliberately incriminated himself in murder over the wavelengths—I truthfully confess that those stains *are* my blood."

Kerry dodged out.

CHAPTER SIX

SLAIN BY THE DEAD

KERRY FADED from a taxi directly before the modernized brownstone front the address of which Eve Vane had given him. He bounded up the stoop, found her waiting just inside the outer door. The monkey-nosed Smitty was with her. They were jittery, but so calm, compared with Kerry's own frenzy, that he knew they had not heard him broadcast his own death sentence. Eve's nervous gesture turned him to the entrance of the first-floor apartment. To her "That's Rhoda Donnell's," he added, "And it's my last chance to crack this case."

A key had been left in the tumbler lock. Kerry eased into a brightly furnished living-room. His drifting examination of it immediately stopped short. A moan haunted his ears. He swerved to the door of the bedroom in the rear. A second groan of pain trailed after the first. Kerry glided over the sill, again halted tightly. Brought up abruptly behind him, Eve and Smitty stared with him at the woman huddled on the bed.

She was tossing with insupportable suffering. Her lids were clamped shut, her fists opening and clenching. Her teeth were sinking into her puffed lower lip. Her print dress was horribly crusted with dried blood. It was torn open at the neck, exposing a ghastly swelling around a black-clotted hole low in her left shoulder. A second bullet had pierced her bloated side.

Her face, twisted with agony, brought no recollection to Kerry. But he saw a swagger-coat crumpled on the floor and, beside it, black leather purse from which the contents had spilled. At once, he picked it up. Inside it were wadded banknotes, feminine necessities, a letter addressed to Rhoda Donnell with a notation in the lower corner—*Apt. A.* Kerry turned back abruptly when the woman on the bed broke into a drone.

"You—you wanted me to come back. You begged me—to

come back. So I came, and now—now I find you with this—this woman. You don't love me. Oh, no, you don't. I'm glad I left—my baggage at the station. I'll never—never live with you again."

Kerry was catching every delirious word on the fly.

"Very well, then," she mumbled. "Choose. Once and for all—we'll settle this—right here—now. That woman—or me. You—did you hear what he said? You get out. Get out and never come back—let him alone. Send her away. Tell her to go. Don't point that gun at me. Oh, God—"

The wounded woman's voice was a fading rush.

"Where—where can I go? Nobody must know—nobody. I don't dare—let anybody see me. This—this isn't my purse. There's a key. It's her address. Driver—listen, driver. Oh, God, I've got to lie down. Maybe it won't hurt so much—in a little while. He does love me. I believe him. He must hate her now—for what she did to me. I can't—stand this— But nobody must know—"

The woman muttered. A spasm shook her racked body. Ease came slowly into it. She lay lax. A sob heaved her brown-smeared chest, then a lesser breath. Agitatedly, Kerry caught her wrist, sought her pulse. He rose, gazing despairingly at Eve. He told her gravely: "She's dead."

"It's murder," Eve said with a shudder. "Who did it, Guy?"

"A corpse killed her."

HE BENT over the woman's limp left hand. A gold wedding-band encircled the third finger. Kerry felt a shudder, as he slipped it off. He peered inside it for initials, found none, replaced it. He picked up the swagger-coat, noted bloodstains inside it. Its pockets yielded nothing. His manner intent, he circled the bedroom. A superficial search gave him no enlightenment. Stepping into the living-room, he found an unsealed envelope on the coffee table. Its face was inscribed *Molly* in a feminine scrawl. Six one-dollar bills were folded inside it.

"That's the woman who bumped into me last night in the court of the Embassy Arms. She had been shot, in the midst of an emotional crisis. She didn't know quite what she was doing, but she had run out of the room where it'd happened. She'd picked up the wrong purse, without knowing it—Rhoda Donnell's. Rhoda Donnell had shot her. Assuming the automatic was full, there've been two bullets unaccounted for until now. They're in the body of the woman on that bed."

"But—"

"You heard her raving. When she ran out of that room, she was desperate that nobody should know what had happened. Wounded as she was, she couldn't go to a hotel or hospital. She'd just come into town, leaving her baggage at the station, so she had no place of her own. In the purse she'd taken by mistake, she found a key and a letter addressed to Rhoda Donnell. She came here. Nobody else but us knows this. The man who killed Rhoda Donnell doesn't."

"Who is she?"

Kerry, his mind clicking, didn't hear. "Use that phone," he directed Eve. "Find out, somehow, if Christy Leach is married. If so, has he been separated from his wife? In any case, where is she? Get busy, Eve." As the girl took up the instrument, Kerry gripped Smitty's arm. "You've got an important job to do. Spot Leach. No matter where he is, find him. Keep out of sight. Tail him until he, somehow, gets close to a radio that's playing and tuned to WUBC. Got that straight, Smitty? The minute it comes about, phone me—here."

Kerry moved about, noting details, while Eve phoned. He was gingerly looking for some clue to the identity of the dead woman on the bed when he heard his secretary ask disarmingly, "Where can I reach Mrs. Christy Leach, please?"

Kerry found no lead that a fugitive could follow down.

"Christy Leach is married," Eve reported presently. "I didn't dare ask too pointed questions of the *Intelligencer's* telephone operator, but I gathered she's a stranger to the staff. Whether separated or not, I couldn't learn. I did get Leach's home number.

There's no answer. Either his wife is quite innocently out some-where, or—"

"I've got the picture," Kerry told her tensely. "I'd have this whole case cracked inside an hour, if Endicott's dogs weren't yapping at my heels. Listen." Ears cocked at the hallway door, he gestured at Eve imperatively. "Get in there—quick."

HE TUGGED her into the bedroom. Closing the connect-ing door all but a paper-thin crack, he peered through. He had caught the tread of a foot outside. Now, he heard the entrance lock turning. The opening door revealed a neatly dressed girl with a coffee-and-cream skin. The Negress came in quietly. Moving toward the bedroom, she caught sight of the envelope lying on the low table. She opened it, counted the six banknotes, slipped them into her bag.

Kerry signaled Eve to remain soundless and invisible, abrupt-ly stepped out. The dark girl started. He went to her saying, "Sit down, Molly." She looked disturbed. "You're Miss Donnell's maid," he asserted. She nodded. He went on briskly: "I'm an investigator. Miss Donnell is in serious trouble. You have your choice of answering my questions here, or at police headquar-ters. You'll be all right, if you're reasonable." Kerry signifi-cantly stroked a twenty-dollar bill.

"But I just come in to clean," the Negress protested. "I come in every day this time to clean—that's all, honest."

"I want you to tell me everything you know about the man Miss Donnell was in love with," Kerry insisted.

Molly sat. She eyed the twenty hungrily, fidgeted. "I never saw him," she said. "I never even heard his right name. Miss Donnell, she call him Bunny. Always it's Bunny. She crazy about him, all right—wild crazy over him. Listen, I won't be arrested, will I? I won't have to go to court?"

"That depends on you, right now," Kerry told her omi-nously. "If you're wise, you'll make it easy for yourself. What's the rest?"

Molly thought. "Miss Donnell go to see him all the time—every night," she revealed. "Sometimes she come in early in the morning. I find her asleep in there, when I come in to clean. Sometimes she still drunk. She talk about Bunny—how she crazy for Bunny. One day I come in, and she all beat up. Her face swell and her eye black. She swear and cry. Bunny did it. But, even after that, she still crazy for Bunny—maybe more so."

"What did she say about that?" Kerry pressed.

"She say he can't get rid of *her*. She say she make him divorce his wife and marry her," Molly went on, round-eyed. "Miss Donnell, she mighty pass'nate. My, she get mad talking about Bunny's wife. She say nobody going to take her Bunny from her. She wild crazy about him."

"You're sure you never saw him? Sure you never heard his real name?" Kerry insisted. "Do you know what number she called, when she telephoned him? Has Miss Donnell a photograph of him here? Didn't she ever mention what he does for a living? Do you know where his home is? Can you tell me anything more about him, at all?"

To all of these questions the answer was, "Naw, sir."

With mingled disappointment and elation, Kerry bestowed the twenty upon Molly. He dismissed her.

"The picture's almost complete," he informed Eve, at last. "Three people are in it, each of them distinct. It's perfectly clear now what happened. We know everything, except the most vital fact—the name of the man."

"Do we?" Eve breathed.

"Certainly," Kerry retorted. "The most important thing about him is that he wasn't in love with Donnell, though he must have had an affair with her, but with his wife—with the woman lying dead on that bed. That man, at this minute, Eve, is in an intolerable position. He saw Donnell shoot his wife, then saw his wife run out—to where? He doesn't know. He doesn't dare ask the police to search for her. He can't let even a hint of what happened come out. All he can do is hunt for her secretly and wait for word from her. Think of the spot that man is in, Eve. He knows the woman he loves is desperately wounded, but she's disappeared, and he can't find her. He must be almost insane with anxiety."

KERRY strode alertly into the bedroom, turned past the corpse to the windows. They looked across a court, upon the rear walls of the houses lining the next street. Uncurtained panes told him that some of the opposite apartments were vacant.

"Skip to the office, but be careful you're not seen," he told her. "Somehow, get access to one of the rooms across the court—the closer the better. Have a special wire strung there right away. I want a man on duty as soon as possible, ready for a broadcast at any minute. He's to bring along two mikes, with the longest cords he can get hold of. You're to stick there with him. The break's sure to come." Kerry's eyes were afire.

"You'd better be right about it," Eve said nervously. "If you aren't, it'll be the last broadcast of Keyhole Kerry."

He nodded grim agreement, gestured her on her way urgently. She eased out. Kerry resumed his search of the rooms, unhopeful of a significant discovery. All the while, his ear was pitched for the ring of the phone bell. With torturous impatience he paced about. He had given Eve a difficult assignment, but he immediately began watching the windows across the court. With no radio in the apartment, he was deaf to any developments in the case that might be piling up on him. Kerry's nerves were raw by the time he glimpsed the first hint of the accomplishment of Eve's orders.

She was looking through bare glass directly opposite the Donnell bedroom. Kerry pried a window open. He legged out, dropped into the court, crossed to a wooden fence. This he climbed. Under Eve's window, he signaled her to raise the sash. The sour face of Kerry's favorite technician appeared in the frame beside hers. Kerry's directions dropped a microphone into his hands. A second mike followed. Trailing snaky black cords, he retraced his steps. With a mike in each coat pocket, and the slinky leads dangling, he put the fence between him and his assistants.

One microphone he lodged carefully in the corner of the court. The other he carried inward through the Donnell window. There he performed a grisly task. He tucked the second mike under the crusted silk of the dead woman's dress. It lay against her unmoving chest. Kerry smoothed the cord behind the bed, hid a length of it under the edge of the rug, adjusted the window drapes to conceal its entrance into the room. Finally, with great care, he draped the swagger-coat over the corpse.

His grim preparations completed, he paused, still alert for the ring of the telephone. On sudden thought, he chanced the blocking of an incoming call by making one, himself. He dialed the number of police headquarters, requested connection with Commissioner Endicott. When a voice asked who was calling, Kerry glibly answered with the name of Christy Leach's chief.

Endicott's authoritative tone boomed.

Kerry talked fast. "Please pardon the necessary, but trifling, deception, Commissioner. This is Kerry. I'm not going to give you time enough to trace this call, so don't bother. I have a question. Just how much importance do you place on my latest flash—meaning the bloodstains I admit are mine?"

"Those bloodstains are going to send you to the chair," Endicott growled.

Kerry hastily severed the connection. His lips bitterly pursed, his face even more haggard than before, the hope of his whole soul fiercely centering upon the stratagem he had planned, he began an indeterminate wait with every empty minute a separate torture.

CHAPTER SEVEN

RADIO TRAP

IT WAS the zing of the telephone bell that shot Kerry's hand to the instrument. Excitement seized him, at its insistent ring. Cautiously, disguising his tone, he asked: "Who's calling?"

Tumbling words answered him. "It's Smitty, boss. Gosh, I couldn't come through any sooner. Listen. I spotted Leach in his newspaper office. He was there for hours. Then a detective came for him and took him down to headquarters."

Kerry moaned at that, chilled with the thought that Endicott had nailed Leach before he could.

"Leach left headquarters just a little while ago," Smitty rushed on. "He went back to his office. Now, he's in a restaurant across the street. Everything's set just as you wanted it. There's a radio near him, and it's tuned to your station. I guess every radio in town is, since this case broke. Now, what?"

"Watch him," Kerry directed. "I'm going on the air, in a minute. Soon as I'm off, I want to know what Leach is doing. If he moves, stick to his heels. Call me back the first chance you get. If Leach heads for this place, give me time to get out before he comes in. I'm depending on you, boy."

Kerry cradled the instrument. He was on the point of a nervous explosion. He had waited interminable hours for Smitty's tip. The court behind the Donnell apartment was night-dark. During the agonizing wait, Kerry had tested the mike circuits and had added two pairs of ear-phones to the tie-up. One was concealed in the corner of the yard, the other lying on the windowsill. Over the second, Kerry had heard from Eve that the police search for him had been intensified, that she had been unable to reach Leach's wife by telephone, that none of their private discoveries had broken in the press.

Now, he took it up again. Bending over the dead woman on the bed, bringing his lips close to the mike concealed under the coat, he directed: "Put me on." The phones brought him the fade-out of a dance band, then, "Take it away." Five seconds later, he clipped out his broadcast.

"Attention, Mr. and Mrs. America. Keyhole Kerry, your scoop-specialist, still being hunted by the law for a murder he certainly did not commit, is for once not bringing you a hot flash. Instead, I have a cryptic message to deliver, which may, or may not, be connected with the baffling Reyburn case. This message is meant for a man whose identity I do not know. He will have no doubt, when he hears it, that it is intended for him. The message, ladies and gentlemen, follows.

"To whom it may concern. Your wife is dying. She has been unable to reach you. She wishes to reassure you that she will never tell what actually happened. She needs you desperately. She wants you to know that she is at the other woman's apartment. She is alone there. I repeat, she desperately needs you.

"That, ladies and gentlemen, is the message that concerns only one of you among millions. I am glad to assist in an emergency, though I do not know what it means. I am completely unaware of the identity of the woman for whom I've sent it. Now, Mr. and Mrs. America, with the police already making an earnest effort to trace this broadcast, I am going off the air, urging you to hang onto this wavelength for what may turn out to be Keyhole Kerry's farewell appearance."

Kerry feverishly slipped the phones off, as the dance band faded in. Sharply anxious for Smitty's next call, he shifted to the outer door to make sure he had left it unlatched. Five endless minutes passed before a ripple of the telephone bell heightened the voltage of Kerry's nerves.

"I lost him, boss." Smitty's voice was mournful. "He heard your flash, all right. He didn't move until you were through, then he scrammed. He dove through the crowd like a football tackle. I'm awful sorry he got away from me, boss!"

Kerry moaned, "Oh, God," and left Smitty hanging to a dead phone.

Kerry stepped back tightly, his swift glance making a last check of every detail. Quickly, he slid over the windowsill. He lowered a Venetian blind to within an inch of the sill, then eased across the court. Settling alertly into the corner, he affixed the ear-phones, took up the mike he had left there.

Eve's strained voice came through: "Guy, you crazy darling, there's a million angles of this thing you can never get out of, no matter what turns up."

"On your toes," he urged. "When I ask for the air, give me plenty of it fast." His sharp gaze turned from the darkened window of the Donnell bedroom to the unshaded ones of the living-room, fastened upon the entrance.

EMPTY seconds became empty minutes. Kerry's anxiety mounted unbearably. Fear haunted him that Endicott's men would somehow manage to trace his wire and pounce upon him before his quarry had time to enter the trap he had set. Through a crack in the fence, he could see Eve hovering in the dark window above, her face a ghostly oval. The line was alive but soundless. Kerry wretchedly reflected that, waiting for the death-house switch to be thrown while the straps of the electric chair held him, could never be worse than this. His every muscle shriekingly ached with tension. Then his breath stopped— because the entrance of the Donnell apartment was opening.

A narrow crack appeared. A shadow moved outside it. The phantom shape became a man, backing in. The shaded lights confused his outlines. As the unknown man eased into the living-room, Kerry whispered into the mike, "Put me on." The furtive caller sidled out of sight, his face still turned away. Kerry's signal came, "It's yours." Eyes fastened upon the blinded window of the bedroom, pressing the phones tight to his ears, Kerry began informing millions of the movements of a man who believed himself to be unobserved.

"Mr. and Mrs. America, attention. Keyhole Kerry urges you

to listen fast to the most remarkable broadcast ever aired. A short time ago, you heard me transmit a cryptic message. That message was based on fact, though it did not originate with a mysterious woman, but with me. It was bait, ladies and gentlemen—bait for a murderer. He is taking it now. He has just secretly entered an apartment where his wife lies dead of two gunshot wounds. He came, believing— Listen."

A voice sounded in Kerry's ear-phones. It was also, he knew, dinning out of countless loudspeakers scattered from coast to coast. The microphone, concealed on the dead woman's body, was picking it up. It was hoarse, frayed with grief. It moaned: "Lucille! Lucille!"

Alert to break off instantly another sound came from the death room, Kerry galvanically resumed. "The voice that just spoke, Mr. and Mrs. America, is that of a murderer. He is totally unaware that you heard it. He is alone in the room with his dead wife, for whom he has been desperately searching. He is stunned with grief to find her dead. I can see him, faintly, bending over her bed. Though I know he has a killing on his soul, I do not know who he is. But, before I give the signal which will enable the police to close down on him, I will present my proof that no one else in the world holds—that he is guilty."

Kerry checked himself, as the voice groaned again: "Lucille! My darling! Oh, God, she was never worth this!"

Grimly exultant that he was holding the nation breathless, as well as the infuriated police and hundreds of frustrated newspapermen, Kerry pressed on. "Last night, an emotional crisis occurred between three persons in a suite at the Embassy Arms. I cannot reveal their names at the moment. I will call them, in the terms of the ancient triangle, the Man, the Wife and the Woman. This scene has already resulted in the death of two of them, and, inevitably, it must mean the Man's doom in the electric chair.

"The Man deeply loved the Wife. For a reason, which I do not know, she had separated from him and had gone to live in another town. He begged her to return to him, but she would not, until last night. Yielding to his pleas, she came unexpectedly to his rooms only to find him with the Woman. The Woman was madly infatuated with the Man, passionately attaching herself to him in spite of his efforts to get rid of her. The meeting of the three was dynamite, and the dynamite exploded. The Man was forced to choose, once and for all, then and there, between the Wife and the Woman. Unhesitatingly, he chose the Wife he loved. Aroused to a fit of jealous rage, the Woman shot her.

"The wounded Wife ran hysterically from the room. She was gone before the Man could stop her. Infuriated, maddened, he tore the gun away from the Woman. In savage retaliation he shot her down. Then, desperate to conceal his crime, he transferred the Woman's body to the apartment of Mrs. Beverly Reyburn. How he was able to do this I will disclose later. Since then, he has been searching for his Wife. I succeeded, without his knowledge, in finding her. By means of my mysterious message, I lured him into the room where he is now kneeling beside her dead body. The police—" Kerry gasped—a sound of sharp dismay that blanketed the country. Tearing off his earphones, he heard the echoes of a Gargantuan voice echoing through the court. Instantly, he realized that one of his listeners, overzealously wishing to catch every one of Kerry's words, had turned to its top limit the volume control of the radio in one of the nearby apartments. His whisper had thundered out. Peering through the crack of the blinds, he saw the man straightening in alarm. Kerry's rasp had drilled into him. Kerry was still unable to see his face, but his fearful exclamation, picked up by the mike hidden on the dead woman, blasted into the court: "Good God!"

Kerry clicked out: "The police will be glad to know that the murderer is"—he had intended to add the Donnell address, but a swift move by the man in the room changed that instantly, and Kerry finished with a screeching—"escaping!"

HE DROPPED the mike and the phones, as he bounded. With his own words echoing deafeningly after him, Kerry flung himself at the window. He glimpsed the man coming erect, stumbling toward the connecting door. Kerry slapped the blind up with a violence that made his quarry a vanishing blur. He sprang from the sill, hurled himself into the living-room. In the dim light, a black figure was darting into the hall. Kerry tackled it.

His flying leap caught it beside the dead woman's bed. His momentum smashed it to the floor. The other man's head hit the floor with a sharp crack. Feeling him go limp, Kerry dragged up. His captive was dazedly squirming, face downward. With one glance at that face promising to dispel the mystery utterly, Kerry's first move was a reach toward the corpse. He dragged the mike from under the coat, brought it to his lips, began speaking even before his hand shot to the fallen man's shoulder.

"Flash. Keyhole Kerry is back, Mr. and Mrs. America, cracking, as he promised to do, the Reyburn murder case. The name of the dead woman, found in the Reyburn apartment, is Rhoda Donnell. For the information of the police, I have just cornered the man who murdered her. His name is Lucius Milbank, manager of the Embassy Arms."

THE ELECTRICAL tension in Studio X, in the Universal Broadcasting tower, was never higher than tonight. Kerry was again on the air.

With fierce persistence he had detached himself from the police who had swarmed into the Donnell apartment, determined to preserve his record of never having missed a broadcast. Two plainclothesmen had dogged him, were waiting in the studio now, but he had managed to make the deadline by the time Milton Raney's overture for *De-Luxe-Lax* was completed. Eve Vane dropped a paper slip before him.

"Flash," broke into the clatter. "Christy Leach, top-flight reporter for the *Intelligencer*, will be delighted to learn—particularly to learn it first from this news-buster—that at Flower

Hospital Mrs. Leach has just presented him with an eight-pound boy."

With a gleeful chuckle, Kerry returned to his account. "Lucius Milbank, as should be evident, Mr. and Mrs. America, was in the perfect position for hiding Rhoda Donnell's body in the apartment of Mrs. Beverly Reyburn. Though he denies it, it can be easily speculated that my first flash on the murder, deliberately falsified in order to confuse the investigation, came anonymously from him. As for my own connection with the case, it is easily explained. Since all news of Mrs. Reyburn came exclusively from me, it is not astonishing that I should have had contact with her, though to what extent I prefer not to disclose. I trust, however, that I will not be sent to the electric chair because, while calling upon her last evening, I suffered a nosebleed—"

Kerry started as Eve Vane slid something else beneath his eyes. It was a sheet of blue-tinted notepaper, signed with an aristocratic flourish—*Mrs. Beverly Reyburn.*

"Flash. I have just received a special-delivery letter from Mrs. Reyburn. Dismayed to find her apartment the scene of a crime with which she had not the slightest connection, she chose to explain to me exclusively. 'Early last night,' she writes, 'I left my apartment in a tremendous hurry. I was most delightfully rushed off my feet by the only man I have ever really loved. He is my boyhood sweetheart and now my husband. Because we wish to live very quietly, I will not tell you my very new name.'

"Keyhole Kerry herewith scoops the world with congratulations to the former Mrs. Reyburn and her bridegroom."

He swung from the mike, gaped at the blue letter, stared at Eve.

"I wrote it, darling," Eve whispered. "For you—and good old *De-Luxe-Lax.*"

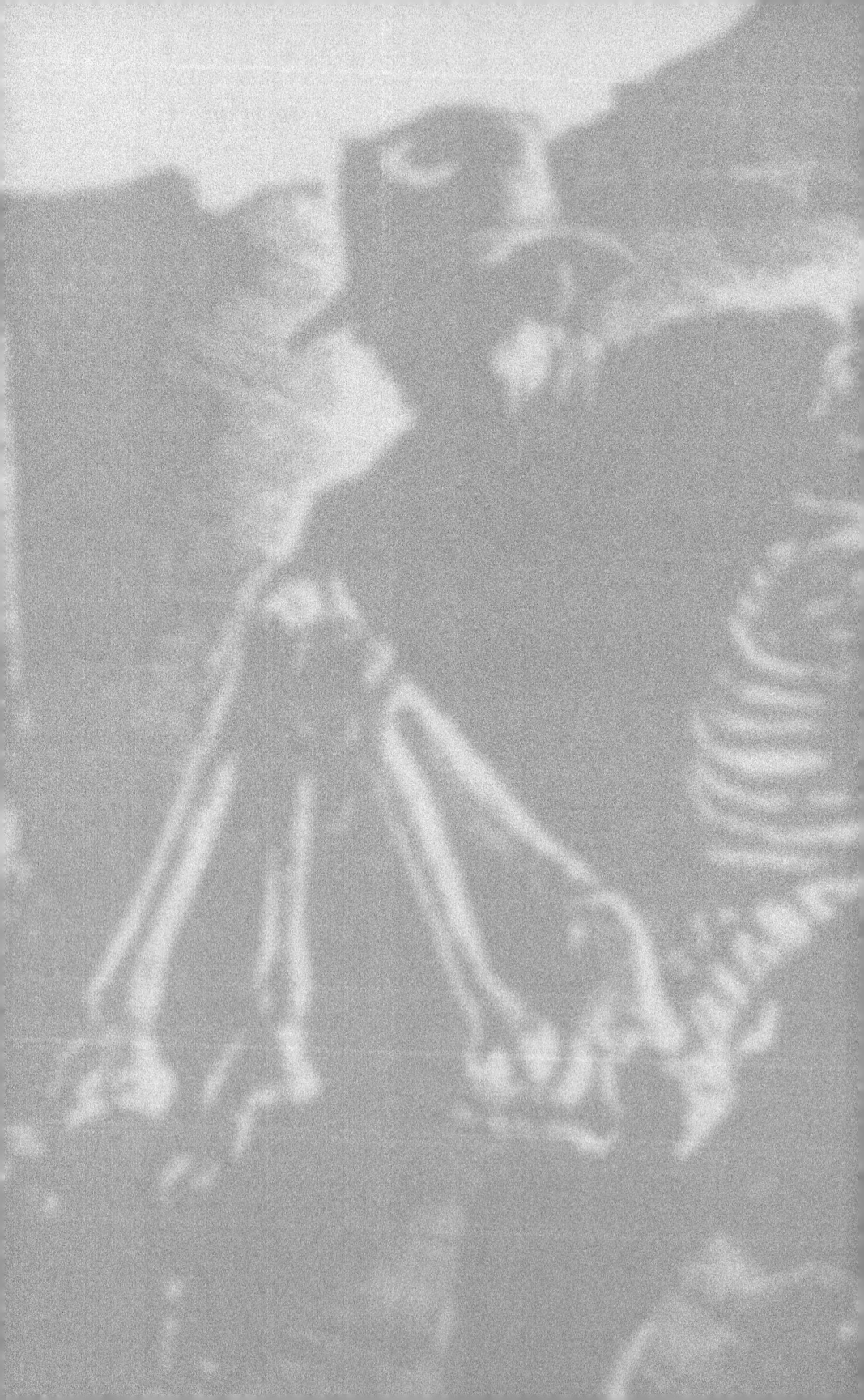

CRIMSON BROADCAST

GUY KERRY, ACE CRIME-
COMMENTATOR OF THE
ETHER WAVES, DIDN'T
KNOW, WHEN HE FRAMED
HIMSELF FOR MURDER TO
CREATE A SPOT-FLASH
FOR HIS BROADCAST,
THAT HIS ONE SURE ALIBI
WOULD BE BUMPED OFF
IN TWENTY-FOUR HOURS.
BUT THAT DIDN'T FAZE
THE KING OF THE KILO-
CYCLES. BEING MURDER
BAIT WAS PART OF HIS
JOB AND MERELY MEANT
HOT NEWS TO BROADCAST
WHEN HE FINALLY PUT
THE PROPER PORTRAIT IN
THE GUILT-FRAME.

CHAPTER ONE

SELF-MADE MURDER

WITH HABITUAL haste, the prematurely white-headed young man swung into the entrance of the Universal Broadcasting Company tower. He was known to millions of radio listeners as Keyhole Kerry, the most galvanic flash-news reporter ever to pervade the ether. Warned by his strap-watch that he was due to hit the mike in less than two minutes, he dodged through the scores of sight-seers in the foyer and headed for the special elevator that would whisk him skyward to Studio X.

As he was about to step into the car, someone unexpectedly thrust a folded bit of blue paper into his hand. Looking up, Kerry saw a young woman hurrying away. Wondering who she was, and why she had passed him the message so furtively, he quickly opened it. It consisted of one line of script that caused his nerves to snap tight—*Sheridan Reese is not dead.*

Kerry felt sorely in need of a few succulent morsels of scandal to whisper to the nation at large tonight. The note seemed to promise exactly the thing he craved—a sensational scoop. He hastened after the young woman with electrically nervous strides.

She was remarkably pretty, strangely pale and had frightened blue eyes. Kerry caught only these details as a new consignment of sight-seers, descending upon the door at that moment, balked his pursuit. He fought his way through them and charged across the sidewalk eagerly, then paused. The moment's delay had given the young woman an opportunity to elude him. She was nowhere to be seen.

Because half the nation was waiting to hear Kerry's latest barrage of spot-news, he reluctantly turned back. All the way up in the elevator the mysterious message tantalized him, but he deplored its lack of authenticity. He thrust it into his pocket as he strode into Studio X.

THE RED second hand of the electric clock was just swing-

The prowler faded away with the skeleton as Kerry tried to ward off the attack.

ing to the zero moment. The tuxedoed announcer, the technicians in the monitor booth and the sound-effects man all gave
vent to a sigh of relief at sight of Kerry.

A willowy, champagne-haired girl pushed the copy for the

broadcast into Kerry's fingers. Eve Vane competently assisted Kerry at his trying task of out-winchelling Winchell, but the strain he put on her nerves was terrific. She suffered an acute attack of the jitters each time he was due to launch himself upon a coast-to-coast network.

Kerry bore down upon the microphone on the desk as Milton Raney, the chubby announcer, was just completing his guileful overture to a cathartic called *De-Luxe-Lax*. The manufacturer of this alleviator of the national ailment was Kerry's sponsor. The moment the dignified Raney retired from the mike, Kerry began his machine-gun delivery in a voice that sounded like a scratchy slate-pencil.

"Good-evening, Mr. and Mrs. United States! This is Keyhole Kerry, your scoop specialist, once more beating the nation's headlines with his exclusive inside chatter. Flash!"

Kerry's words sped out against a background of noises which simulated the activity of a busy newsroom. He gloried in the reputation that his red-hot stuff usually made the *Parade of Time* program sound like last year's almanac, and other news commentators seem like sleepy professors in an ancient history class. But tonight something was lacking, the edge was off Kerry's characteristic zest.

Reaching the point when Raney took over the mike to croon his blandishments concerning *De-Luxe-Lax*, Kerry morosely wagged his head.

"Eve," he whispered, "my stuff isn't up to standard tonight. If I can't burn the ears off the great American public, I'm not happy. And if I don't pull off another sizzling scoop pretty soon, people will begin to say that I'm washed up. Something sensational has got to happen—and if it doesn't break of its own accord, I'll *make* it happen."

"No, Guy!" Eve protested, a terrified light springing into her eyes. "Don't do that—not again! Please!"

Kerry swung back to the mike. In his staccato twang, he ripped off one item after another. Each was exclusive, but to

Kerry they seemed trifling compared with the startling revelations for which he had become famous. His dejection increased.

While he talked, he removed from his pocket the bit of blue paper that the furtive young woman in the lobby had left in his hand. He fingered it speculatively, then abruptly, with a gesture of desperation, he abandoned his prepared copy.

"Flash! Attention, all New York City newspapers! Your radio oracle is again the first to announce a stop-press item. It concerns the case of Sheridan Reese. Some months ago, Sheridan Reese, the scion of a fine old family, disappeared. Weeks passed—anxious weeks for his bride, the former Enid Martin, song-bird of the Broadway night-spots.

"Then the forearm of a man, in an advanced state of decomposition, was found floating in the East River. Fingerprints were obtained from it, and duplicates of these prints were found in the non-criminal file of the United States Department of Justice. The arm, which seemed to have been torn or hacked from the elbow, was identified as that of Sheridan Reese.

"Still later, a man's body was recovered from the East River. It was battered and badly decomposed, and one of its forearms was missing. There was, and is, no doubt that the forearm previously found belonged to this cadaver. This, then, ended the search for Sheridan Reese.

"The direct cause of Reese's death was uncertain, but it was generally believed that he had been struck down by a hit-and-run driver, and that his corpse was thrown into the river as a means of avoiding prosecution. But only your prophet of the wavelengths is in a position to reveal what may be the startling truth in this case."

KERRY took a steadying breath, knowing that Police Commissioner Endicott—to whom Kerry was an unbearable gadfly—was noting down his every word at headquarters.

"This radio newshawk, ladies and gentlemen," Kerry raced on, "consistently checks and double-checks every item he broadcasts, in order to make certain that it is authentic. But this information was passed to me only a few minutes ago, and in a strange way. The local gendarmerie will be interested to learn, I'm sure, that though Sheridan Reese was given a fine funeral, and interred in the family crypt, there is strong reason to believe that he is not actually dead!"

Kerry delightedly imagined millions of gasps arising simultaneously from coast to coast, epithets exploding in the office of Commissioner Endicott, and moans of despair being uttered by the city editors and newspaper reporters to whom his name was anathema.

He was about to continue when Eve Vane tapped his shoulder. Glancing up, he saw a red light glowing in the soundproof telephone booth in the corner. Since the instrument was provided for the reception of last-minute beats, Kerry gestured to Raney to take the mike, and dove into the cubicle.

"Make it fast!" he urged over the line.

"Phipps speaking," a cautious voice answered. "I've got something hot."

Paul Phipps was one of the espionage agents whom Kerry maintained on his personal payroll. A reporter on the staid *Herald,* Phipps was in a perfect position to tip Kerry off to news-breaks of national interest which could not possibly appear in the headlines until hours later.

Watching the second hand of the clock, Kerry urged: "Let's have it!"

"I'm in the city-room," Phipps said quickly. "I just took a call from some man who swore he was going to kill himself. He sounded like he meant it, and he said his suicide would make front-page stuff. Then I heard a shot—and that was all."

Sparks jumped along Kerry's nerves. "Go on! What's his name? Where did he call from? I need this flash!"

"Wouldn't give me his name," Phipps hurried on. "Said we could find him at One-sixty East Thirty-eighth. Then—bang! I think that bird actually killed himself right while he was talking to me."

"Meet me at that address as fast as you can get there!"

Shouldering from the booth, eyes afire, Kerry nudged Raney aside and snatched up the mike.

"Attention, Mr. and Mrs. United States! Flash! I have just received a startling tip-off by telephone. This call came from a man who refused to give me his name. He declared that he was about to commit suicide. I actually heard a shot fired, then I could get no answer. I am now tracing that call." This was stretching the truth a bit, but Kerry had no intention of allowing anyone to beat him to the source of this news. "Keep your radios tuned to the wavelength to which you are now listening, until Keyhole Kerry, your newshawk of the kilocycles, returns with further information that will beat the world—at any moment!"

Kerry relinquished the mike at the last second. As Raney began a closing paean to *De-Luxe-Lax*, he hurried to the door. Eve caught his arm, in an attempt to caution him, but he shook himself loose and ran out, leaving her with turquoise eyes anxious.

KERRY'S taxi swung to the curb directly in front of a brownstone house in the Murray Hill district. As he hopped out, leaving a banknote in the driver's hand, he saw a thin young man just rounding the corner. He paused warily at Kerry's side on the stoop.

"It'll be tough on me if anybody sees me with you, Kerry," Paul Phipps said, nervously fingering his small mustache. "Any newspaperman who tips you off stands a damn good chance of getting his throat cut by his city editor. If I didn't need the money—"

"You know you can count on me in a pinch, Phipps," Kerry answered impatiently. "Never mind about that now. I've got a dead man on my mind."

Kerry pushed at the door which swung open. At the front of the hallway, Kerry found another door standing ajar. He looked into the small apartment beyond and nodded with grim satisfaction.

"There he is," Kerry murmured.

As Phipps paused behind him, Kerry gazed curiously at the corpse on the bed. The body was that of a man in his middle thirties. One of his legs dangled to the floor. His hair was stiff and flaxen. His swarthy face was unknown to Kerry. The head was twisted on the pillow. The bullet had made an ugly hole behind the right ear, and an automatic was lying near the limp right hand.

Noting that the telephone had spilled off the standard beside the bed, Kerry made a quick circuit of the room. The dead man's coat was hanging on a chair. In the inside pocket was a wallet in which were a few banknotes and a Connecticut driver's license bearing the name Henry Colvin. Unhesitantly, Kerry confiscated it.

On the table was an uncorked bottle of ink, and a pen, its nib still wet. Turning to the corpse, Kerry discovered that its right forefinger and thumb were smudged with black. He looked about for whatever the dead man had been writing, but found nothing.

Then his eyes lighted with elation. Kerry was itching to put this flash on the air but, with a grin at Phipps, he began busying himself in a strange manner.

First covering his fingers with his handkerchief, he picked up the automatic and stuffed it into his hip pocket.

"Hold on there, Kerry," Phipps protested. "You don't intend to take that gun away from here, do you? Removing evidence is a serious offense!"

Feverishly intent, Kerry produced from his vest pocket a pair of shell-rimmed eyeglasses, which he rarely wore because he was too impatient to waste time putting them on and taking them off. Now, to Phipps' amazement, he lifted the dangling foot of the corpse and placed the glasses on the floor beneath it.

He thrust the dead man's shoe forcibly downward upon one of the lenses. The glass splintered. Kerry picked up the frame and returned it to his pocket, leaving the glittering fragments on the floor.

"Kerry," Phipps inquired uneasily, "what the hell are you up to?"

Again covering his hand with his handkerchief, Kerry picked up the telephone and made sure it was still in working order. "I've got to flash this murder right now," he said.

"Murder?" Phipps said. "This is an out-and-out suicide!"

"Maybe it *was* a suicide," Kerry said delightedly, "but it's a murder now!"

KERRY spun the dial, calling a special number of the Universal Broadcasting Company. An answer came from one of two men who were constantly on duty in the master control-room, at the behest of Kerry's sponsor, to receive his calls at any hour of the day or night. Eagerly he directed: "Put me on."

De-Luxe-Lax not only paid Kerry a staggering stipend under an iron-clad contract restricting his hair-raising performances to the air-waves, but expensively provided him with an extraordinary arrangement whereby he could break into any other program at any time. Calling from any telephone, he could, using it as a microphone, almost immediately hit the ether. In response to Kerry's request, the wavelengths were now being cleared for him.

"Take it away!" his cue came.

He waited impatiently five seconds, then began firing. "Attention, Mr. and Mrs. United States! This is your scoop specialist, Keyhole Kerry, returning as promised with a startling flash. For Commissioner Endicott's information, he will find the dead body of a man known as Henry Colvin in Apartment One-A, at One-sixty East Thirty-eighth Street, Manhattan. For the commissioner's further information, this man may not be, as I was first led to believe, a suicide. The evidence, ladies and gentlemen, points to murder!"

Kerry could almost feel the electrical reaction that must be answering this breathless announcement—rage in the city-rooms, and blasphemous consternation at police headquarters.

Kerry rushed on elatedly: "I have reason to believe that there is a startling underlying significance to this man's mysterious death. I will soon have further information for you and you and you. Hang onto your radios, Mr. and Mrs. United States, for Keyhole Kerry, your oracle of the kilocycles, promises to pop up with another flash within a very few minutes!"

Transported to the seventh heaven of a newshawk's delight, Kerry replaced the telephone and gripped the befuddled Phipps' arm.

"Let's go!" he urged. "There'll be a prowl-car arriving in less than two minutes."

He steered Phipps from the apartment, closing the door with a hand still wrapped by his handkerchief. They ran down the stoop, swung around the corner, crossed the street and paused in the dark doorway of a store.

"Kerry, you've gone nuts!" the reporter said. "What the hell have you got up your sleeve, anyway?"

"God, this is wonderful—just what the doctor ordered, Phipps!" Kerry answered gleefully. "Don't you get it? I've framed a murder on myself!"

CHAPTER TWO

JAIL BAIT

EVEN SOONER than Kerry had expected, a blue prowl-car veered around the corner and squeaked to a stop in front of 160. Two uniformed men charged out of it and bounded up the stoop. Kerry chuckled, his enthusiasm undampened by Phipps' anxious stare.

"You know that a suicide isn't half as interesting as a murder, Phipps," he explained rapidly. "That's why I took the gun away—

to make this one look like a killing. Then I thought of an even better idea—a way of turning it into the most sensational murder in years. There won't be a dearth of hot exclusive news any longer, thank God, because I've made it seem that I'm the murderer."

This was Kerry in his most daring vein. His creed was to get the news first, no matter how, and if the world failed to supply him with electrifying flashes, he boldly manufactured them.

"Good Lord!" Phipps moaned. "You mean you want the cops to nail you for murder?"

"Don't you see how it will shape up? I'll have the inside track on the news of how the police are closing in on me. I'll broadcast a play-by-play account of the chase. I'm going to build it up to the limit, Phipps—short of the electric chair. But naturally, I'm leaving myself an out."

"Meaning me?" Phipps demanded.

"Yes," Kerry said. "You're a witness to the fact that Colvin killed himself while I was broadcasting tonight, and that he was already dead when I reached the apartment. I want you to keep absolutely mum until I say the word, then you'll broadcast a statement that'll clear me."

"That means my finish in the newspaper game!" Phipps protested. "They'll blacklist me. I'll never be able to get another reporting job."

"I'll make you my assistant," Kerry promised. "It'll mean more money for you, a chance for bigger things in radio. It's the chance of a lifetime for both of us, Phipps! Now, you'd better hop over there and watch developments. Get going!"

Still anxious and bewildered, Phipps trotted back to the apartment where the dead man lay. Kerry remained in the obscure doorway until a massive sedan, escorted by motorcycles with howling sirens, swung into the side-street. Recognizing it as Commissioner Endicott's official car, Kerry advanced then. Seeing Kerry, the commissioner paused on the stoop, glaring furiously.

"Good-evening, Commissioner," Kerry said affably. "As you see, I had the straight dope, as usual, and had it first. It's really not much of a murder, and I think we'll be able to crack it in short order."

"We!" Endicott exploded. "Kerry, I'm fed up with your damned interference. For your information, I can run my department without any help from you. You're going to tell me where your tip came from, and then you're going to stay strictly out of this case. Start talking right now, Kerry—where did you get your information?"

"You know I never reveal my sources, Commissioner," Kerry answered. "I tell the whole world everything I know as soon as I learn it, but I never tell a soul where I get it. In this case, though, I can say that my tip was anonymous."

"Kerry," the commissioner growled, in the tone of a man tried to the limit of his endurance, "you'll tell the truth, or I'll drag you down to headquarters and grill it out of you."

"You've tried that already, and it hasn't worked," Kerry retorted. "If you ever get really rough with me, I'll broadcast the whole thing blow by blow. But we're wasting time, aren't we? Let's get inside, and find out—"

Endicott gave Kerry a push. "You're not going inside. From now on, you're on the outside of this case. When the breaks come, you'll get the news last, understand? When I'm through with you, you'll feel like you've been pulled through a keyhole backwards!"

The commissioner and his men tramped into the death room. With a grin, Kerry trudged away through the growing crowd of the curious that his flash was bringing to the scene. He signaled a taxi, and directed the driver to take him to the U.B.C. tower.

AN ELEVATOR soared Kerry to a floor high in the sky-scraper. Pushing into his little office, he at once bolted the door. The room was walled with autographed photos of celebrities, crowded with file-cabinets, crammed with littered desks. In one of the chairs a gangling boy was slouched.

He was cotton-headed and simian-nosed, and his name was Smitty. He was Kerry's messenger and aide-de-camp at all hours of the day and night.

"Where's Eve?" Kerry asked quickly.

"She's home, chief," Smitty said. "She always has a spell of nervous indigestion whenever you start busting loose like you are tonight. She said to call her if you want her."

Kerry nodded, then rummaged about until he found a box that had contained typewriter paper. Again covering his hand with his handkerchief, he removed the death gun from his pocket. After making a note of its serial number, he placed it in the box and stuffed paper around it. He was tying the lid down when a knock at the door surprised him.

Cautiously opening a crack, he saw Paul Phipps. Phipps sidled nervously in and Kerry again bolted the door.

"What the hell, Kerry!" Phipps began breathlessly. "You didn't plant that blotter, too, did you?"

"What blotter?"

"Endicott found it. It had been used—probably by the dead man—to blot an envelope. The address was smeared over by other writing, but the name was clear enough. Kerry, that envelope was meant for you."

"Where is it?" Kerry asked quickly.

"No sign of it. Colvin must have mailed it before he called me and shot himself."

"I'll be damned!" Kerry exclaimed, his eyes dancing. "If he wrote me a letter before he bumped himself off, it must be damned important. I'll be watching for it to arrive—it'll make a swell flash."

"Maybe," Phipps said doubtfully, "but how will it look, coupled with that broken lens you left in the place?"

"That'll make it all the better. It helps the frame-up. It'll be easy enough to explain later. After all, hundreds of people write me every day." Taking up the box, he swung around to Smitty. "Beat it down to Grand Central with that," he directed, "and check it. Bring the claim ticket to Eve's apartment. Get going, Smitty!"

As Smitty left, Kerry perched at his desk, taking up the microphone that was always there, in readiness for a flash at any time. He pressed a button that activated a signal in the U.B.C. monitor-room, and slipped on a pair of ear-phones. Five seconds after he heard his cue— "Take it away!"—his rasping voice lightninged from coast to coast.

"Attention, Mr. and Mrs. United States! This is Keyhole Kerry, making good his promise to bring you further developments in the Colvin murder case. The police, personally directed by Commissioner Endicott, are now at the scene gathering evidence. Though the commissioner refuses to admit me to the apartment where Colvin's corpse lies, I am able to inform you of their findings—and more!

"Though they have not been able to unearth the murder weapon, they have discovered two important clues. The first is that Colvin wrote a letter to this correspondent, and mailed it, a few moments before the death bullet drilled into his brain. When this letter reaches me, I will promptly flash to you whatever information it contains. The second clue, which the police are now puzzling over, is the fragments of an eyeglass lens found beside the corpse."

Phipps was listening, as motionlessly intent, Kerry knew, as his millions of fans in every state in the Union.

"The police believe, ladies and gentlemen, that the owner of the broken eyeglass lens is the murderer of Henry Colvin. Their theory is that the glasses were broken during the struggle in which Colvin was murdered, and that the killer fled in desperate haste, leaving the fragments behind. The Homicide Squad is already making an effort to trace that man through the prescription for the lens. Ordinarily they might learn his identity sometime tomorrow. But, ladies and gentlemen, if Commissioner Endicott is listening, he will learn that man's identity right now!

"The suspected murderer whom the commissioner is seeking—the fugitive who left the broken lens under the victim's heel—is none other than this correspondent, Keyhole Kerry!

"Your seer of the ether is signing off in great haste, Mr. and Mrs. United States, because he has no intention of letting the gendarmes collar him for a first-degree homicide! Within a very short time he'll be the quarry of a city-wide search but, nonetheless, he'll be back on the air soon with another spine-tingling revelation!"

HAPPILY, Kerry swung from the microphone to find Paul Phipps gaping at him. "My God, Kerry!" Phipps exclaimed aghast. "You're sure as hell asking for it!"

"Certainly!" Kerry agreed. "The oftener I wave the red flag in front of the bulls, the more hot flashes I'll get out of it. I'm playing this thing so I'll be one jump ahead of Endicott all the way, but I'm depending on you for important help, old man. Hop back over to that apartment, stick on Endicott's tail and keep me posted on what's happening."

"I can't do that, Kerry," Phipps protested. "Endicott fired me out. That's why I risked coming over here. The only way—"

A jangling sound from the telephone interrupted. Snatching it up, Kerry heard a girl's voice—quiet, afraid.

"Mr. Kerry?"

"Yes. Who's calling?"

"I—I'm the young woman who gave you that note about Sheridan Reese."

Instantly Kerry pressed the opportunity. "Who are you? How did you get hold of that information? How do you know Reese isn't really dead? If he isn't, whose body is in his casket? Where—"

"Don't ask questions now, Mr. Kerry," the girl's anxious tone interrupted. "The quickest way to learn all the answers is to meet me at the Reese crypt in Woodlawn Cemetery in an hour."

"The Reese crypt in Woodlawn Cemetery in an hour," Kerry repeated eagerly. "But how do I know this isn't a gag? If you're acting in good faith—"

"I think you'll find, Mr. Kerry," the girl broke in quietly, "that this is a murder."

She hung up.

Jubilantly, Kerry swung around to Phipps. "Good Lord! For weeks nothing has been happening, and suddenly I've got two murders on my hands—even if I did fabricate one of them myself." Glancing at his strap-watch, he asked: "Isn't there some way you can stick close to Endicott, Phipps?"

"He's keeping reporters at a distance until he gets around to giving out a statement. But there's one lead I can hang onto, Kerry. Colvin's body has already been carted to the morgue, and Endicott has asked for an immediate post-mortem. I'll camp there, and maybe I can pick up something special."

"On your way," Kerry directed urgently. "If you grab off something hot, call Eve. I'm going to her place right now. We've got to move! If Endicott heard that last flash of mine he's got a squad of detectives closing in on me right now."

He dodged from the office with Phipps. An elevator dropped them to the street level and as Kerry left the car he became certain that his hunch was correct. He saw two burly men tramping into the lobby. Their bulldog shoes and beefy faces proclaimed them to be detectives.

Kerry turned his back on them, tugged Phipps along as he strode toward the opposite entrance. The complexities of the great foyer, and the confusion of people always milling about in it, enabled him to reach the street without being spotted. "Stay with it, pal!" he urged Phipps, as he trotted toward a taxi. Happy in the knowledge that his elusiveness would feed the fires of Endicott's wrath, he directed the driver to Eve's apartment.

EVE ANSWERED her bell with a glass of bicarbonate in

her hand. Dyspepsia is the occupational disease of radio broadcasting, and Kerry's high-pressure tactics made Eve's case especially noteworthy. Her lovely eyes were full of alarm, but before she could speak, footfalls scampered close and Smitty bounded in.

"Here you are, chief!" Smitty said, proffering to Kerry the claim-check for the murder weapon.

Kerry gestured it away. "I don't dare carry that around with me," he said quickly. "If Endicott found it on me, I'd be sunk deeper than I care to go. Keep it, and take damn good care of it."

"O.K., chief," Smitty said and tucked the tag snugly into his pocket.

Leading Eve into her charmingly modern living-room, still giving her no opportunity to speak, Kerry produced a slip of paper from his pocket.

"This is the serial number of the gun in the Colvin case," he informed her rapidly. "Your job is to check it, and find out who that gun belongs to. Turn your wiles loose on our pal, Inspector Tarrant, and you'll soon have the dope."

Inspector Tarrant was another secret source of some of Kerry's inside information. A good cop of the old school, Tarrant was nonetheless hostile to Commissioner Endicott, because be believed that he, instead of Endicott, had merited the appointment to the commissioner's chair. Whenever he could, without disrupting an official investigation too violently he took keen delight in sharpshooting at Endicott from ambush.

"I'll do it right away, Guy," Eve said, "but—"

"Another thing—damned important," Kerry cut in. "Just before Colvin died, he wrote me a letter. It's probably full of hot stuff. I want you and Smitty to spell each other at the office until that letter arrives. Colvin may have sent it special delivery, so you'd better hop down there right away. As soon as that letter comes—"

"Guy, wait—listen!" Eve begged. "My stomach is all tied up

in knots from worrying about you. I wish I were back with my fans and bubbles. I don't know why I was ever idiot enough to let myself fall in love with a maniac like you. Guy, what in the world are you up to?"

"Darling," Kerry told her with a broad grin, "I'm having the time of my life. I'm a fugitive from justice. Within a few hours, a whole army of cops will be turning this town inside out, trying to find me. Endicott will begin bellowing that my flight is a confession of guilt. I'm going to egg him on until he works up a hell of a strong case against me. Isn't that wonderful?"

"Oh Guy, you crazy lunatic!" Eve wailed. "You know he's dying to give you the works, and you're deliberately baiting him. You know all the papers will help him. This case will be tried in the headlines, and you'll be pilloried. They hate you so much, they'll swoop down onto you like vultures and—"

"All the better!" Kerry exulted, "I'm going to lead the cops in the merriest chase they've ever been through, I'm going to goad Endicott to the point where he'll actually have me indicted for murder. I'll build it up into the biggest murder case of the century, Eve. Then, when it looks like it's all over except for throwing the switch, with Keyhole Kerry strapped in the sizzle-seat, I'll vindicate myself and blow up the works right under 'em. Eve, darling, don't you think it's the swellest thing that ever happened?"

"I think you're out of your head, Guy Kerry," Eve moaned. "What if something goes wrong?"

"Nothing will," Kerry said confidently. "At the very last minute I'll prove, beyond a doubt, that the murder they're trying to nail me for isn't a murder."

The purring of the telephone interrupted. Eve caught up the instrument, then pushed it at Kerry, wailing: "For you, you madman!"

In answer to Kerry's twang, the wire brought the voice of Paul Phipps.

"I'm calling from the morgue," Phipps said in a strained tone.

"They've just finished the post. It shows that the bullet went into Colvin's head at a sharp downward angle. The gun was fired from above and to the rear. The assistant M.E. swears that Colvin couldn't possibly have held the automatic in that position and fired it himself."

Kerry stiffened.

"In other words, that tip I got over the phone was all wet," Phipps continued. "And you can't make a new flash out of this, because you had it right in the first place, even though you didn't know it. Colvin did not commit suicide."

Suddenly pale, Kerry gulped at Phipps an order to stay on the job, then, lowering the instrument, he stared at Eve bewilderedly.

"My God!" he blurted. "I've framed myself for a real murder!"

Kerry saw indications of imminent hysterics in Eve's eyes. "Oh, Guy!" she gasped. "What can we do now?"

He felt the same sting of panic, but he braced himself. "Sit tight, and make the most of it," he said. "This is tougher than I'd meant it to be, but it's still the swellest set-up I've ever had. Why, it's even better than it was before! And I can still squeeze out of it. When Phipps calls again, tell him for God's sake to take good care of himself—I need him for an alibi."

"Guy, you fool! I—"

"Don't go to pieces, Eve. The worse this gets for me, the better it'll be in the end—I hope! Skip down to the office and keep an eye out for Colvin's letter. I'm on my way to a cemetery."

CHAPTER THREE

GRAVEYARD RENDEZVOUS

PUZZLING OVER the case, Kerry traveled by taxi to a parking-space near the U.B.C. tower. There he transferred to his roadster. Driving rapidly, he reached Woodlawn Cemetery at almost precisely the appointed time.

Gloomy quiet shrouded it as Kerry prowled, seeking a way in. Having negotiated the fence at its easiest point, he began feeling his way into the deeper darkness among the tombstones. Not knowing where the Reese family crypt was located, Kerry was obliged to grope along the black paths of an eery maze of monuments that looked like a white company of motionless ghosts.

Suddenly he was chilled by a muffled scream. Kerry dodged in the direction of the cry, stumbling over graves. Suddenly he saw a light appear. The beam of an electric torch played across the marble front of a dwelling of the dead. Its bronze entrance was swinging open. Kerry scarcely had time to glimpse the name graven above it—*Reese*—before a girl ran out.

She sped past the man holding the torch. Turning quickly, the man ran after her. They paused breathlessly a short distance from Kerry. Watching them with alert amazement, Kerry saw the girl clinging to the man. She spoke breathlessly, and the man muttered reassurance. Suddenly, at a sound which came from the Reese crypt, the man swung his light back to the open bronze door.

"Somebody just came out!" he exclaimed.

Swift footfalls, almost soundless, were fading into the sepulchral quiet. Kerry moved toward them. A rustling of leaves urged him into a run. He was suddenly conscious that, while he was chasing the prowler, someone else was also pursuing him. The next moment a hand gripped Kerry's shoulder from behind and he was dragged to a stop.

He was striving to tear himself loose from a crushing embrace when a blinding light shot into his eyes, and a girl's voice exclaimed: "Stop, Rex, stop! That's Mr. Kerry!"

Kerry's captor promptly released him. The gleam showed him Rex's ruggedly masculine face and sharp blue eyes. As the girl stepped closer, turning the light down, the glow revealed her also. Kerry recognized her at once as the young woman who had passed him the blue note concerning the questionably dead Sheridan Reese.

"Rex, the—skeleton is gone!" she said in a gasp.

With an urgency that permitted no explanation, Rex loped off. His light flashed among the tombstones as he skirmished deeper into the cemetery searching for the dark form of the fugitive. Kerry looked wonderingly at the girl but she was too urgently concerned to offer him enlightenment. She turned quickly, hurried to the Reese crypt and disappeared inside.

Following her, Kerry stopped short in the doorway, eyes taking in a startling scene. Set into one wall of the marble room was a pattern of small bronze doors. Each of these bore a name-plate. One of them yawned, disclosing a cold recess in which a casket had reposed. The name on it was *Sheridan Reese.*

The casket which had rested in the hollow was now on the floor, its lid removed. On the stained satin lining, and also scattered on the floor, were dry brown bits of stuff—apparently decomposed human flesh. Several small bones lay nearby. The largest fragment of the vanished skeleton lay directly beneath the open recess. It was an arm, broken off at the elbow. And in the curled, fleshless claw was a murderous-looking knife.

"I thought—" The girl spoke in a terrified whisper, staring at Kerry. "I thought the skeleton was trying to kill me!"

IN SPEECHLESS amazement Kerry absorbed the rest of the scene. Standing opposite the rifled casket was a tripod to which a camera was affixed. On the floor beside it was a device for firing flash-bulbs. The bulb in the socket was smashed, and smoky fragments of it were scattered about. The girl, now gaining control of herself, began unscrewing the camera from the tripod. Kerry's questions were forestalled by quick footfalls outside and Rex reappeared.

"He got away, Sheila," he said. "Did you get a picture?"

"I don't know," the girl answered, hastening at her task.

"We'd better get out of here, before the caretaker or the cops grab us," Rex urged. "Come along, Kerry."

Kerry had every intention of going along. Accustomed to the realism of every-day news-busting, he was entranced by the ghoulish details of this affair. Rex and Sheila hastened from the crypt, closed the massive door, and hurried along a dark path. Thoroughly delighted, Kerry kept pace with them, carrying the girl's camera case.

He helped boost Sheila over the fence. Once they had made good their escape from the graveyard, he led them toward his roadster.

"May I drive you somewhere?" he inquired.

The girl assented quickly, adding that they had come up in a taxi, and gave Kerry an address near Washington Square. She sat snugly between Kerry and Rex, the latter's arm tightly around her as Kerry started off.

"Chin up, sweet," said Rex. "It's all over now."

Kerry felt the girl trembling against him. He gave Rex's reassurance a moment to take effect, then asked: "Are either of you named Reese, by any chance?"

"No," Rex said. "Sheila's name is Forbes—Mrs. Robert Forbes."

Kerry's nostrils dilated with the scent of scandal.

"My name is Grant," Rex went on. "I'm a licensed private detective. I've been working on a case for Sheila. I hope tonight's job winds it up."

"So do I," Kerry said, pressing the roadster to a swifter clip. "You wouldn't have invited me to that graveyard if you hadn't wanted to let me in on it, Grant. Let's have it."

Sheila Forbes said: "You see, my husband disappeared months ago. All this while, Rex and I have been trying to find him. For a long time we were working absolutely in the dark. The Missing Persons Bureau couldn't find even a trace of him. Then Rex and I became desperate and we began working on the idea that—"

"One moment," Kerry interrupted incredulously. "You, Rex,

were desperate to find the missing husband of this lovely girl you're crazy about?"

"Damn right," Rex Grant said as the car swung around a corner. "Bob Forbes was a good-for-nothing. Sheila married him when she was just a kid—of course, she didn't realize then that he'd turn out to be a rotter, content to let her support him. She's a first-class fashion photographer, and he'd been living off her for years, like a damned leach."

"He knew Rex and I were in love—we didn't try to conceal it," Sheila said quietly, "but he wouldn't divorce me, and he was very careful not to give me any grounds for suing him."

"Because she was his meal ticket," Rex Grant said. "After Bob Forbes had been missing a while, Sheila and I became convinced that he was dead. We have a damned good reason for wanting to prove it. If we can't prove it, we'll have to wait seven years, until Forbes can be declared legally dead, before we can be married. But if we are able to establish the fact of his death, then we can be married immediately—and that's what we've been trying our damnedest to do."

KERRY'S hands tightened on the wheel. "Did you expect to find Bob Forbes' corpse in Sheridan Reese's casket?" he demanded.

"Yes," Grant said.

"Did you find it there?"

"Yes," Grant said again.

Kerry's nerves turned into high-tension wires. "What! Can you prove that?"

"I don't know," Sheila Forbes said distractedly. "Rex and I are both sure it was Bob's body in that coffin, but if I didn't get a picture—"

"Your flash-bulb went off," Kerry interrupted. "Why are you doubtful about having a picture?"

"It happened so unexpectedly. I was so terrified—"

"Listen, Kerry," Rex Grant broke in. "Somebody knew we

were going to the Reese crypt tonight—and knew why, what's more. The skeleton was stolen in an attempt to prevent our identifying it as Bob Forbes'. There's some murderous scheme behind everything that's happened. But to hell with that. All I want to do is prove that Bob Forbes is dead. And we're not sure that we can, now that the skeleton is gone."

"You see," Sheila Forbes said quickly to Kerry as he steered the car through midtown Manhattan, "we forced open the door of the crypt and then opened the casket. It was a ghastly job, but we had to do it. As soon as I saw the skeleton, I was sure it was Bob's."

"How?" Kerry asked.

"When Bob was younger," the girl answered, "he worked in a lumber camp one summer, and broke his leg. It was never set properly. It made him limp, and he used that as an excuse for shirking any activity except dissipation. The right leg of the skeleton had been broken and badly spliced in exactly the same place. I'm sure of what we saw, but—"

"We went back to the car to get the camera case, Kerry," Rex Grant said. "Then I watched outside the crypt, while Sheila went about taking a photo of the skeleton. Suddenly I heard her scream—"

"I was all set to fire the bulb," the girl hurried on, "and suddenly I was frightened out of my wits. I realized that the right forearm of the skeleton was missing. It had been there, but now it was gone. Then I saw the arm—coming out of the empty recess. The fleshless fingers were gripping a knife, and it reached toward me. I was already so overwrought—I jerked, and the flash-bulb went off—then I screamed and ran out—"

"Someone had sneaked into the crypt while we were away, getting the camera case, Kerry," Grant explained. "We must have come back before he had time to take the skeleton out, so he had to hide. He used the skeleton's arm and a knife to scare Sheila off, then he ducked out fast with the rest of it. God knows if we'll ever see it again. I hope she got a picture!"

Sheila pointed to a small apartment house. "That's where I live. I'm going to develop the film right away. Please wait and see it, Mr. Kerry. I want you to know the truth, and to broadcast it. Then maybe someone will come forward with some new information that will help prove that Bob is dead."

Stopping the car, Kerry said anxiously: "Lord, I've got to hear the rest of this. But what led you to the Reese tomb? If it was Bob Forbes' skeleton you found, how did it get inside Sheridan Reese's casket? And in that case, where the hell is Sheridan Reese?"

"Let's get that film into the developer before we do any more talking, Kerry," Rex Grant urged.

Jubilant as he was over this break in the Reese case, Kerry deplored the fact that it was distracting him from the more important complications of the Colvin murder. Instinctively he looked for a telephone as he entered Sheila Forbes' apartment. He found none until he followed the girl and Grant into the darkroom in the rear.

THE INSTRUMENT sat among a professional array of photographic apparatus and supplies—tanks, a printer, an enlarger, chemicals and stores of sensitized materials. Kerry took it up and asked, "May I?" While Sheila Forbes deftly made preparations, he twirled the number of his office on the dial. The troubled voice of his secretary answered.

"Eve—" he began.

"Wrong number!" Eve snapped.

Kerry alertly broke the connection. He had called the phone on his desk. Now he dialed another number—that of an instrument in a soundproof booth buried among the file-cabinets. As the distant bell purred, he watched Sheila Grant.

She extinguished the white light and turned on a red bulb. In its dull glow, she removed the slide of the film-holder, slipped the film out, inserted it into a hanger, and dipped the hanger into a tank.

Again Eve answered. "Yes?" she whispered.

"What the hell's the trouble there?" Kerry demanded.

"The trouble here is cops. Two detectives are camping in this office, waiting to put their hooks in you. One of 'em is trying to force his way into this booth right now. I'll keep him out, if my foot doesn't break. Guy Kerry, you're in the soup."

"Listen, Eve!" Kerry protested. "Has Colvin's letter come?"

"No, but—"

"Did you check the serial number of that gun?"

"I did, I did, and you'd better listen to me!" Eve wailed. "Inspector Tarrant gave me that dope before I left my apartment. It knocked me off my pins. Ever since then, I've been rushing around like a wild woman. First I beat it out and got a photo of the man who owned that gun. Then—"

"Eve! Who is he??"

"That gun belonged to Sheridan Reese!"

Kerry took a tighter grip on the phone. Peering at Sheila Forbes and Rex Grant as they bent intently over the tank, he urged in a tense tone: "Go on, go on."

"Then I ran over to the morgue and took a good look at the man known as Henry Colvin," Eve resumed breathlessly. "I'm surprised you didn't recognize him. His hair is bleached, his mustache is gone and his face is tanned, but there's not the slightest doubt about it, Guy. Henry Colvin is Sheridan Reese."

Staring hard through the ruddy glow at Sheila Forbes and Rex Grant, Kerry asked: "Anything else?"

"My God, isn't that enough?" Eve moaned. "Do you realize the jam this puts you in, Guy? Reese was supposed to have been killed months ago, but all this time he's been alive, disguised, hiding. You've turned suspicion on yourself as his murderer. Don't you see that this brings a new element into the case— something that was lacking before—your motive for killing Reese?"

"My—what!"

"I can tell you exactly how Commissioner Endicott will tie all this in," Eve rushed on. "He'll say that you—the master-mind who knows the most intimate secrets of everybody's private life—you knew all along that Reese was alive. He'll say you were forcing Reese to pay you blackmail to keep quiet. He'll say you bled Reese to the limit, until Reese became so desperate he was going to expose you. Then, to prevent that, you killed Reese and tried to cover yourself with a couple of phony flashes about a suicide."

"Oh God!" Kerry groaned. "I've got a horrible feeling you're absolutely right. Listen, Eve. Does anybody else know who Henry Colvin really is?"

"Not another soul, so far—thank Heaven!" Eve muttered.

"Then stay right where you are, darling," Kerry directed her grimly. "Keep an ear cocked on the radio and wait for the fireworks!"

KERRY lowered the phone, his eyes still fixed on the girl and Grant. In the sepulchral red shine, their faces looked ghostly. Sheila Forbes had lifted the hanger from the developer and was gazing at a dim image on the dripping film.

"I did get it!" she exclaimed. Immersing the film again, she said breathlessly. "It'll take a few more minutes."

"While we're waiting," Kerry said levelly, "you can explain why you expected to find Bob Forbes' remains in Sheridan Reese's casket."

"We realized that Forbes and Reese had both disappeared on the same night," Grant answered. "And we remembered that Forbes knew Sheridan and Enid Reese, and often went on drinking bouts with them. I questioned Enid Reese, and she said that her husband and Forbes hadn't been together that night, but she sounded to me as if she were lying. I was damn sure the two cases connected up somehow."

Kerry asked incisively: "But did you forget the fact that the body dragged out of the East River was identified as Reese's by means of his fingerprints?"

"It was," Grant admitted, "but that could have been managed simply enough. Reese's prints were in the non-criminal file of the Department of Justice in Washington. I presume you know about that file. People are encouraged to send in their prints. The idea is to use them in cases of accidents and disasters, to identify bodies that might otherwise never be recognized. It's a fact that ten thousand people a month are sending their prints to the F.B.I. voluntarily.

"You simply send a penny postcard to Washington, asking for a file card, and back one comes. You follow instructions, put your prints on the card, and ship it in. In Reese's case, somebody pulled off a slick trick. Somebody sent in Bob Forbes' prints under Sheridan Reese's name. Naturally, then, when Forbes' body was pulled out of the river, it was identified as Reese's."

"We felt absolutely sure that that was what had been done," Sheila Forbes added, "because I remembered, one morning not long before Bob disappeared, finding him in bed dead drunk, with ink smudges on his fingertips. And he couldn't remember where he'd got them."

"I'll be damned!" Kerry murmured.

Again Sheila Forbes lifted the hanger from the developing tank. Now the image on the film was clear and strong.

"Yes!" Rex Grant exclaimed. "There's the old break in the right thigh-bone. It's perfectly plain. That was Bob Forbes' skeleton. See for yourself, Kerry."

Kerry peered at the image, noted the unmistakable enlargement of the bone at the point of fracture, and reached automatically for the telephone—but checked himself.

"I'll shout this to the whole cockeyed nation soon," he promised, "but until then I want you to keep it strictly under your hats. Agreed?"

They nodded. Kerry muttered that he had a job to do, and left, leaving them gazing after him uncertainly.

CHAPTER FOUR

A DATE AT THE MORGUE

KERRY HURRIED to his car and started off. Then, remembering that his roadster was well-known, and that he was the subject of a concerted police search, he sought a parking-lot. He swung into the nearest, on Madison Avenue. Pausing briefly in its office hut to consult the telephone directory, he hailed a passing cab, sent it toward the address of Enid Reese.

When it stopped at a brownstone front, Kerry directed the driver to wait. In the vestibule he punched a call-button labeled with Enid Reese's name. Finding the entrance ajar, he strode directly toward the door of her apartment on the first floor.

It was open an inch. A young woman was warily looking out. She stiffened with alarm at sight of Kerry. Suddenly she shut the door in Kerry's face.

Conscious of quick voices and hurried movements inside the door, Kerry twisted the knob, then knocked. He rapped imperatively until, moments later, Enid Reese opened the way. Kerry strode in, glanced around the room, then turned to a connecting door and thrust it wide.

A chill draft poured in through an open window in the rear, billowing the silken curtain. Kerry bounded to it and put his head out. He saw a dark movement at one of the fences that divided the court within the block of buildings. It was a man, scrambling to the rear entrance of one of the other houses. Kerry tensed with an impulse to give pursuit but, realizing he could not overtake the fugitive, turned back to confront Enid Reese.

The former night-club thrush was dark, beautiful, luscious of body—and trembling with fright.

"Whoever that man is who scrammed out of here," Kerry

commented acridly, "he couldn't have thought I was your husband. Or could he?"

Enid Reese stammered: "There—there was no one!"

Kerry stepped closer. "Let's skip it," he said. "I think you know who I am, Mrs. Reese. I have a taxi waiting. I want you to come with me—and I strongly advise you to do what I ask."

"But—why?"

"Because," Kerry answered, "in a few minutes I'm going to tell millions of people what has actually happened to Sheridan Reese. And if you're innocent of being a party to a criminal conspiracy, not to mention one or two murders, you'll want me to have the facts straight."

For a moment Enid Reese stared at him, pale and transfixed. Suddenly she caught up her mink coat and her hat, closed a white fist on her gloves. Kerry grimly escorted her out to the taxi.

Settling beside her on the seat, he directed the driver: "Take us to the morgue."

Enid Reese gazed at Kerry wide-eyed as the cab started up. "What—what do you want?" she asked breathlessly.

"Information," Kerry answered succinctly. "Start at the beginning. The Reese family disapproved of Sheridan's marrying a night-club singer, didn't they? He married you anyway, and that estranged him from his father and mother, didn't it?"

"Ev-everybody knows that."

"Sheridan had always been a playboy, squandering his very generous allowance, hadn't he? When that allowance was cut off, he had to buckle down to work in a brokerage office, didn't he?"

"Every—everybody knows that, too."

"And he hated it. He couldn't make a go of it. You were running deep into debt. But when Sheridan Reese's death was established, and his big insurance policies were paid, you came into an easy fortune. And so did Sheridan Reese! But everybody doesn't know *that!*"

Enid Reese twisted her gloves and stared at Kerry in silent terror.

"I want to know how much of a part you played in his neat little game. You'd better tell me the facts right here and now, because if you deserve a break I'll give it to you—and the police will pound the truth out of you anyway."

ENID REESE melted back into the seat and sobbed into her handkerchief. Kerry let her. The cab was nearing the morgue when she looked up, her pleading eyes dewed with tears.

"I—I'll tell you the truth," she whispered. "I really thought Sherry was dead. I didn't—didn't even know the body had been identified as his, until the police notified me. It wasn't until weeks later that I heard from him."

"You mean that this grisly plan of his was all a surprise to you?"

"Of course!" Enid Reese blurted. "He phoned me—told me he'd done it to get the insurance money. He said that after a time we could meet in some foreign country and go on living together in luxury. But it was too soon yet, and in the meantime he needed cash. I began sending him money regularly, but never seeing him. Can—can the police do anything to me for that— for not telling them, as soon as I found out Sherry wasn't really dead?"

Kerry said to the driver: "Stop here." As the cab swung to the curb, he said: "But how long is it since your husband returned to town? Why did he risk coming back?"

"But—I didn't know!" Enid Reese said. "Where—where is he?"

Grimly Kerry pointed to a somber building standing directly ahead. "In there," he said. "He was murdered tonight. His body is awaiting identification. But before you go in, I want to know if there was a reason anyone could have had for—"

"Oh-h!" Enid Reese cried softly. "Sherry—Sherry!"

Then, frantically, so frantically that Kerry could not restrain her, she sprang out of the cab, ran, sobbing, toward the morgue. Eager as he was to follow, Kerry did not dare show himself. In a feverish hurry, he paid the cab driver and ran along the side-street in search of a telephone.

He found one in a corner drug store, spun off his special number and urged his technician: "Put me on!" He could imagine millions of listeners expectantly bending their ears to their radios as the current program faded. His signal came—"Take it away!"—and five seconds later his twang blanketed the nation.

"Attention, Mr. and Mrs. United States! Your newshawk of the kilocycles, Keyhole Kerry, is bringing you one of the most amazing flashes of his career. Listen carefully, for I must be brief. I must finish before police headquarters has time to trace this wire and surround me with cossacks. I am still a hunted fugitive, being sought for tonight's murder of a man who was believed to have died many months ago—Sheridan Reese!

"Sheridan Reese, ladies and gentlemen, not Henry Colvin, is the name of the dead man to whom I directed the police earlier this evening. Behind this startling revelation lies a daring, cold-blooded, murderous intrigue which your scoop specialist is exclusively revealing now."

KERRY was watching the entrance of the store, alert for an invasion of furious blue-coats. "The truth is this—Sheridan Reese fabricated his own death. Because he needed a body to be buried as his, in order to make his plan work, Reese murdered a friend of his. Then, changing his appearance and his name, he effaced himself from the New York scene. The body that was later dragged out of the East River, so battered that it was unrecognizable, was identified as Reese's solely because Reese had cleverly contrived to substitute a friend's fingerprints for his own in the non-criminal file of the F.B.I. The name of the poor devil who was buried as Sheridan Reese, in the Reese family crypt, was Robert Forbes.

"At this very moment, Mrs. Reese is at the city morgue, identifying the body of her husband—by whom she is now a widow for the second time. The important question now is, Why was the 'dead' man killed tonight?

"A short time ago, Reese returned to New York and rented a furnished apartment under the name of Colvin. I think he risked coming back because his plan had met with some unexpected complication. Possibly some interloper, who was aware of Reese's machinations, was demanding a share of his loot as the price of silence."

Eyes still on the door, Kerry was poised to bolt at any instant.

"Police Commissioner Endicott is becoming convinced, ladies and gentlemen, that I am that interloper. You have probably noticed that, so far, I have not said one word as to whether or not I am actually guilty of tonight's murder. I have a strong reason for avoiding that point. My reticence is necessary to my method of handling my part in this affair. But—"

Kerry's apprehension was making his nerves unbearably tight and hot.

"But I promise you and you and you that when the proper moment comes, I will speak. In other words, I will take good care that no one scoops me on my own story! Until that moment comes, ladies and gentlemen, Keyhole Kerry is again becoming a fugitive from justice. Good-night!"

Kerry clattered out of the booth and dodged from the store. Halfway up the block, he abruptly sidled into the nearest shadowed doorway. He watched a prowl-car streak to the corner and buck to a stop. At the same time a second police roadster howled down from the opposite direction. Four uniformed men, their guns drawn, charged into the store that Kerry had just vacated.

Delighted yet chilled, the man who gloried in the attention of a nation took to his heels, grimly seeking dark obscurity.

CHAPTER FIVE

GOOD-BYE, ALIBI!

KEYHOLE KERRY paced back and forth across the little room. Murky morning sunlight shone in the window. The clock on the table pointed to a few minutes before nine. Kerry's unshaven beard bristled, and his eyes were red-rimmed after a sleepless night. For hours he had been waiting for the telephone to ring, but it was remaining nerve-rackingly silent.

The instrument was listed under a false name. Under the same *nom-de-guerre*, Kerry had rented this small office, in an unfrequented building, months ago. He had wished a safe retreat, in cases of emergency, such as the present predicament. And no racketeer on the lam had ever planned a hide-away more shrewdly. Only Eve knew the number of the phone, and she never rang it except from a public pay-station. The fact that she had not called was grinding on Kerry's frayed nerves.

When, at last, the bell sang out, he snatched the instrument up.

"Guy," came Eve's weary tone, "I couldn't call sooner. I've just come from an all-night session at headquarters. I've been through hell for you, Guy. Endicott shouted me into a state of exhaustion. I didn't tell him anything, but I didn't need to—he has plenty of ideas of his own. Have you seen the morning papers?"

"I haven't dared to go out after them, for fear of missing this call. What about Reese's letter?" Kerry demanded. "Did it come?"

"No, Guy. I went through the morning mail five times, but it isn't there. Reese couldn't have mailed it to you at U.B.C. He must have sent it in care of the *De-Luxe-Lax* Company, and the plant, for God's sake, is 'way over in the wilds of Jersey. I've sent Smitty over in a taxi. But the letter may not be there either, Guy. We may never see it now."

"I know," Kerry moaned. "Two different things could have happened to it. The cops may have intercepted it. Or, the murderer may have found it in Reese's room and destroyed it. And I need that letter!"

"If you ever get out of this, Guy Kerry," Eve blubbered, "I'll be the most surprised woman who ever suffered a nervous collapse."

"I still have my out," Kerry said grimly. "O.K. Eve. Back on the job, and call me the instant there's a break."

Kerry hurried from the telephone and out of the building. At times like this, he was profoundly gratified that his face was not one-millionth as familiar to the world at large as his sandpaper voice. He gathered an armful of papers, scurried back to his desk and eyed the ominous headlines.

Eve's doomful prophecy, concerning Endicott's theory, had come true. The front pages prominently featured the commissioner's belief that the murder had sprung out of a certain radio reporter's blackmailing activities, which Endicott had apparently suspected for years. Black type accused Kerry, by innuendo, of having known of Reese's plan from the beginning, of having victimized Reese, of having murdered Reese to save himself from exposure.

"Damn it!" Kerry exploded. "I invited 'em to call me a killer, but when they call me a crooked reporter, that's going too far!"

HE READ that the police check-up had verified the fact that the broken eyeglass lens actually belonged to Keyhole Kerry. The entire force was ransacking the city, striving to flush him out of hiding. Mrs. Enid Reese, after having been questioned, had been released under bail, on a writ of habeas corpus obtained by her attorney. A statement made by Mrs. Reese only added to Kerry's anxiety—

> My husband had begun asking me for more and more money. He said he needed it desperately. He said that he was being forced to pay over huge sums to somebody who had learned of his plan, and that if he didn't pay, this person would expose him.

Kerry took up the telephone. Calling the city-room of the *Herald*, he asked for Paul Phipps. Phipps' tone dropped cautiously at the sound of Kerry's voice.

"Lord, Phipps! I just wanted to make sure you're all right. Whatever you do, don't step in front of any taxis. Before very long, I'll want you to broadcast your alibi for me, because this is getting to be too damned much of a good thing."

"The sooner the better, Kerry," Phipps answered warily. "As the situation stands now, we don't dare press it too far. Whenever you want me, just say the word, and we'll blow up Endicott's case against you."

"Right. Stay there in that office," Kerry directed Phipps, "until I call you again. Then come running."

Again Kerry paced the floor. Time crawled. An hour crept by, then another. With each passing minute, Kerry's anxiety mounted. It was almost noon when the telephone rang again. Catching it up, Kerry again heard Eve's tired voice.

"Smitty just got back from the *De-Luxe-Lax* plant with a batch of mail for you, Guy," she told him, "but Reese's letter isn't there. It isn't, it isn't!"

"Oh God!" Kerry moaned. "Keep looking for it, Eve. It may turn up yet. In any case, call me back now and then. It won't be long before I put on a broadcast that'll prove me innocent and make Endicott look like a dunderhead."

Kerry felt the pressure of that necessity bearing harder and harder upon him as the day dragged on. He kept pacing the office. At intervals Eve called to say that the Reese letter was still unaccounted for. He forgot to eat. His hunger for news on the case was sharper. Dodging out and back with the latest editions of the afternoon papers, he scanned every line.

Enid Reese's statement was now followed up with another, more explicitly damning to Kerry—

My husband didn't tell me the name of the man who was demanding hush-money from him, but he hinted that this man was in a powerful position in radio, daring and dangerous, and able to make the facts public at any time.

Kerry grimly mulled over those words. He was still marching off the length of the secret office when darkness closed down. Again Eve phoned, to tell him distraughtly that there was still no Reese letter in sight. With sudden decision, he called the number of the *Herald* city-room and again got Paul Phipps on the wire.

"This has gone far enough, Phipps," he began grimly. "Being accused of blackmail is something I didn't count on. The mere hint of it is poison to me. When the radio audience begins to believe that my racket is crooked, then I'm finished. I've got to prove my integrity right now. I want you to skip over here pronto—"

"Wait, Kerry!" Phipps broke in.

"We can't wait any longer!" Kerry snapped. "If I don't crash through now—"

"But I've had another tip!" Kerry quieted tensely at that, and Phipps hurried on. "It just came by phone a minute ago. A man's voice—the same voice that tipped me about the so-called Colvin suicide."

"What did he say?" Kerry demanded quickly.

"He said he wouldn't talk over the phone. He said he wanted to see me personally. He said to come over to the end of East Fifty-fourth Street right away. That must mean something, Kerry. The end of East Fifty-fourth Street is where Reese's body was pulled out of the East River."

"On your way!" Kerry urged. "I'll be over there myself, as fast as I can travel."

"If that man's on the square, we certainly need him, Kerry," Phipps agreed. "In fact, you're going to need all the help you can get. We've just heard from headquarters that the D.A. is going before the Grand Jury now to ask for an indictment charging you with the first-degree murder of Sheridan Reese. He's sure to get it. What's more, the *De-Luxe-Lax* Company has just issued a statement saying that if blackmail charges are substantiated against you, they'll rule you off the air."

The shock of that caused Kerry to totter a little. "You're going to alibi me on the air, Phipps," he said grimly, "as soon as we've followed through on that unknown man's tip. For God's sake, get over there—get going!"

KERRY slammed the telephone down and left the office. Emerging from the building, he clambered into a taxi, his nerves aflame with impatience. Traffic was at its thickest. Theater, dinner and movie crowds were making midtown Manhattan a nightmare of congestion. In desperation, Kerry abandoned the taxi while he was still blocks from the East River.

Striding swiftly, he followed the dead-end street. Here it was dark and quiet. The sluggish East River blackly reflected the lights of Brooklyn. A freighter, gliding alongside Welfare Island, hooted mournfully. The street met the water at a short ramp and a small pier, shrouded with murk. Kerry approached it rapidly—until, suddenly, he stopped short, every nerve cold.

He heard two quick gunshots. The flash of the weapon sprang out of the darkness at the brink of the river. In the instant of light, Kerry saw a face—the face of Paul Phipps. Phipps' lean figure was outlined dimly against the wavering reflections on the water. Kerry shouted at him but Phipps did not answer.

Kerry sprang down the ramp. He thought he heard quick, fugitive movements somewhere in the gloom. He was still yards from Phipps when a light appeared. It was the gleam of a flashlight held in Phipps' hand. It swung down; and Phipps dropped it. Continuing to burn, it threw a glow upon Phipps. Kerry saw him tottering—saw glistening crimson on his neck and collar.

Before Kerry could reach him, Phipps toppled—fell loosely over the edge of the pier and smacked flatly into the river!

Kerry shot one wild glance around, saw nothing, then ran and dove. Fully clothed, he flung himself into filthy water. It was like rancid ink. Kerry groped crazily under the surface, trying to find Phipps. He bobbed up, gagged once—for a sewer was pouring into the river directly under the pier—then forced himself down again.

Moments later he flung his arms around a tarry piling and clung. Lack of sleep and food, and the reek of the water, overwhelmed him. As soon as he was able to breathe, he kicked toward the bank. He pulled himself aboard a moored sand scow, tottered up the ramp, then propelled himself on buckling legs along the street.

Stumbling into a public garage, ignoring the stare of two mechanics, he grabbed up the telephone. Spinning the zero, he gulped out a demand for connection with headquarters. Dripping, spitting out nauseating stuff, he spoke in a choked whisper.

"Get an emergency wagon to the end of East Fifty-fourth! A man's just been shot and thrown into the river!"

That, he knew, would be enough to throw the rescue squad into instant action. They would rush to the scene with fire-engine speed. Kerry clung to the phone. The two mechanics had heard him, and were hurrying out of the garage, toward the pier. Grasping the opportunity, Kerry spun off his special number.

"Put me on!" he gasped; and after "Take it away!" came, he began a frantic sputter.

"Attention, Mr. and Mrs. United States! Keyhole Kerry is bringing you a new and startling flash in the sensational Reese case. A police emergency car is now speeding to the end of East Fifty-fourth Street in an attempt to rescue Paul Phipps, a newspaper reporter. Apparently Phipps was shot, and perhaps killed, just before he fell into the East River, by some participant in the two previous murders. Listen, ladies and gentlemen!"

Kerry turned the transmitter toward the street to catch the mounting screech of a siren. The sound shrilled louder and a green car sped past. As it faded, Kerry resumed.

"You just heard the emergency wagon rushing to the scene. I will endeavor to report to you the result of their search. Hang onto your radios, Mr. and Mrs. United States, for I'll soon be back with a flash concerning the fate of Paul Phipps!"

KERRY dropped the instrument and ran from the garage. He saw that the police car had stopped, that its crew were running down to the pier. A searchlight glared out over the water, and revealed men and women hurrying to the spot from the surrounding streets. Deciding that a direct approach might mean his own capture, Kerry hurried to First Avenue, shifted to Fifty-third, then turned again toward the river.

The pier at the end of Fifty-third was longer. Already men were gathering on it, to watch the operations a block away. Other people, having caught Kerry's flash, were craning out of the windows of the surrounding apartment buildings. As the crowd thickened, Kerry carefully kept himself in the dark background. He shivered in his wet clothes, and a sickness of heart seized him. Minute by minute, as he watched, the despondency within him grew.

The crowd was already beginning to disperse when Kerry hastened away. On First Avenue he ventured into a bar. He shut himself inside a telephone booth, again dialed his special number and moaned: "Give me the air!" During the five-second wait, after he heard "Take it away!" his face became even more haggard and his shoulders more heavily laden with despair.

"Flash, Mr. and Mrs. United States! Keyhole Kerry is back. The search for Paul Phipps is being abandoned. The attempt to recover his body from the East River has failed. Perhaps it will never be found. Only two persons in the world can say what happened to him tonight, ladies and gentlemen—your scoop specialist, and the man who is responsible for his disappearance. The time has come when I must reveal all I know about this case."

A small radio behind the bar was twanging out Kerry's voice and a score of men, all unaware that the broadcast was originating within a few feet of them, were listening raptly.

"Paul Phipps was one of my assistants. He went with me last

night to the room, where I found the disguised Sheridan Reese dead. He had promised to testify, over the air tonight that while examining the deathroom, I dropped my eyeglasses accidentally. He was the one living person who could have proved that I am innocent of both blackmail and murder. Now he cannot speak in my defense. It is obvious that a diabolical plan lies behind what has happened tonight. It is this, ladies and gentlemen—the man who really killed Sheridan Reese has taken this means of destroying my alibi and fastening his own guilt upon me."

Warily watching the street door, Kerry rushed on: "I dare not say more now, Mr. and Mrs. United States. At this very moment, the Grand Jury is indicting me for the murder of Sheridan Reese. If I don't flee from this telephone at once, I will certainly be captured by the gendarmes, and all my efforts to prove my innocence will be balked. Keyhole Kerry, your fugitive newshawk, is now heading—not for the electric chair, I hope!—but for the tall timber!"

CHAPTER SIX

TOP-HAT PAY-OFF

HAUNTED BY the fear that the arm of the law was reaching closer and closer to his neck, Kerry hurried into his hide-away. Startled, he found both Eve Vane and Smitty there. The radio was playing, the whitenesses of their faces testified that they had heard Kerry's latest flash. Eve at once began pushing a bit of paper at him.

"I found it, I found it!" she said in a sick wail. "The Reese letter!"

Kerry snatched at it. He unfolded a closely written sheet and, while river water dripped from him, read the message rapidly.

Exclusive information for Keyhole Kerry—

Investigate the case of Sheridan Reese. You will find material for plenty of sensational news flashes. Use every effort to verify the following:

Enid Martin was not in love with Sheridan Reese when she married him. She was, and still is, the love-slave of another man whose identity I do not know. I will call him Mr. X.

Mr. X encouraged Enid Martin to marry Sheridan Reese in the hope that, through her, he would share in the Reese fortune. This plan failed when Sheridan Reese's marriage alienated him from his family. Enid Reese, still secretly dominated by the avaricious Mr. X, then urged upon her husband a plan whereby he was to play dead, so that she could collect his huge insurance policies. This money, she said, they would share. Financially desperate, and blindly deluded by his wife, Reese put this scheme into operation—a plan involving fraud and murder.

Enid Reese duly collected. But she sent no money to her "deceased" husband, who was in hiding. The real motive behind her plan thus became evident. It was Mr. X, not her husband, who was to share with her this ill-gotten fortune. Working together with devilish cleverness, Enid Reese and Mr. X had jockeyed the "late" Sheridan Reese into a situation that paid them handsomely and at the same time left him, they thought, with no possible comeback, because he was "dead."

They were wrong. Though I hope to be able to continue to hide and elude the law, I am determined to make them suffer for their treachery, even though it may mean my own doom. Therefore I am sending you this absolutely true statement.

Sheridan Reese.

Kerry stared at Eve.

"I decided to look through all the mail one last time, Guy," she said breathlessly. "I found it in the very first batch that had come this morning. It was stuck to the back of a package of books, and I'd missed it. I couldn't get you on the phone, so I rushed over here. Thank Heaven—"

"Lord!" Kerry gasped. "This explains why Reese came back to town. He must have known somebody else was getting the money he'd counted on. He must have tried to find out from his wife who Mr. X is. Mr. X became afraid that Reese would blow up the works. Also, Mr. X must have heard my first flash, about Reese's being still alive. So he killed Reese, for two reasons.

First, to protect himself. Second, to make sure of the insurance money, which he would otherwise lose."

"Of course!" Eve exclaimed. "That's the reason behind the tip-off. Mr. X wanted it known, as soon as possible, that Reese was really dead. And naturally, he wanted it to look like a suicide—Reese blowing his brains out through fear of being caught. Then Mr. X coached Enid Reese in a story that would incriminate her as little as possible, and at the same time stick you for the murder. Why, that little— Oh Guy!"

"Mr. X has certainly put Keyhole Kerry behind the eight-ball," Kerry said grimly. "He robbed me of my alibi. He's responsible for what happened to Paul Phipps tonight. There's only one way I can save myself from the chair now—and that's to find out who Mr. X is, and pin this whole thing on him. Lord! He's the rat who scrammed out of Enid Reese's apartment last night, and I might have collared him then!"

"Guy, what—what can you do?"

"I've got to think of something—I've damned well got to," Kerry said. He thrust the letter back at Eve. "Keep that, and guard it with your life. I need every particle of evidence I can get my hands on. That gun may help. Mr. X's fingerprints may be on it. Smitty, beat it down to Grand Central right now, and get it back."

"Sure, chief!" Smitty said alertly. He thrust his hand into the pocket where he had stowed the claim-check, and suddenly his face went deathly white around his freckles. "Oh gosh!" he gulped. "Gosh—it's gone!"

Kerry grabbed him and probed into the pocket so violently he almost ripped it off. Smitty staggered as Kerry and Eve searched into every pocket he had, almost pulling him apart in the process. When they finished, they were stunned.

"Mr. X was watching you, Smitty," Kerry said in a grating tone. "He followed you around. He watched his chance and picked your pocket. I hope to God he hasn't yet had a chance to get that gun out of the checkroom. Beat it down there and see if you can find it, Smitty. Get going!"

SMITTY went out with desperate haste. While Eve's terrified eyes clung to him, Kerry tramped back and forth across the office. He asked once, "Did you make sure nobody followed you here?" and Eve murmured, "I'm positive nobody trailed me." Abruptly Kerry turned to the telephone, dragged out the directory, found a number, then spun the dial.

Eve stood transfixed, watching him. When Kerry spoke, it was in a low, cautious whisper that lacked all resemblance to his normal scratchy voice.

"Enid?"

"Yes?" Enid Reese's voice returned.

"We've got to get out of town."

After a hesitation, Enid Reese whispered in turn: "But—why?"

"Kerry just received the letter. Kerry knows all about it. It won't be long before he puts it on the air."

"But the letter—it couldn't have said—"

"It said enough. They'll catch us sure, if we don't get away. How soon can you leave?"

"Right—right now."

"Good. Get out of that apartment immediately. Make sure you're not trailed. Be at the Fort Lee ferry in exactly an hour. I'll be on the first ferry that pulls out after the hour. Once we're across the state line, in Jersey, I'll join you. It's our only chance.

"I—I'll be there."

"If the phone rings again, don't answer it."

Quietly, Kerry hung up. His eyes held a desperate light.

Eve gripped his arm. "I know what you're trying to do. This will prove that Enid Reese was up to her neck in the scheme. You're going to try to force her to tell you who Mr. X is. But why the ferry? Why—"

"So she wouldn't suspect a trick. I told her that Keyhole Kerry has the letter. She, as well as everybody else, knows my tactics—

how I've used a microphone as a trap, in several cases. She'll reason that I couldn't corner her with a wire on a ferry-boat in the middle of the Hudson River—but she'll be wrong."

"With things in as big a mess as they are, I'm ready for anything, Guy," Eve said miserably. "Go on, go on."

"I want you to hop over to U.B.C. Get hold of the top-hat broadcasting dingus—understand? Collect a technical crew, and take that contraption up to the ferry. Be there in plenty of time. I've got a little errand to do, before I join you there, but—"

"There'll be cops watching the ferry, Guy!" Eve objected. "Cops looking for you!"

"I'll have to risk that," Kerry said quickly. "Run along, Eve!"

Kerry hustled her out. He picked up the telephone. He was hotly anxious to make the Reese letter the subject of a flash but, wary that it would urge Mr. X to make an escape, he did not dial his special number. He spun off another taken from the directory, and a man's voice answered: "Grant Detective Bureau."

Kerry immediately hung up. He took a trench-coat from the closet, covered his wet clothing with it, put on a dry hat, and left the office.

SINCE the Grant Detective Bureau was not far, he walked— swiftly. Reaching the fourth floor of a building on Broadway, he opened a door and walked directly to a desk.

Rex Grant was sitting at it. In another chair, beside Grant, was Sheila Forbes. They looked surprised and uneasy. Kerry promptly picked up the telephone, dialed his special number and, when his watchdog answered, said: "Hang onto this line."

"What's up, Kerry?" Grant asked.

"The game," Kerry answered laconically. "Grant, you look like the answer to this radio reporter's prayer. Take that puzzled expression off your face, and don't waste time asking me what the devil I mean. I'm going to tell you that, right here and now.

"In the first place, you're a private detective, a man whose business is digging up information. Also, you're a slick thinker who figured out a cute trick about substituting one set of fingerprints for another. You're an attractive boy whom a woman would easily fall for—even a married one—and you know all the Broadway night clubs inside and out. Moreover, for a long time you've been wanting to get rid of the husband of the woman you love. Do you begin to get the drift of what I'm driving at?"

"Damned right I do!" Grant growled.

"I thought so," Kerry said, holding the open telephone ready. "Enid Reese has been in love with you for a long time. You're crazy about Sheila Forbes, but that's beside the point—you had Enid Reese under your thumb. You cooked up the plan for Sheridan Reese's 'death,' and you did it for two reasons. One, to grab onto plenty of money. Two, to get rid of Bob Forbes. But when it dawned on you that you couldn't marry Sheila until you proved that Forbes was dead—"

"Rex!" the girl broke in, her tone frightened. "What is he saying!"

"You're the mug who's been hanging this thing onto me, Grant," Kerry said. "You tried to clinch it tonight by getting rid of Paul Phipps. If you think you can squeeze out of this, just start talking, because in two seconds I'm going to spill the whole works on the air."

Grant smiled, then he chuckled, and his chuckle erupted into a laugh.

"Sorry, Kerry," he said. "I heard your first flash about Phipps. It came over the radio in the office of the police commissioner. I was talking with Endicott at the time—coming clean about having been a ghoul last night. If you doubt me, I suggest that you phone Endicott."

Kerry's shoulders sagged as he stared. He didn't doubt Grant. He had less than no desire to telephone the commissioner. He lifted the telephone, said, "Never mind," then went to the door with dragging steps. On the sill he paused, looking back.

"Well, I didn't really think you'd done it," he said. "From the first, I had the impression that you're a pretty good egg."

HE TRUDGED to the elevator and out into the street. While a taxi carried him northward, he reflected that he was perilously near the end of his rope. But he was still grimly hopeful when he reached the ferry station.

Leaving his taxi, he strode until he caught a signal from a car parked near the ferry entrance. Crowding into it, he found two technicians, a pile of clothing, a confusion of radio apparatus, and Eve.

"Guy!" Eve choked. "Smitty phoned just before I came here. He says the box is gone from the checkroom, and that somebody used the stolen ticket to claim it."

Kerry's moan said that he had expected this. He noted that one of the technicians was testing a sensitive receiving-set equipped with a loop aerial. From the set, a wire ran out of the car, into the nearest store, and connected with a telephone line leading to the U.B.C. control-room. The other man was doing strange things with the pile of clothing.

Kerry struggled out of his trench-coat and peeled off his wet suit. Carefully he put on a pair of dark trousers, a dickey, a white vest, then a tail-coat. The technician stuffed small but powerful batteries into his pockets, then made connections with a tiny microphone concealed in Kerry's white tie, and with a compact transmitter concealed inside a top-hat. When Kerry emerged from the car, carrying a stick that was in reality an antenna, he was actually a fashionable walking broadcasting-station.

This strange contrivance had been used a number of times for broadcasts originating among crowds in the open. It was the oddest *tour de force* that radio engineering had yet developed, but no one before Keyhole Kerry had ever thought to use it in an attempt to unmask a murderer.

Kerry walked away from the car, swinging the electrical walking-stick and counting in a normal tone of voice. When the technician at the receiving-set in the car signaled that reception was satisfactory, he hurried back.

"The trouble with this contraption," he said uneasily, "is that it feels too damned much like the electric chair!" He glanced at his strap-watch. "Time's up. The next ferry is it. Eve, darling, pray for me."

Taking a deep breath, Kerry sauntered toward the ferry. Blue-coats were standing about. Several men, who looked like detectives, were watching the crowds. Boldly, hoping that his unwonted garb was an effective disguise, Kerry mingled with the scores who were pressing toward the incoming ferry. When the gate opened, he drifted with them, glancing about for Enid Reese.

He did not glimpse her.

Kerry found a dark spot on the deck. Passengers herded to the rails. Cars rolled aboard. Moments passed while the ferry filled, with the Jersey lights twinkling on the water. Kerry's eyes hunted for Enid Reese all the while, in vain.

Knowing that the technicians and Eve were listening in the car, that his control man in the master monitor-room was ready to switch him onto the network at his signal, he kept saying in a low tone: "I hope you can hear me. God, I hope you can hear me."

The gate clattered shut. The ramp was pulled up and the ferry began churning out of the slip. It chugged out into the current and the darkness on the deck became heavier. Kerry left his obscure position. Quietly strolling the deck, he looked sharply at every face. Dread crept into his heart—dread that Enid Reese had refused the bait, that something had warned her away. Then he saw her.

Kerry said quietly: "Put me on."

ENID REESE was standing anxiously at the rail. Her worried eyes were turning expectantly—searching, Kerry hoped, for the man known as Mr. X. Her glance passed over him as he turned his head. Judging that the air was his by now, Kerry spoke again.

"Attention, Mr. and Mrs. United States! Keyhole Kerry, your headline beater, is speaking to you over a special short-wave hook-up. Because the police are still hunting for me, I prefer not to reveal where I am, until later. I am standing, however, within a few feet of a woman who is fleeing New York City at this very moment, in great fear that she will be charged as a party to the murder of which I am accused."

Enid Reese left her position, hurried along the rail, and paused at a spot where passengers were few. His eyes fixed upon her, Kerry sauntered in that direction.

"That charge, when it is made, ladies and gentlemen, will be absolutely true. The woman is the widow of Sheridan Reese. She has come here to meet the man who planned, first, Sheridan Reese's fake death, then his actual murder. She is guilty of assisting at every step of this multiple crime. I am about to accost her, in the hope of frightening her into making a damaging admission. You and you and you, numbering millions, ladies and gentlemen, are witnesses to this attempt. Listen!"

Kerry crossed the deck. He paused at the side of Enid Reese. As his hand took her arm firmly, she looked up and gasped.

"Good evening, Mrs. Reese," he said grimly.

Enid Reese stifled an exclamation.

"I'm afraid I haven't done you justice, in my estimation of you, Mrs. Reese," Kerry went on as her eyes opened roundly. "When I questioned you last night, I thought you were a sensitive, timid little thing. Now I realize, instead, that you're avaricious, cold-blooded, and an excellent actress."

"Why!" the woman exclaimed. "Why—how *can* you say a thing like that?"

"Thanks for proving my point about acting ability," Kerry said with a grim smile. "I can say a thing like that because you helped plan the murder of Robert Forbes. Because, after you put your husband in the position of a living dead man, you deliberately betrayed and abandoned him. Because, when he returned to protest your treachery, you encouraged another man to murder him—the man you're waiting for now."

Every word of this, Kerry hoped desperately, was flashing across the country—but he could not be sure.

Enid Reese was looking at him narrowly. "You know a great deal, don't you, Mr. Kerry?" she asked in an edged tone.

"Enough to send you to the chair, Mrs. Reese," Kerry answered levelly. "You see, the letter your husband wrote me before he was killed reached me tonight. It damns you utterly—you and the man who murdered him a few minutes after he mailed it. Mrs. Reese, you have only one hope of saving yourself. That is, to throw yourself on the mercy of the court, to plead that you were forced, like a slave, into committing these crimes, to—"

"You can't prove Sheridan wrote that letter!" Enid Reese blurted wildly. "He's dead—you can never prove it!"

"His handwriting—"

A swift step sounded behind Kerry. Startled, he twisted about. He saw a dark figure darting from the shadow of the deck-house. An arm was reaching high, the hand gripping an automatic. The man hurled himself upon Kerry, whipping downward viciously with the gun. Kerry jarred against the rail—and his top-hat full of transmitting apparatus fell off his head.

IT DROPPED to the length of its flexible cord and dangled as Kerry caught at the arm wielding the gun. He tried to see the face of his attacker, but the mid-river darkness baffled his eyes. He was conscious that Enid Reese was standing by, watching the struggle with merciless coldness. Striving to preserve the working condition of the transmitter, Kerry was desperately hampered. Wrenching away, he shouted.

"Attention, New York police! Order Enid Reese stopped at the Jersey end of the Fort Lee ferry! Her confederate is also aboard! He's beating me with a gun—I'm trying to catch sight of his face—"

Kerry's voice became a moan. A savage side-swipe of the gun had caught him on the temple. He staggered against the rail, feeling powerful hands gripping him. He was heaved up, pushed. Aware that he was being spilled overboard, he seized one of the other man's arms. He clenched it with all his strength as he fell.

The other man plunged over the rail with Kerry. They struck the water with a loud, flat splash. And at that instant, Kerry realized, as the river water penetrated the coils and condensers, that his transmitter went dead.

He rose to the surface first. Dizzy blackness surrounded him. Reflections traced crazy patterns around him. He saw a head pop up from the water, then caught the glint of the gun that the other man was still gripping. Kerry ducked down. The queer, muffled sound he heard was the explosion of the weapon. He kicked, felt the other man's body, drove his fist into it as hard as the water permitted.

Bobbing up, he struck again, at the dim face. The gun swung at him, and he grabbed it. Closing both hands upon it, he twisted. He splashed back with the gun. Because the other man was kicking at him viciously, he whipped the weapon down at the almost invisible head. The crack of the impact was sharp and solid. Kerry grabbed the other man's collar as he was going down.

He found himself holding onto an unconscious body. The ferry had churned on its way. The Jersey shore was close, but Kerry's wire was near the New York slip. He began swimming frantically toward it, towing his captive. His hope of complete vindication gave him the strength to make it.

The other man was reviving when Kerry splashed into the slip. Men shouted at him from above. A police-boat swerved in. When they reached for his prisoner, Kerry let them have him, but he began to climb. He persisted until, pulling on a lowered rope, he managed to scramble onto the pier. A police-man reached for his arm, but he shook free. He stumbled, gasping, toward the broadcasting-car and realized that Eve Vane was running frantically beside him.

"We got all of it, Guy!" she was puffing at him. "All of it until we heard a loud splash. Did you take him, Guy, did you take him?"

With water streaming from him, Kerry reached into the car for the microphone.

"Attention, Mr. and Mrs. United States! This is Keyhole Kerry, climbing up out of the Hudson River, where he was thrown by a vicious attack on the part of the man who really murdered Sheridan Reese. I was able to subdue him and drag him to the shore. I have already turned him over to the police. I hereby accuse him of being the master-mind behind the entire Reese affair. His name, Mr. and Mrs. United States—the name of the man who will rightfully go to the electric chair in my place—is Paul Phipps!"

THE LITTLE studio high in the U.B.C. tower was again filled with an electrical tension. It was the hour of Keyhole Kerry's regular program. His machine-gun delivery was ringing out over the entire nation. The technicians, the announcer, Eve, Smitty, and two detectives, watched him intently as he fired words into the mike.

"When I leave this studio, ladies and gentlemen, I will be hustled down to police headquarters. But I will not be going to face a murder charge. As you already know, Paul Phipps and Enid Reese are already in custody and will be indicted for the first-degree homicide of Sheridan Reese. It seems, however, that Commissioner Endicott is a bit uncertain about one or two points of the case—and so I am going down to headquarters to help clear them up!

"But first I tell my story to you and you and you. It was Paul Phipps whom Sheridan Reese designated as Mr. X in his letter. Phipps gave me his first fake tip on Reese's death in the hope that I would help establish it as the suicide it was not. Immediately I became involved, he exerted himself to tie me into the case so that I could never get out. Through another fake tip, he lured me to the East River and staged a scene which, he hoped, would convince the whole world that he was a victim of the murderer instead of the murderer himself. He did this, ladies and gentlemen, not only to cover the disappearance he had long been planning, so he could enjoy the proceeds of his crime, but also to destroy my alibi.

"When I phoned the home of Enid Reese last night, in a planned endeavor to force a confession from her before the radio audience, Paul Phipps was there. Like the shrewd woman she is, she led me on, planning to trap me instead. Phipps boarded the ferry, knowing I would be there. He meant to kill me because I was the greatest threat to the final success of his plan. Suspecting that I was broadcasting Enid Reese's words, he was forced to strike on the spot—with the very same gun he had used to kill Reese! It is damning evidence against him. The hottest possible news, ladies and gentlemen, brought to you by your scoop specialist!"

The inexorable clock warned Kerry that he was almost at the end of his allotted time.

"A final flash, before I sign off. Rex Grant, the private detective, and Sheila Forbes, the fashion photographer, will become one before the new moon!

"Keyhole Kerry, your scoop specialist—and provedly a man innocent of the slightest suspicion of blackmail or murder—is very gratefully saying good-night—until the next sizzling flash!"

He turned from the mike as Raney began crooning dignified blandishments concerning his sponsor's product, and found Eve Vane sitting weakly in a chair. In one hand she had a glass full of a cloudy solution, and in the other a little tin box. "What's this?" Kerry demanded.

"I'll die, I'll die if I don't swallow both of these right this minute, damn you, Guy Kerry. This," she said, gesturing with the glass, "is bicarbonate, and *this* is a double dose of good old *De-Luxe-Lax.*"

MAESTRO OF MURDER

WHEN GUY KERRY, *DE-LUXE-LAX'* GIFT TO THE ETHER WAVES, STARTED OUT THAT SWELTERING AFTERNOON TO DIG UP MATERIAL FOR A SPOT-NEWS FLASH HOTTER THAN THE WEATHER, HE NEVER GUESSED HE WAS ON THE WAY TO HIS OWN KIDNAPING— OR THAT ONCE THE VICTIM OF A SNATCH HE'D FIGHT TOOTH AND NAIL TO PREVENT POLICE, TROOPERS AND G-MEN FROM RESCUING HIM.

CHAPTER ONE

THE CORPSE IN
THE GREEN COUPE

IT WAS hot in Manhattan. The sweltering night was driving throngs to the beaches, into air-conditioned movies and to countless Tom Collinses. More millions, who had to stay on the job went through the motions torpidly. Keyhole Kerry, however, was not a case in point. Electrically nervous as always, he turned from breezeless Central Park and strode purposefully along a sultry canyon that branched east off Fifth Avenue.

The stifling heat did not retard Kerry in his ceaseless pursuit of spot news. His sandpaper voice was known to the entire nation as that of the ace newshawk of the air. His specialty was sensational scoops. From him, the gossip-hungry public heard startling inside stuff and succulent scandal more exciting than any other radio reporter could achieve. His mad task of out-winchelling Winchell had turned his hair prematurely white. It kept him hopping at all hours. Even tonight, when all New York lolled in the doldrums, he was hard on the scent of an exclusive flash.

A cotton-headed, simian-nosed lad kept pace with him until they reached a dark doorway, then they side-stepped together into the shadows. The boy was of indeterminate age, and was called Smitty. If he had any fuller name, no one had ever thought to inquire about it. He assisted Kerry by running errands and keeping his big ears unfurled for stray bits of chit-chat. Tonight he was inordinately proud because Kerry was pressing him into service on an important lead.

"Keep your eye on that stone house across the street, Smitty," Kerry directed him.

Narrow and white, the house sat against the side of the snooty Trafalgar Hotel. Mosaic glass windows two stories high, like those of a chapel, dominated its staid façade. From these, lights shone in a brilliant spectrum, but all the other windows were secretively dark. At the curb, a massive black sedan was sitting, and a uniformed chauffeur was standing at attention near the entrance.

"Within an hour, Smitty," Kerry said quietly, "one of the most important concerts of the year is going to be broadcast from that place—but nobody is supposed to know where it will originate."

"You mean another of the Jan Nordham organ recitals that the studio has been making such a fuss over, chief?" Smitty inquired.

"I do," Kerry answered. "U.B.C. has put out carloads of publicity about the series of programs, but at the same time, for some strange reason, Nordham himself has been kept wrapped up in a hell of a lot of mysterious secrecy. The whole world listens to him play, but he's being guarded closer than a king. There's something damned queer about this set-up, Smitty. I want to get the inside stuff. If anything unusual happens, tip me off pronto."

"O.K., chief," Smitty said eagerly. "What about that bird who just got out of that green coupe—the guy who's just now ringing the bell?"

"I'll look into him myself," Kerry said. "On your toes, now!"

LEAVING Smitty on watch and obscured by the humid gloom, Kerry strode on. He crossed the street at the corner, carefully observing the caller who was waiting at the entrance of the Nordham home. The chauffeur, he saw, was eyeing the

Kerry dodged out of the closet in the confusion.

young man warily. As the door opened, Kerry effaced himself by flattening against the closed freight entrance of the Trafalgar Hotel. From this point of vantage he listened.

"I'm Hugh Sheldon," the caller announced in an uneasy tone. "I must see Miss Nordham—at once. It's important."

A bald butler, whose face was square and hard, gazed inscrutably at Sheldon. "I'm sorry, sir," he said coldly. "I informed you, the last time you called, that Miss Nordham does not wish you to be admitted."

Kerry saw Hugh Sheldon's eyes take on a determined glitter. He was handsome and blond, obviously British—and nettled. "Look here," he said. "I don't understand this, and I don't like it. You're a new man, so perhaps you don't know that I'm engaged to marry Melody Nordham. I don't believe she's refused to see me. I'm just as certain that her father wouldn't order me kept out. There wouldn't be any reason for it. Whether you like it or not, my good man, I'm coming in."

He stepped to the sill but immediately the butler thrust him back. The force of the push tottered Sheldon on his heels. At the same time, the chauffeur took an ominous step closer. Hugh Sheldon peered at the two with stiffer determination.

"There's something damnably wrong here," he said tersely. "I haven't been able to reach my fiancée on the telephone. This is the third time you've stopped me at the door. Well, I've had enough of it. I'll not waste another moment arguing. I'm going to the police."

Kerry saw the butler's eyes narrow and the chauffeur's chin lift to a threatening angle.

"I shouldn't advise that, sir," the butler said gutturally. "It would be most unwise."

"Your saying that gives me all the more reason for informing the authorities at once," Hugh Sheldon asserted.

He turned away and, as he strode to his coupe, the chauffeur stepped quickly into the house, and the butler suddenly closed the door.

Keyhole Kerry scented a flash hotter than the weather. Intent upon learning Sheldon's story, he started toward the young man's car. Before he could reach it, its motor awoke and it swerved from the curb. Kerry called once, "Wait! Sheldon!"—cautiously, so as not to attract attention from the Nordham house—but the young Englishman pressed the coupe toward Fifth Avenue at an anxious speed.

With a signal to Smitty, warning the boy to remain at his post, Kerry broke into a run. He had left his roadster parked on the Avenue. By the time he reached it, Hugh Sheldon's machine was blocks away.

Kerry spurted off through a red light but thick traffic, flowing sluggishly on both sides of the street, immediately cut him off. Jockeying for position, he soon found an opening and stepped on the gas pedal. He was still accelerating when another car, traveling at an even faster clip, whizzed past him.

Kerry recognized the massive sedan as the vehicle which he had seen sitting in front of the Nordham house, but he had no opportunity to glimpse the occupants.

He urged his roadster after it. The next moment he was stamping on the brakes and muttering blasphemy. The lights had changed, cross-traffic was streaming out of the park, and the sedan was continuing while Kerry sat balked.

It was away again before the street in front of Kerry was clear. Abandoning all caution he streaked ahead. He could not see Hugh Sheldon's green coupe, and the black sedan had weaved itself into a long advantage. Fuming and perspiring, Kerry drove his damnedest, but it was not until he reached Fifty-ninth Street that he again glimpsed Sheldon's machine.

THE BEACON had just turned from red to green, but Sheldon's car was not moving. Cars behind it began blaring their horns, but the black sedan was not one of them. It had vanished. Kerry swung to the curb as the traffic cop began shrilling on a whistle. Bouncing out, he zigzagged through the stalled cars toward Sheldon.

He was standing rigid, looking in the window at the slumped figure at the wheel, when the patrolman bawled over his shoulder: "C'mawn, c'mawn, get goin'."

"The only place this chap is going, officer," Kerry said, "is to the morgue."

Hugh Sheldon's hands had dropped limply into his lap. His head was hanging forward. From three small holes in the region of his left temple, blood flowed, rapidly coagulating. The squawking auto horns were playing a discordant requiem for the Englishman.

"Mother of God!" the cop blurted.

Sparks were jumping along Keyhole Kerry's nerves. His one thought to hit the ether with this news-beat as fast as possible, he spun away from the car. Elbowing through a gathering crowd, he sought a telephone. He loped into the cafeteria in the center of the block and slammed into a booth.

He spun a special number on the dial. The moment a voice answered, he urged: "Put me on!" The voice was that of one of two watchdogs who were constantly on duty in the Universal Broadcasting Company tower, ready to receive Kerry's calls at any hour of the day or night. His "Put me on!" was a demand for the entire coast-to-coast U.B.C. network—a demand that was always immediately granted.

KERRY'S commercial sponsor not only paid him a staggering stipend, under an iron-clad contract that restricted his performances to the air-waves, but provided him with an extraordinary arrangement whereby he could use any telephone, anywhere, as a microphone. Other programs welcomed his intrusions, for the expectancy of catching Keyhole Kerry with a new red-hot flash kept millions listening to the entire hook-up continually. At this moment, Kerry knew, the ether was being cleared for him.

"Take it away!" rang over the line.

Kerry impatiently waited five seconds, then began firing words into the transmitter at a speed that made all other news commentators seem tongue-tied by comparison.

"Attention, Mr. and Mrs. United States! This is Keyhole Kerry, your scoop specialist, bringing you another sizzling flash.

Not even the police are learning sooner than you and you and you that a young man named Hugh Sheldon was murdered not more than two minutes ago while sitting in his car at the corner of Fifty-ninth Street and Fifth Avenue!"

Delightedly, Kerry imagined countless gasps arising from a myriad of throats, and vehement oaths bursting from the mouths of hundreds of newspapermen in the metropolis—city editors and reporters to whom his name was anathema, because his swift technique made their fastest extras seem as musty as last year's almanacs.

"The police will be glad to learn from your radio oracle, ladies and gentlemen," Kerry raced on, "that Hugh Sheldon was murdered by the occupant of a big black sedan which lost itself in traffic immediately after the death shots were fired. I do not know who killed Sheldon, but I strongly suspect that he was murdered in order to prevent his going to the police to demand an investigation of a matter which was of important private concern to him.

"Since Sheldon did not live to reach the police, I am going to undertake to investigate the matter myself. Obviously this is a dangerous mission, but I hope to have several startling revelations for you soon. In the meantime, Mr. and Mrs. United States, keep your radios tuned to this wavelength, for in a very few minutes I'll be back on the air with my regular program of exclusive inside chatter. Until then, Keyhole Kerry is signing off—and hoping to keep out of range of the killer who took such ruthless means of shielding himself!"

He broke the connection, then spun the dial again. The number he called this time was that of his office. The strained voice of a girl answered.

"Eve!" he said. "Get busy on this break pronto. Find out Sheldon's address. If you can't get it from the telephone company, try the Motor Vehicle Bureau. Connect with somebody where he lived, and pump them for all you're worth. You ought to have something important by the time I reach the studio—something for a new flash."

"Guy—listen!" his secretary said anxiously. "Did you mean what you just said on the air—that the man who murdered Sheldon might go gunning for you next?"

"It seems too damned likely for comfort, Eve," Kerry answered. "Drastic measures were taken to silence Sheldon. There are big names involved in this. Some big, crooked scheme is under way. It's made to order. If I don't have the inside track on it all the way, it'll be because a bullet stopped me from trying."

"The only objection you would have to being murdered," Eve said distraitly, "is that you wouldn't be able to broadcast the flash yourself!"

"Get busy with the phone, Eve," Kerry urged. "I'm beating it to the studio right now."

He dodged out of the restaurant, ran down the street to his car and headed for the Universal Broadcasting Company tower. As he nosed through the curious crowd that had massed at the intersection of Fifth and Fifty-ninth, Kerry shot a grim glance at the car in which Hugh Sheldon sat dead.

CHAPTER TWO

DARK RHAPSODY

RADIO BROADCASTING is a business productive of frayed nerves, chronic indigestion and temperamental collapses, but all other programs seemed almost languid in comparison with the hair-trigger tension under which Keyhole Kerry's regular barrage of inside stuff was launched upon the ether. Tonight the agony of it was even greater than usual.

The big electric clock above the monitor booth in Studio X swung to the deadline second, when the most widely listened-to quarter-hour on the air must begin, but Keyhole Kerry had not yet appeared.

Plump Milton Raney, the announcer, perspiring in spite of the million-dollar cooling system, began crooning into the mike his overture to *De-Luxe-Lax*. The manufacturer of this alleviator of the national ailment was Kerry's sponsor. A sound-effects man began tapping at a typewriter and ringing a telephone bell to simulate the activity of a busy newsroom. And Eve Vane, Kerry's secretary—willowy, champagne-haired and luscious—was experiencing an acute attack of the jitters, as she always did when Kerry was about to hit the air.

Raney was just finishing his blandishments concerning *De-Luxe-Lax* when Kerry swung in the door. In one swift, continuous motion, he plucked a roll of copy from Eve's trembling hand and planted himself in front of the mike on the desk. A dizzy sigh of relief rose around him. Immediately he began his staccato delivery in his slate-pencil rasp.

"Good-evening, Mr. and Mrs. United States! Your newshawk of the kilocycles—who is very proud of the fact that he has never missed a scheduled program—is back again with more sizzling spot-news, exclusive flashes and juicy tidbits of gossip."

Eve Vane, still quaking, signaled him with her turquoise eyes that the information he had requested her to unearth was contained in his copy. He seemed concerned with a more pressing matter. Without glancing at his notes, he sped on.

"As soon as I go off the air, at the conclusion of this program, ladies and gentlemen, the whole world will begin listening to another memorable organ recital by Jan Nordham, whom many acclaim as the greatest living musician. It is not generally known that the source of this series of magnificent broadcasts has been kept shrouded in deepest secrecy. Yet it is true that Jan Nordham plays his masterly concerts—for which he receives the highest fee ever paid a radio artist—in strict privacy and under guard.

"No member of the U.B.C. staff is permitted to be present. The program is monitored, and the announcements are made, here in the U.B.C. tower. Not even the highest officials of this broadcasting company have seen Jan Nordham since his recent return from Europe. All negotiations were conducted through Nordham's manager, Murray Drew. While you listen to Nordham's beautiful renditions, you may wonder, as I have, at the reason for his cloak of mystery."

THOSE in the studio were raptly intent upon Kerry's extemporaneous item, and so, he hoped, were millions of others scattered from border to border.

"This situation is particularly intriguing, Mr. and Mrs. United States," Kerry hurried on, "because it offers such startling contrast to Jan Nordham's earlier concerts. His last broadcast over this network was two years ago. At that time he used the organ in the hugest studio in this building. An audience of several thousand was present at each program. Jan Nordham gloried in their acclaim. He publicly said that their enthusiasm was an inspiration. Yet tonight—as he has done consistently since returning from two years of complete isolation abroad—he will play in solitude, behind doors at which sentries are posted to prevent, by force if necessary, any intrusion."

Kerry took a very necessary breath.

"For the first time, ladies and gentlemen, I am going to make a number of startling revelations concerning Jan Nordham. This information is the result of my own investigation. It is fragmentary and indefinite, yet it is the best that weeks of hard-driving endeavor could produce. Attention!

"It is believed that about a year ago Jan Nordham suffered a serious illness or a serious accident. Whatever happened to him, the nature of it has been kept carefully from the whole world. My every effort to learn this has been frustrated. At any rate, Jan Nordham recently returned to the United States, with his daughter, under closer cover of secrecy than even the Lindberghs managed to achieve. But, ladies and gentlemen, even more mystifying is the fact that Jan Nordham's favorite and most promising protégé is missing!"

Eve Vane made a startled sound—which, Kerry hoped, was being echoed from coast to coast.

"In an effort to learn more about the great musician," Kerry hurriedly explained, "I attempted to get in touch with Miss Alicia Ballard. Alicia Ballard is the attractive young woman whom Nordham once declared to be the finest artist of her generation. She was closer to the master organist than anyone else, except his daughter. On one program, in fact, she played a duet with him—an unparalleled distinction. But, Mr. and Mrs. United States, I have been absolutely unable to locate Miss Ballard."

Kerry began to shuffle through his notes as he continued his rapid-fire delivery.

"Alicia Ballard has disappeared. It is a startling fact that she vanished only a few days before Jan Nordham's first concert in the present series. She left no forwarding address, but told a few friends that she was going abroad. However, I have searched the passenger lists of all ships which sailed at that time—and her name is not included in any of them. Furthermore, my inquiries at the State Department have brought to light the even more significant information that Alicia Ballard is not the possessor of a passport. The truth is, ladies and gentlemen, that Miss Ballard is strangely *but willingly* missing!

"If Alicia Ballard is now within the sound of my voice, I urge her to communicate with me as soon as possible.

"I do not suggest, ladies and gentlemen, that Alicia Ballard's disappearance has anything to do with the secrecy surrounding Jan Nordham—but I do believe it means something important. I am not hinting that there is anything wrong about Jan Nordham's seclusion—but I am sure there must be a newsworthy reason for it. Being notoriously lacking in respect for anyone's personal privacy, I have pledged myself to find out the truth behind this fascinating situation and, at the proper time, to reveal it to you and you and you.

"Hang onto your radios, Mr. and Mrs. United States. I'll be back in a jiffy, with more exclusive inside chatter."

As he swung from the mike, Raney took it up to resume his

beguilements concerning *De-Luxe-Lax*. Flipping through his notes, Kerry retreated into a corner with Eve.

"Guy, you've passed up the hottest angle of all," Eve said in a whisper that the microphone could not catch. "You didn't mention that Hugh Sheldon's murder connects directly with the rest of it."

"I'm keeping that under my hat," Kerry told her. "If I spilled it now, the papers and the police would get at Nordham and shove me out in the cold. As it is, I have the inside track—an exclusive lead. When the time is ripe, I'll spring it, and when I do it'll be a bombshell. What did you find out about Sheldon?"

"He moved into the Carlton Hotel the same day that Jan and Melody Nordham arrived from Europe," Eve said. "He had tags on his baggages showing that he came over on the same ship. I checked with the steamship line and discovered he had a cabin adjoining the Nordhams'. He seemed to be rich, cultured and altogether a fine chap."

KERRY nodded. "Hugh Sheldon was engaged to Melody Nordham. That's a flash in itself—nobody else knows it—but I'm keeping that mum for a while too. The picture's pretty clear. Sheldon and Melody Nordham met while Jan Nordham was in retirement in England. Sheldon must have known the answers to all these puzzling questions about Nordham. In fact, he was about to find out a damned sight more—about something that happened since they came to New York—and that's why he was rubbed out. Eve, I tell you there's something big behind this—"

Raney was signaling frantically from the mike. Kerry hopped back to it. Resorting to his written copy, he machine-gunned items into the ether. As he talked, he fidgeted, which Eve fearfully recognized as the symptoms of his burning impatience to be off on the trail of even more sensational news. The second hand of the electric clock was swinging toward the end of his allotted period when he again abandoned his copy.

"Concerning the murder of Hugh Sheldon, ladies and gentlemen, there are no new developments at the moment. The police are launching a routine investigation and beginning a search for the sedan from which the murderer fired the shots. I anticipate that they will make scant headway. My latest information from headquarters is that the murder weapon was a twenty-two. Since no reports were heard at the time of the killing, the gun was probably fitted with a silencer.

"Keep your radios tuned to this wavelength, Mr. and Mrs. United States, for I promise to serve up soon a sizzling platter of new inside stuff on this reprehensible crime. Keyhole Kerry, your headline beater, is signing off until the next exclusive flash—which may come at any time!"

Milton Raney began murmuring his closing paean to *De-Luxe-Lax* as Kerry swung from the mike. Kerry started toward the door, but as he gripped the handle, Eve stopped him.

"Guy, you can't go running around loose with a murderer on your trail," she protested.

"If I don't keep on the move, Commissioner Endicott will collar me and waste a lot of precious time trying to bully me into telling the rest of what I know," Kerry explained impatiently. "In another minute, Nordham will begin his recital. I'm on my way to his home."

"But nobody's supposed to know where he lives," Eve said. "How did you find out?"

"Easy. I had Smitty trail the technician who set up the mike. I think I know a way of getting into the place. If I can sneak inside, I'm sure to grab onto something worth a flash. Camp in the office, Eve. I may need you."

"What you need even more, Guy Kerry," Eve said with a wail, "is a bulletproof vest."

Striding galvanically, Kerry hurried to the elevator. When the panel opened, a man emerged from the car. He paused at sight of Kerry, then, as Kerry stepped in, he jerked around and followed.

"Mr. Kerry!" he said anxiously. "I'm Leonard Ballard, Alicia Ballard's brother."

WHILE the car descended, Kerry eyed him alertly. He had strong, square shoulders, a trim mustache and keen, dark eyes set deep under bushy black eyebrows. "Go on," Kerry urged. "Where's your sister?"

"I—I don't know. That's what I want to find out. I was in a bar across the street a few minutes ago, and I heard you broadcasting about her. I thought you might know something more than you put on the air—something that might help me locate her. It's been weeks since she went away. I'm half out of my mind with worry. If only—"

"Why haven't you gone to the police?" Kerry asked incisively.

"She asked me not to. You see, at the time she disappeared, I got a note from her. She wrote that she was going to be gone for a while—but she didn't say where—and she told me not to worry and not to do anything about it. I thought it was damned strange. I'm too anxious to let it slide any longer. If there's anything you can tell me, Kerry—"

"I've broadcast everything I know about her," Kerry said. "Have you any idea what's behind it?"

"I'm completely at a loss—completely."

"In that case," Kerry answered, as the car stopped, "get in touch with me later. I'll do my best to find your sister, but at the moment I have an important appointment."

He strode from the elevator, crossed the huge lobby without a backward glance, and hurried to the parking-space near the U.B.C. tower where he kept his roadster. Driving rapidly up Fifth Avenue, he noted that the intersection at Fifty-ninth Street where the Sheldon murder had occurred was no longer the focal point for a curious crowd. He swung to the curb near the Nordham home, strode along the cross-street and sidled into the doorway where Smitty was still faithfully keeping watch.

"Anything brewing?" Kerry inquired.

Smitty mopped sweat from his liberally freckled face. "Everything's been quiet as a tomb, chief," he answered, "except that a few minutes ago the organ began playing."

Kerry could hear, faintly, the strains of the mighty pipes beyond the great colored-glass windows.

"Nordham's recital is under way," he said. "Every selection you hear means another bag of money in Nordham's pocket. Stick right where you are, Smitty, and keep your eyes peeled. I have a bit of peeking through keyholes to do."

When he left the doorway, his gaze was directed at the big black sedan that was again sitting in front of the Nordham house. The hard-faced chauffeur, Kerry saw, was once more posted at the entrance, like a watchful gorilla. Kerry noted the license number of the sedan as he strode into the exclusive Hotel Trafalgar.

To the haughty clerk at the desk he said: "I made a reservation by phone early this morning in the name of Vane Smith. You have the room ready for me."

"Yes, sir. In the location you stipulated, sir. The west side of the hotel, on the sixth floor. Will you sign, please?"

Kerry signed the false name, paid the outrageous rental in advance because he was carrying no baggage, and was escorted to Room 630 by a bellhop with an elevated nose. Once the door was bolted, he opened the window and gazed down at the black roof of the Nordham home. Satisfied that it was easily accessible, as he had anticipated, he took up the telephone and called the number of his office.

"Eve," he said quickly, when his secretary answered, "call your pal Inspector Tarrant at headquarters and get him to check this license number for you. Nine-X-nine-nine-seven-nine. I'll hold on until you have it."

HIS IMPATIENCE to get under way sharpened while he waited. At last Eve announced: "That car is registered in the name of Jan Nordham."

"Good Lord!" Kerry blurted. "That's the murder car—the sedan used by the mug who killed Hugh Sheldon. And it's another piece of information I'm keeping under my hat until later."

"This sounds dangerous, Guy," Eve said with a catch in her throat. "What are you up to now, you lunatic? Please be careful!"

"I'm about to do a job of breaking and entering," Kerry informed her. "Stick close to that telephone, Eve. Anything can happen now—and it probably will!"

Having broken the connection, he attacked the bed. Tearing off both sheets, knotting them together and tying one end of the rope to the radiator, in the traditional manner, he crawled out on the sill. He lowered himself hand over hand. Reaching the Nordham roof, he turned to a triangular hut built at the rear. It was the exit of the fire-stairs, and Kerry murmured silent gratitude for the city ordinance that required it.

From his pocket Kerry brought a strong screwdriver, with which he had provided himself for this illegal purpose. As he pried at the frame of the skylight he felt, through his feet, the vibrations of the organ being played below. The wood of the window sash was soft with age. Kerry loosened it without difficulty. Crawling through the opening, he heard clearly the voice of the organ reeds singing a Bach fugue.

Kerry ventured down the dark stairs. They led him into a gloomy hallway where the song of the organ sounded even more majestic. Peering down the stairwell, he saw indistinct shadows moving—servants, he surmised, who were guarding the doors of the studio. Avoiding them, Kerry turned farther to the rear of the dwelling. When he risked opening a small door, the tones of the great organ beat upon him mightily.

Quickly he stepped into a dark recess, closing the door tightly. He was in the space behind the pipes. Feeling caught in a harmonious storm, he looked around curiously at musical mechanisms which were working strangely in unison, electrically activated by the great musician's deft fingering of the keyboards. The banks of tubes shielded the console from Kerry. He could not see Nordham playing. But, elated at the prospect of discovering the world-famous artist's secret, he began to prowl, seeking a spy hole.

He froze when the organ, after a vibrant burst, became silent. Far away, in the U.B.C. tower, Kerry knew, an announcer was speaking over the network. In a moment the air began vibrating with the strains of an étude by Chopin. Kerry resumed his prowling, but he moved carefully and slowly, because of the confusing gloom and the clutter of mechanisms that sprang without warning into activity around him.

Jan Nordham's concert was nearing its end when Kerry ventured to open a small door on the opposite side of the recess. Jubilantly he saw that it gave upon a narrow balcony that encircled the studio. Ducking below the rail, he crept along it. The great, high-vaulted room was dark except for the iridescent shine of the lights at the colored windows, and the glow reflecting from the music on the easel of the console. Now sure of a clear view of the master at the keyboards, Kerry lifted his eyes.

He crouched still and startled, gazing at the strangest scene he had ever beheld.

THE GREAT Jan Nordham, garbed in tails, was swaying on the bench as he fingered the keys—but he was not the Jan Nordham that the world had known. His legs were stumps that ended bluntly in leather boots at the knees. Kerry was stunned by the revelation, by the realization that the renowned musician was totally unable to actuate the pedals of the footboard—and yet the deep bass tones were rumbling out in perfect concord with the treble.

A girl was supplying the bass accompaniment which Jan Nordham himself could not render. She was seated on the floor behind the great musician. With her hands she depressed the various pedals as his skilled fingers flew. Unknown to the world, these latest concerts of Jan Nordham had in reality been duets, played secretly, with overtones of suffering!

Then, as Kerry's widened eyes became accustomed to the weird lighting of the guarded studio, he grasped the details that made the scene even more grotesque.

The girl at the pedals had something fastened over the lower part of her face—a gag! Her own voice was forcibly stifled while she gave utterance to the majestic tones of the organ! Absorbed as she was in her playing, her eyes remained fixed on the back of Jan Nordham's head, and in them shone terror. Her movements were strangely restricted—and then it was that Kerry saw the chain.

She was pinioned to the huge instrument—held there by links of steel, which gave her only enough play to manipulate the pedals.

The fear in her eyes came from the fact that Jan Nordham himself was playing under a constant threat. Above his wing collar, and encircling his throat, was a noose! It was drawn tightly around his neck. The dark line of the rope rose at an angle above him and reached the balcony at a point almost directly opposite Kerry.

There on the balcony a man was standing—the bald, brutal-faced butler. His eyes were fixed upon the organist, and in both his big hands he was gripping the other end of the rope that was noosed around Jan Nordham's throat!

In this nightmare scene, Keyhole Kerry saw a sensational flash. He was seized with an impulse to rush it into the ether as quickly as possible. Yet the macabre grotesquery of it held him motionless.

As he stared, the last chord of Jan Nordham's last selection throbbed from the pipes. For several long beats, the beautiful harmony swelled out. Then, abruptly, it ceased—and, mingling with the echoes, came a choking cry of terror.

Simultaneously, three things happened, things that shocked Kerry so sharply that he jerked erect.

Jan Nordham, with a sure, swift motion, plucked from his left sleeve a long-bladed knife. With a deft slash he cut the cord which held the gag in the girl's mouth. Then he swung the knife upward toward the rope, at the same time twisting to shout at the microphone which was hanging from the roof of the studio. Instantly, the man on the balcony lunged back, pulling the rope taut. Dangling by the neck, the organist was lifted from the bench. Strangling, he struggled frantically to escape the tightened noose, kicking with his stump legs—

And at that instant all the lights went out.

CHAPTER THREE

THE REEDS SANG OF DEATH

KERRY BROKE into a run. The curved rail guided him around the balcony toward the bald hangman. He was conscious of swift movements below, as if a squad of men were rushing into the dark studio. Unseen doors slammed, admitting brief streaks of light. Kerry flung himself at the spot where the murderous butler had been bearing back on the rope—but he stumbled and groped through empty air.

Bright light suddenly struck him full in the eyes. Almost blinded, he scarcely discerned the dark figures closing in around him. His arms were grasped with such strength that he could not shake himself loose. He was dragged from the balcony, through a door, across the hall. He was just becoming able to see his captors when he was thrust into a small room.

Once free of the crushing hands, he spun about. The door was closing, but through it he glimpsed three men whose hard faces looked merciless. Guns were in their hands. Kerry tried hard to see those weapons clearly. He hoped to find that one of them was a .22 with a silencer attached. The swift shutting of the door left him uncertain, but all the guns had seemed to be of heavier caliber.

Breathing hotly, Kerry tried the knob. The door was fast. Footfalls beat away down the hall as he gazed about the room. It was small and comfortably furnished, and it lacked windows. Kerry felt that he could shout himself hoarse without even a whisper being heard outside the walls of this strange house. Grimly, he sat on the bed, staring at the door, waiting—and itching for a microphone.

His nerves felt like incandescent wires all the while that sticky, heavy silence lasted.

Then deliberate footfalls approached his door. A key turned in the lock. Kerry rose to confront the man who stepped in. The visitor was trimly garbed and his manner was cool. His skin was drawn tightly over high cheekbones. From his appearance, he might have been either a business man of distinction or a criminal of rare and ruthless cunning. He eyed Kerry with disdain.

"You realize, of course," he began in a modulated tone, "that you could be arrested and jailed for breaking into this house."

"O.K.," Kerry said heatedly. "Call the cops. The quicker the better!"

He was answered by a suave smile. "You are Keyhole Kerry, are you not? I am Murray Drew, Mr. Nordham's manager. I hope that it will not be necessary to prefer charges against you but—"

"I'll be damned!" Kerry exclaimed. "You're supposed to be looking out for Mr. Nordham's interests, but you come in here acting as though I were the worst offender in this mix-up. You're not trying to gloss matters over, are you? Where's Mr. Nordham? Why was he playing with a noose around his neck? Why was that girl chained to the organ? In other words, what the hell's going on here?"

Murray Drew frowned at him. "A noose?" he said, "A girl

chained? I'm afraid I don't understand, Mr. Kerry. Has the hot weather made you ill, by any chance?"

"I'm certainly hot enough," Kerry retorted, "but I'm not out of my mind, if that's what you mean. I saw Nordham dragged off the organ bench when he tried to shout something into the microphone. Both Nordham and the girl acted as if they were in terror of their lives. I'm damned well going to find out exactly what it means."

Murray Drew shook his well-groomed head. "I still don't understand. I assure you, nothing of the sort happened—nothing even remotely resembling what you say."

KERRY'S fists clenched as he stepped closer. "Don't try to tell me I was seeing things! Why is this house full of gorillas with guns? Why is everybody being kept away from Nordham and his daughter? Who—"

"Mr. Kerry," Drew interrupted decisively, "there are excellent reasons why Mr. Nordham has taken such care to seclude himself, and why we have kept the truth about his—ah—condition from the public. I realize that this, to you, constitutes important news. But I want you to understand the situation clearly. Accordingly, I think it best that you see Mr. Nordham and his daughter personally, in order that he may reassure you."

"I'd like nothing better!" Kerry declared.

"This way, please," said Drew.

He gestured Kerry from the room. Wonderingly, Kerry followed him down the stairs to another room at the front of the house. Kerry was amazed to find that the armed gorillas were nowhere in evidence now. The house seemed peaceful, yet Kerry felt a strange tension in the air. When he stepped into the library, he immediately sensed that he had entered upon a scene that was being expertly staged for his special benefit.

Jan Nordham was seated in a huge chair near a mammoth fireplace. A blanket was wrapped around him below the waist. His eyes were luminous and dark, his face bore the stamp of fine character, but its lines expressed suffering and fear. Seated beside him, on a hassock, was the girl. She was remarkably attractive. Hers was the delicate face of a sensitive artist. Yet she seemed to be controlling herself with difficulty, fearful that she would yield to an almost overwhelming dread.

"Mr. Nordham," said Murray Drew quietly, "this is Mr. Kerry."

The great organist extended his powerful right hand. "Good-evening," he said in a throaty tone. "Mr. Kerry, this is my daughter, Melody."

Nodding to Kerry, the girl rose, took a chair beside Jan Nordham. She gazed at Kerry intently and Kerry, mopping at his face, sat down to study them.

"Mr. Nordham," Murray Drew explained with a smile of tolerance, "Mr. Kerry is under the impression that there was some sort of disturbance just as you terminated your concert."

"Disturbance?" the organist said in a puzzled tone. "Why, not at all. It ended exactly the way all my radio concerts do—I simply finished. It's strange that you should think otherwise."

"And nothing out of the way happened?" Kerry said grimly.

The girl answered: "Of course not. Nothing at all." She continued to gaze intently, as if with covert significance, at Kerry.

Kerry, shrewdly picking up the cue that had been given him in this piece of carefully but quickly planned dramaturgy, said: "Then I guess I *was* seeing things."

"I'm afraid so," Jan Nordham said. "But I'm glad of this opportunity to talk with you, Mr. Kerry. You see, I listened to your broadcast concerning me tonight. I think it best that I tell you the facts outright. Not because I wish them publicized—far from it. In fact, I want to appeal to you to cooperate with me in keeping the truth secret—concerning my—my affliction."

The steady eyes of the girl disturbed Kerry. He realized suddenly that she was attempting to communicate with him—make him aware of something without Murray Drew's knowledge. Nodding Jan Nordham on, he quickly glanced at her. She was sitting with one hand pressed to the cushion of her chair. As Kerry's eyes flicked toward her, she turned her hand slightly, so that Drew would not see. In it she was holding concealed a folded paper.

Instantly, once she was sure that Kerry had seen it, she thrust it down under the cushion, and her hand rose empty.

"You see, Mr. Kerry," the organist was saying, "a year or so ago I suffered an accident on my estate in Sussex. I was chopping down a tree. It fell at an unexpected angle and struck me. In fact, it"—the musician's fine face grew darker in its lines—"it crushed both my legs so badly that it was necessary to amputate them. You understand, I'm sure, how tragic it was—because it seemed that I could never play an organ again."

THE GIRL rose from her chair and placed her hand on Jan Nordham's arm. "I'm so happy that I've been able to bring you back to your music, Father," she said.

Jan Nordham nodded, smiling wanly. "Without you, it would have been lost to me," he said. To Kerry, he went on: "The way my daughter and I play together would seem grotesque to the world. If it became known, my recitals would appeal more to the morbidly curious than to lovers of great music. I am not a freak, Mr. Kerry—I am a musician. For this reason—because my music must always be more important than this grotesque manner of playing it—I have done my utmost to keep my condition a complete secret."

Kerry rose. Casually, yet with his nerves tightening, he transferred to the chair which the girl had left.

"Does this explain the whole set-up?" he asked. "The guards, the gun—everything?"

"It does," Jan Nordham answered. "My precautions may seem excessive, but I have found them to be necessary. Being a famous man yourself, you know how difficult it is to avoid celebrity-seekers, autograph-hunters—even criminals who sometimes select victims of prominence. I appeal to you, Mr. Kerry, not to divulge my condition to the public. I implore you to respect my confidence."

Kerry said promptly: "I'll do that, Mr. Nordham. Hot news means as much to me as your music does to you, but it's part of my creed never to broadcast an unjust flash, never to do harm needlessly. I'm damned glad you told me this before I busted loose with the nearest microphone." He gazed at Murray Drew. "I understand now. From now on, I'll know how to handle this matter."

He pushed himself up from the chair, and his hand slid into his pocket with the girl's note.

"Excellent, Mr. Kerry," Drew said affably. "Mr. Nordham, I'm afraid, is a bit tired after his concert. You won't mind?"

"Not at all," Kerry agreed. "Good-night, Mr. Nordham. Good-night, Miss Nordham. If you'll listen to my broadcasts as they come along, you'll hear me make amends."

Whereupon, to Kerry's surprise, Murray Drew coolly escorted him to the door. The bald butler who had choked Jan Nordham with the noose, now politely bowed Kerry out. The chauffeur, who had aided in capturing him, allowed him to pass almost unheeded.

Kerry walked casually past the murder car sitting at the curb, but as soon as he was away from the Nordham house, his stride quickened electrically.

He made a gesture which, he hoped, Smitty would interpret as an order to remain in the doorway across the street. His hand closed hotly on the note in his pocket as he swung into Madison Avenue, dodged into the nearest lighted doorway—a stationery shop. Wedging himself into the telephone booth, he immediately dialed his special number.

"Hold it a minute," he said, when his technician's voice answered.

He unfolded the note, and as he rapidly read it, the temperature of his nerves climbed feverishly.

Mr. Kerry—

Mr. Nordham and I have just been given instructions as to what to do when we meet you. I hope desperately that you will not be deceived, but in case the stratagem succeeds, I am writing this explanation in great haste and at great risk.

First, believe nothing that you may hear us tell you, except the matter of Mr. Nordham's affliction and his wishes concerning publicity about it.

Second, I am not Mr. Nordham's daughter, Melody Nordham. I am being forced to pretend to you that I am, but in reality I am Alicia Ballard.

Just before Mr. Nordham's series of concerts began, I was kidnaped. Both moral and physical force were used to bring and keep me in this house. I have obeyed the criminals' demands for the sake of Mr. Nordham and his daughter. He is compelled to comply with the kidnapers' orders through his great anxiety for Melody. At the very beginning, she was seized by this same gang of crooks—

Elated, yet chilled, Kerry skipped to the rapidly scrawled conclusion of the note.

You dare not act until Melody is found and safely returned to her father. Otherwise these men will murder her. They will stop at nothing—even this note may cause my death, if they discover that I have written you. You are also in great danger. If you reveal that you know too much for these crooks' safety, they will not hesitate to—

Kerry could hold himself in no longer. "Put me on!" he rasped over the wire.

Waiting with torrid impatience for his signal, he heard nothing else—not the footfalls in the store, nor even the clatter as the door of the booth began to open. With eyes only for the startling note, he did not see the black shadows that closed in on him, nor the gun clubbing down at his head.

Without warning, Kerry's skull exploded. "Take it away!" grated out of the dangling receiver even as he fell unconscious from the booth.

CHAPTER FOUR

NO RESCUE WANTED

"FLASH! THIS is Keyhole Kerry, your clairvoyant of the kilocycles. A few minutes ago I was bashed on the head by a crowd of desperate crooks who invaded a stationery store on upper Madison Avenue in order to corner me and prevent my making certain startling revelations concerning the Sheldon murder case!

"Flash! Though my memory of this incident is confused, I dimly recall being bundled into a car and transported to another part of the city. I remember a moment when raw whiskey was poured on me. In this way my assailants were able to pretend, convincingly, to anyone who chanced to see them hustling me from their car, that I was staggering drunk. I have been hidden in a building, the address of which I do not know. I feel certain that the murderer of Hugh Sheldon is responsible for engineering this snatch.

"Attention, New York police! Attention, Federal Bureau of Investigation! Attention, Mr. and Mrs. United States!

"Flash! God, my head hurts!"

Keyhole Kerry deliriously imagined that he was hearing his own voice blaring from the nation's loudspeakers, but in reality he was mumbling to himself.

As his consciousness brightened, he lay still, trying to steady his senses. Soon, his head throbbing, he propped himself on his elbows and looked around.

He was lying on a bed. At the foot of the bed a man was sitting—the Nordham chauffeur. The man had removed his tunic, and his collar was open. In one hand he had a fan, which he was waving at his sweaty face, and in the other he was holding an automatic that looked as big as a howitzer. He was gazing at Keyhole Kerry in an ominous way that made it clear he would disapprove of any move that Kerry might make.

Behind the man with the gun were two windows. The windows were wide open, but no breeze was stirring the curtains. The sky was still black, and the heat was still smotheringly oppressive.

"Lie down!" the chauffeur ordered.

Kerry willingly complied. His head remained on the pillow a long time, while it painfully cleared. In another room nearby a radio was playing. His captors, Kerry knew, were letting it run in order to catch any news bulletins that might warn them of danger, but while Kerry listened, no bulletins were read. He felt chagrined at the thought that the world at large was probably still unaware of his abduction—but as soon as he began to contemplate the news possibilities in his otherwise deplorable situation, he felt decidedly better.

When footfalls came into his room, he struggled to a sitting position. Murray Drew was now standing beside the armed chauffeur. His bearing was no longer conciliatory. Instead, he looked relentlessly evil.

"As a business manager, Drew," Kerry remarked wryly, "you did a good job of giving me the business."

"You asked for it, Kerry," Drew said.

KERRY nodded, and his head throbbed so that he immediately wished he hadn't. "I'm sorry I can't speak as well for your ability as a stage director. The scene you put on for my benefit, with Jan Nordham and Alicia Ballard, didn't happen to fool me. But for that matter, I didn't fool you, either, by pretending to believe it. You saw her pass that note, didn't you—or did someone else?"

"I wouldn't advise you to talk much, Kerry," Drew suggested significantly.

"You were taking no chances," Kerry went on. "If you had succeeded in deludring me, you'd have let me remain at large—

but you would have kept watch over me. When you saw me heading for a telephone, you knew you'd have to take drastic measures, and you did. I've only myself to blame. It's just that it's almost impossible for me to restrain myself when I get near a transmitter with a hot morsel of news."

"From now on, we'll do our best to help you control yourself in that habit, Kerry," Drew said levelly.

"How long are you going to keep me here with this baboon and his artillery?" Kerry inquired. "Or am I slated for the morgue?"

"That's up to you," Drew answered. "You'd better realize at the outset that we have nothing to lose by killing you—you or anyone else concerned. Each of us can fry only once, you know—but we're going to take great pains to avoid that possibility. So I wouldn't advise you to try shouting out the window for help, or trying to get near a telephone, or making any kind of a disturbance whatever. If you did, you might get the cops up here—but when they arrived, you wouldn't be interested."

Kerry managed a grin. "Mr. Drew," he said, "you don't realize how grateful I am to you for snatching me. After all, my business is news. I'm always happy to announce hot flashes, but I'm even more delighted at the opportunity to make 'em. When it becomes known that I've been kidnaped, it'll make a whale of a story."

"It's not going to become known just yet, Kerry," Drew said.

"The bigger the story grows," Kerry went on, "the better I'll like it, naturally. I want to build it up to the limit. I wouldn't for the world spoil its possibilities by trying to get myself rescued right away. I won't attempt to call out the marines just yet, you see, so don't worry. The only thing I don't like about it is the fact that I won't be able to put the break on the air myself."

"Damned right you won't," Drew asserted.

"That being the case," Kerry suggested hopefully, "you wouldn't be averse to spilling the inside dope, would you? What's this all about?"

Murray Drew smiled thinly and turned to the chauffeur. "You're to keep an eye on him all night, Sam, but not in here where he might pump you. Go out and close the door and watch from the other room. If he tries a fast one, give it to him, and don't waste any time about it." His snaky smile widened, disclosing gleaming teeth. "Pleasant dreams, Kerry. If there's anything else you want, just ask for it."

"O.K.," Kerry said promptly. "How about a live mike?"

"If you ever see another microphone, Kerry," Drew said, "you'll be a damned sight luckier than you have any reason to expect."

Drew signaled Sam from the room, then followed and closed the door. Kerry heard a bolt click into its socket. He got out of bed, grimacing with pain, and searched through his pockets. They had been emptied. The note that Alicia Ballard had passed to him was gone. By this time, he realized, it had been destroyed.

Hoping grimly that the girl had fared better than her message, Kerry ventured to the connecting door. He pressed against it and found it immovable. Kerry thereupon resorted to the keyhole. Through it he viewed an area of the adjoining room. Within his angle of vision, the chauffeur was watchfully sitting, eyeing the door and fondling the big automatic.

KERRY turned to the window. The street lay far below. Directly opposite him stood a tall warehouse. All its windows were black. The sign painted across it was too dim to read in the darkness.

Kerry tried to orientate himself—but within his range of vision there was no spire or other metropolitan landmark to hint his location. The signpost on the street corner was indecipherable in the distance. An elevated track was visible, almost two blocks away, but it was of no aid to identifying the neighborhood. Turning his attention to closer things, Kerry saw that a narrow stone ledge ran across the front of his prison, just below the windowsills, and he began to speculate.

He went back to the bed and lay down. Beginning to get

used to smelling like a distillery, he listened to the muted radio. An announcement told him that it was tuned to his own station, WUBC, and that before long the day's program would end. Itching for a chance to get at a telephone before the network signed off, Kerry crept back to the keyhole.

Sam was still sitting in the chair on the opposite side of the next room, the huge automatic still in his hands, but his head was lolling and he was blinking sleepily.

Kerry prowled about his cell. Outside the windows, the metropolis baked in dark silence. Except for the radio, the crooks' apartment was quiet. Kerry's nerves, however, were not. His impatience was even hotter than the night. He was burning to shout these developments into the ears of the nation.

Over the radio, the final program of dance music began. At the end of a half hour, Kerry realized urgently, the U.B.C. antenna would go dead. As one melody tinkled after another, he warily observed Sam. He noted through the keyhole that the big bruiser was sitting laxly in the chair, torpidly dozing. Now only ten minutes of broadcasting remained, and Kerry decided to chance his stratagem.

Going to the window he removed his shoes, then carefully climbed out on the sill. Balancing himself precariously, he ventured upon the narrow ledge. He supported himself on his toes, spread-eagled his arms and perspired. Sweat drenched him as he sidled along an inch at a time. The distance from his window to that of the next room seemed to him to be at least six miles. In reality it was six feet. Once he reached his objective, Kerry crouching down, panting.

Sam was still sitting tilted back in the chair, as Kerry had last seen him. From some point beyond, the radio was still playing. Easing in, over the sill, Kerry sought a telephone. There was none in the living-room. Venturing past the slumbering Sam, Kerry peeked into the dark foyer.

There was a desk there and on it a phone. Kerry promptly reached for it. He was elatedly lifting the instrument when he heard a slight noise. The sound had come from the door at Kerry's side.

The knob was turning. Slowly it revolved clockwise, then twisted back, but the door did not open. Reluctantly Kerry put the telephone down. He closed his hand on the knob, felt an automatic bolt withdraw as he turned it, then opened a crack and peered through.

Suddenly he snatched the door open wider and reached out. His hand clamped on a thin shoulder. Dragging a small figure inward, he quickly and quietly shut the door. At once he clapped his hand over the open mouth of his startled captive. Smitty's eyes popped at him.

"Don't make a sound!" Kerry whispered.

But as soon as he removed his hand, Smitty gasped: "Gosh, chief, I thought maybe some crooks had grabbed you! I couldn't figure out—"

Instantly Kerry stifled Smitty's rush of words. "Pipe down!" he breathed. When Smitty nodded compliance, he added: "Stay right here and watch sharp. For God's sake, if I don't get this on the air inside one minute, the station will sign off!"

THE BEWILDERED Smitty watched him as he circled the foyer. Opening another door, he found a closet. Delightedly, he caught up the telephone and backed in. He signaled urgently to Smitty, closed the door, snapped on a light and rapidly spun the dial. As soon as his special number answered, he rushed out his signal.

"Put me on, put me on quick!"

The closet door shut away the sound of the radio in the apartment, but Kerry knew that the dance program was being faded. His cue came— "Take it away!" During the necessary wait of five seconds Kerry almost jumped up and down with wild impatience, then his twang began machine-gunning into the transmitter.

"Attention, Mr. and Mrs. United States! This is your scoop

specialist, Keyhole Kerry. Listen fast, for this flash may be forcibly interrupted at any second. If you hear any sounds of violence, it will mean that desperate measures are being taken to silence me. I am actually risking my life by speaking to you because I have been kidnaped and am being held prisoner. The murderer of Hugh Sheldon, fearful that I will explode his criminal intrigue, which cost Sheldon's life, has taken this ruthless means of—"

Outside the door, Smitty's voice rang: "Chief! Chief!"

Immediately Kerry nudged the closet door open. He saw black figures hurrying into the dark foyer. The metallic glitter of guns struck his eyes. One of these was being pushed into Smitty's stomach, and Smitty was being slammed against the wall. Seizing the opportunity offered by the swift confusion, Kerry dodged out of the closet. Ducking under the arms that grabbed for him, he dropped the telephone onto the desk and threw himself into a driving line-plunge toward the living-room.

Sam was just snapping out of his doze. As his eyes flickered open, Kerry swept one hand across the lamp on the table, smashing it to the floor. The room went black as Sam sprang up. Kerry side-stepped the chauffeur and bounded to the window. He climbed out on the sill and began negotiating a return trip over the narrow ledge—this time with desperate haste.

He heard the mêlée in the foyer become rougher. Somebody shouted hoarsely for light. In a moment a gleam shone out the window by which Kerry had just left. Sidling even more rapidly, risking a fatal plunge to the sidewalk far below, Kerry achieved the next sill. With sweat trickling over his body, he dropped in. As he reached the foot of the bed, the connecting door flew open.

Murray Drew, clad in a bathrobe and slippers, charged in. He had an automatic in his hand. Behind him Sam appeared, weapon pointing at Kerry. Kerry ignored it, but gave close attention to Drew's. He wanted to see that it was a .22 with a silencer attached, but his hopes were dashed. Drew's weapon was a .45, and looked even bigger.

"I heard noises," Kerry said innocently. "Anything wrong?"

"You're going to hear another noise, like a gun going off, if that flash makes any trouble, Kerry," Drew said ominously.

Sam blurted: "It couldn't've been him, speakin' on the radio—it couldn't! He couldn't've been anywhere near that phone! I was sittin' out there, wide awake, alla time. Besides, the door was still bolted when we come in here just now. Boss, you've been dreamin'!"

DREW made a threatening gesture that silenced Sam. Though the signing-off hour of WUBC had passed, the dance music had continued. A moment ago it had faded, now an announcer's voice spoke rapidly. Holding his breath, Kerry listened.

"Ladies and gentlemen, you just heard an interrupted news broadcast by Keyhole Kerry. His absence since early tonight, when he aired certain startling information concerning the Hugh Sheldon murder, convinces us that his flash, concerning his abduction, is absolutely authentic. Realizing that his life is in danger, we have immediately called upon the police to search for him. In consideration of the vital seriousness of this development, Station WUBC will continue broadcasting tonight indefinitely, in order to provide you with the latest news concerning the kidnaping of Keyhole Kerry as rapidly as the developments break."

Kerry grinned delightedly. "Good old Milton Raney," he said. "Pinch-hitting for me and *De-Luxe-Lax* like a veteran!"

Drew stepped close, planting his automatic against Kerry's chest. "The first thing they'll do is try to trace that call," he said tersely. "If they manage to, Kerry, they'll find you, all right—but they'll find you very damned dead."

"If that's not bluff," Kerry demanded, "why don't you bump me off right now?"

"Our little deal won't be completed for another week, Kerry,"

Drew answered through thinned lips, "and at the moment I'd rather not take the risk and trouble of disposing of your body. But I'll damned well inconvenience myself to that extent if you force me to."

"Somehow," Kerry said soberly, "you convince me."

THERE was a scuffling of feet at the door. Drew growled, "Bring him in, Nate," and a burly, neckless man appeared, gripping Smitty's arms. The man was one who had done guard duty at the Nordham home. His push sent Smitty staggering to the bed where he sat down violently. His right eye was already beginning to turn black.

"Gee, chief!" he gasped, mopping his beaded face and blinking at Kerry. "I had a chance to get you out of here, and you wouldn't let me take it!"

"Sorry, Smitty," Kerry answered, still keenly aware that Murray Drew was covering him with the automatic. "I know your intentions were of the best, but under the circumstances—"

"Just after you came out of the Nordham place, chief," Smitty hurried on, "a couple of big bruisers dodged out and went after you. I saw 'em carry you out of the stationery store and put you in a car. I thought I'd better find out what they were going to do to you, so I trailed the car in a taxi. I covered this building a while, and then I saw you looking out the window, and I came up thinking I'd pull off a swell news-beat by rescuing you. Gee, chief!"

Kerry put his arm across the lad's shoulders. "The hell of it is, Smitty," he said, "I don't want to be rescued—yet."

"Huh?"

"Of course not!" Kerry explained. "I want to stay kidnaped until I become a seven days' wonder. I want this case to build up into the biggest front-page story in the country. The longer I stay missing, the better it'll be. If a bunch of G-men come wading in here right now, wanting to pull me out, I'd do my damnedest to resist them. But thanks, anyway, Smitty. You meant well."

"What Eve says is right, chief," Smitty remarked incredulously. "When it comes to getting news, you're certainly nuts!"

Murray Drew's icy eyes had sharpened. He was listening through the door. Again the dance music was fading from the radio. As Milton Raney's voice returned, Kerry felt a sharp chill—for he saw Drew's finger tightening on the trigger.

"We bring you a special news bulletin, ladies and gentlemen," Raney said dulcetly. "As the first step toward attempting to locate Keyhole Kerry, who was kidnaped tonight, and who is being held prisoner somewhere within New York City, we undertook to trace the telephone wire over which he gave you his sensational flash. We regret that we must report failure. The connection lasted for such a brief period that locating the source of Kerry's call is impossible. We confess ourselves absolutely in the dark as to his whereabouts, and as to the identity of his abductors. However, every effort is being made to find Kerry. We will continue to broadcast developments as they arise, in order to be the first to give you the latest flashes on the kidnaping, as Keyhole Kerry would have wished."

"My God!" Kerry protested. "That's good work, but Raney doesn't have to speak of me as if I were already under the sod!"

A sharp, triumphant gleam had come into Murray Drew's eyes. "Nate," he directed his henchman, "stay right in this room and watch them. Sam, go back and keep an eye on the door. This is the last time I warn you, Kerry. If you try one more wise stunt, your announcer pal's manner of speaking will be only too appropriate."

"I believe it," Kerry admitted.

Murray Drew strode from the room. Sam resumed his watchful post opposite the doorway. Nate, who looked as if murdering a radio reporter would be a matter of the utmost indifference to him, planted himself in a chair and rested his automatic on his paunch. His porcine eyes glittered threateningly at Kerry.

"There's nothing to be uneasy about, pal," Kerry assured him, settling comfortably on the bed. "We like it here—so far!"

CHAPTER FIVE

NO NEWS IS BAD NEWS

DURING THE rest of that night, and during the days and nights that followed, the radio in the hide-away played continually. Though the crooks maintained their grim watchfulness relentlessly, so that neither Kerry nor Smitty was able to make a single unobserved move, they elatedly listened to the bulletins that were broadcast at frequent intervals.

"A significant angle of the Kerry kidnaping," the instrument announced, "is the fact that no ransom demand has been made. This circumstance strengthens the theory that Kerry was seized in order to silence him, because he had discovered that some daring criminal project was under way, and because the crooks need time to complete it.

"Various clues have proved to be dead-end leads—for instance, the investigation of the disturbance in a small stationery store on upper Madison Avenue. Every effort is being exerted by the New York police, and by agents of the Federal Bureau of Investigation, to locate Kerry and his assistant, known as Smitty. So far, however, they have produced no results."

"Thank God for that!" Kerry told Smitty fervently. "For once, I'm glad Commissioner Endicott hates my insides. He's probably not trying very hard. Very likely, he's hoping I'll never turn up again."

"But look, chief," Smitty complained. "How long do you want to stay locked in here, anyway, with a battery of cannons pointing at you?"

"Obviously, my wishes in the matter aren't the only important factor, Smitty," Kerry answered, "but until now I have no real cause for complaint."

The radio continued: "The criminal intrigue which brought about Kerry's abduction is also connected with the murder of Hugh Sheldon. The police investigation of the killing has brought nothing of importance to light."

A later announcement rang ironically in Kerry's ears.

"Alicia Ballard, whose disappearance Keyhole Kerry was the first to disclose, is still unaccounted for. In an attempt to gain information concerning her, Police Commissioner Endicott today arranged an interview with Jan Nordham, the great organist, through Murray Drew, Nordham's manager. After talking with Nordham, and Nordham's daughter Melody, the commissioner confessed he had learned nothing that might prove of value in the search for the missing girl."

Hearing that, Kerry was filled with a fine frenzy to get into the immediate proximity of the microphone.

"Oh God!" he burst out at the startled Smitty. "That's priceless! If I could only hit the air right now with the truth! Time and again, Endicott has done his damnedest to muzzle me, and this would show him up for the dunderhead he is. Think of it, Smitty. He arranged that interview through a crook who's up to his neck in the Sheldon murder. He talked with Nordham by permission of Nordham's kidnaper. He went to that house trying to find the very girl he spoke with and he came away without suspecting it. God, if I could only get my hands on a mike, if I could only get to a phone!"

IT KINDLED the smoldering spark of his news zest. Content until now to let the story of his kidnaping build up into a national sensation, he suddenly found himself afire with the desire to supply the climax by breaking it himself. The restraint under which he suffered served only to fan the flame. Yet, with the eyes and the guns of his captors turned constantly upon him, he found his burning urge balked.

He took to prowling his cell, his every movement electrically nervous. He snatched glimpses out the window at every opportunity. He studied his guards, carefully noting their weaknesses, their lapses of attention. On Nate he kept an especially sharp eye, not only because Nate looked the most merciless, but because now and then he swigged from a pint flask of rye that he packed on his hip. Kerry caught sounds from the other rooms, denoting comings and goings. All the while he paced about with the ceaseless tension of a caged maniac.

After their dinner tray had been brought, he found a chance for a covert whisper to Smitty.

"Somebody besides us is being kept locked up in this apartment. I've seen 'em taking another tray to and from a room down the hall that runs off the foyer. I'll be my last cent it's Melody Nordham."

Smitty was more concerned over Kerry's own plight. "I was just thinking, chief," he answered quickly. "If they keep you here much longer, you'll miss your regular program, and it'll be the first time."

Kerry nodded grimly, then he alertly lifted his head. "It'll be just one week from the night they snatched me. On the same night, Jan Nordham gives the last concert in his series. That must be what Drew meant when he said their job wouldn't be finished until then. Smitty, they're planning to wind up the deal and scram!

"If I break my record by missing my program," he concluded, "it'll be because Drew kept his word and drilled me full of little round holes."

"But we can't get out of here, chief!" Smitty said anxiously. "We don't stand a chance."

"It's up to me—"

At that moment Nate loomed through the doorway with his gun in one hand and his pint flask in the other. "Here, youse!" he bawled. "Break it up!" And as silence fell, he sent a stiff shot of rye sluicing down his thick throat.

On the radio, the most persistent topic, except for the abduction of Keyhole Kerry, was the weather. Announcers in air-cooled studios informed the sweltering metropolis that the heat wave was continuing. The humid air was as cloying as mucilage. Kerry's guards, torpid as lizards, but still watchful, kept the windows open, but no breeze alleviated the oppressive sultriness.

The windows, however, occupied Kerry's shrewd thoughts. In spite of Drew's threats, he mulled over another stratagem, spurred by the realization that the deadline for his regular program, as well as for the criminal's intrigue, was nearing inexorably.

Tonight the heat was downright stupefying. Of those inside the hide-away, Kerry alone was alert. Without appearing to do so, he watched every move of his captors. Nate, stripped of his shirt, made frequent trips to the refrigerator for ice cubes. He drenched the cubes in rye and drank liberally. His intention was obviously to cool his fat hulk, but the effect of the alcohol was to make him even hotter. With secret elation, Kerry watched this cycle operate. At last, long after WUBC had ceased broadcasting, when Nate was the only member of the gang in evidence, the inevitable came.

More numbed with liquor than asleep, Nate sat slumped in the chair in Kerry's room, his hand curled around the butt of his automatic, both resting on his belly.

"Watch him, Smitty!" Kerry cautioned.

TAKING off his shoes, he went silently to the connecting door. It was bolted on the other side. Kerry drew a deep breath and resorted to the ledge outside the windows. Again poising himself on his toes, flattening himself against the sheer wall, he sidled across to the sill of the next room.

The living-room was deserted but, Kerry knew, other members of the cabal were in the bedrooms. Careful to make no noise, he crawled in. Immediately, he ventured into the foyer. Even before he turned to the telephone, he tried the outer entrance.

Though he had opened it easily during his previous excursion, it would not open at all this time. Kerry soon found the reason. The lock had been changed. It was of the type that required a key from the inside as well as the outside. That key, of course, was in Murray Drew's possession. Realizing that, Kerry felt ruthlessly trapped.

But, still gambling on his subterfuge, he took up the telephone, swung into the closet and closed the door.

At his first attempt to spin the dial, he muttered maledictions. It would not turn. A patented lock had been affixed to it. This too had been provided by Drew, of course, for the definite purpose of frustrating Kerry, should he somehow manage to reach the instrument again. The delay it caused him, however, was not appreciable. He tapped the contact bar ten times in quick succession, which produced exactly the same effect as spinning the zero.

When the operator answered, he did not ask for his special number. It would have availed him nothing. WUBC had ceased broadcasting for the night. Even the Midwest and Pacific Coast stations in the network, Kerry knew, had signed off by now. He called, instead, the number of Eve Vane's apartment.

While the distant bell rang, he listened through the door, realizing that discovery would turn blazing guns upon him.

"Eve!" he whispered, as soon as his secretary's sleepy voice answered. "I want you—"

"Guy! Guy, darling! Where are you? Are you all right? I've been going crazy with worry—I've been out of my mind. Oh, I'm so glad to hear from you—"

"Then, good Lord, listen!" Kerry said imperatively. "I've got to talk fast. Be sure you get everything straight. Above all, understand that you must not notify the police. Don't tell the cops where I am. Don't tell the G-men. Don't call out the National Guard. Don't tell anybody—not anybody at all. Have you got that straight?"

"Yes, Guy," Eve said quickly. "But why—why?"

"Because, I've got to keep my own snatch exclusive," Kerry hurried on. "If the cops came barging in here, I'd get pumped full of lead pronto. Even if I managed to side-step the bullets, I'd lose my hold on the story. Endicott, damn him, would drag me straight down to headquarters, to question me, without giving me a chance at a mike. He'd hold me there until all the papers had the whole story ahead of me. I'd get scooped on my own kidnaping—me, the scoop specialist. I'd rather die than have that happen."

"Guy, you crazy fool—"

"Listen!" Kerry insisted. "Locate the Metropolitan Warehouse. I'm in an apartment directly opposite the top floor of it. Get hold of a couple of technicians and go there. Take along a parabolic mike—understand? String up a wire and have it ready at all times. Aim the mike directly into this apartment. You'll have to open one of the warehouse windows, but for Lord's sake, keep out of sight—don't show yourself to anybody in this place. Got all that straight?"

"Yes, Guy, but—"

"We'll have to communicate by means of signals. When you see me put my hand to my ear, listen in, but don't broadcast it. When the time's ripe, I'll put my hand to my mouth—then put the mike on the air and let 'em have the works. In the meantime, I'll try to ask you questions, to make sure everything is O.K. Answer by putting something small on the windowsill—one object for yes, two objects for no. All clear?"

"Yes, but—"

"One other thing. Bring a pair of strong binoculars. Study the faces of the men you see in this apartment, particularly a mug named Drew. Send somebody down to headquarters to look through the rogue's gallery. The idea is to learn who Drew really is, as well as the others. If you can put any flashes about that on the air, without tipping my hand, have Raney do it. If I'm lucky, this will add up to the most spectacular broadcast I've ever pulled off. Even if I'm *not* lucky, the radio audience will be able to hear the reports when Drew begins sharpshooting at my heart."

"Guy!" Eve wailed. "If you'll only let me—"

"No!" Kerry blurted. "Whatever you do, don't get any help

until the very last minute. I've got to keep hold of this story, Eve. Why, I don't even know all of what this set-up means yet. I absolutely must learn the rest of it, if possible. But I do know the crooks are planning to skip tomorrow night, and I'm going to do my damnedest to collar 'em before they can get away. It may be the last of Keyhole Kerry, Eve—but it'll be worth it. It's the only chance I've got, anyway. Can't talk any longer. Get going!"

Kerry broke the connection.

CAUTIOUSLY, he opened the closet door. The apartment was still quiet. Dripping with perspiration, Kerry replaced the telephone and glanced around. Eager as he was for more news, the moment's opportunity for a further investigation seemed too good to pass up, in spite of the hazards of discovery. Silently, he began toeing down the gloomy hallway.

He dodged past the open door of a room in which Sam was dozing. When he paused, he was at a door that was bolted. The bolt had been recently installed. Kerry released it, looked through a narrow crack into a dark room—then, quickly, he stepped in and shut the door behind him.

A frightened sound came out of the darkness. Kerry heard a quick, fearful movement. The light of a bedside lamp gleamed at him. In its shine, a girl was huddling on the bed. She was wearing only stockings and a slip. Her face was soft, beautifully modeled, her eyes shining with dreadful uncertainty. At once Kerry strode to her and clicked off the light. In the hot darkness, drenched with the perspiration of anxiety, he stood motionless.

Then, quickly, he sat on the bed beside the girl. "We can't waste words," he cautioned her. "If any of these rats happen to see that that bolt is loose, it'll mean curtains for both of us. You're Melody Nordham, aren't you?"

"Yes," the girl whispered.

"How long have they kept you locked up here?"

"Weeks."

"Since before the series of concerts by your father started?"

"Yes."

"Tell me quickly—"

"They—they brought me here by force. Father has been so horribly worried about me—that's why he didn't notify the police. I know his only thought is to get me back home safely. But he didn't have enough money to pay a ransom. He had to arrange the new series of recitals in order to get enough to pay them. Tomorrow night is the last program. Oh, I hope when it's over, they won't harm him—"

Kerry's hand closed warningly on the girl's arm. Her rush of words stopped. Listening, Kerry heard new sounds—indefinite but portentous.

"Chin up!" he whispered, then jerked to his feet. Hurrying to the door, he looked out. He sidled into the hall, closed the bolt, then hastened along on tiptoe.

From some uncertain point, the vague movements and voices continued. Feverishly anxious, Kerry didn't devote so much as a second to identifying them. He dodged across the living-room and back to the window. As he climbed out on the sill he heard, from somewhere, the sound of a latch clicking. With reckless haste, hugging the side of the building, he inched himself along the ledge.

Ducking into his room, he found Nate still in an alcoholic daze and Smitty staring round-eyed. Nate stirred slightly as he crossed to the bed. The noises in the apartment were louder now. They were nearing the door of Kerry's cell and caused Nate to awaken. The next moment the latch clicked, the door opened, and three men entered the room.

Murray Drew and Sam were gripping the arms of a third man, whom they were forcing along between them. Their guns were prodding into their captive's sides. Kerry immediately recognized the dark, deep-set eyes, the bushy brows and the trim mustache of the prisoner. This was the man who had introduced himself to Kerry as the brother of the missing Alicia Ballard.

DREW and Sam thrust him toward the bed. He spun on them, his eyes flashing, but their guns held him in check.

"You're going to stay here a while, Ballard," Drew said. "Kerry will tell you the sort of behavior I expect from you. He'll also tell you what to expect if you don't conduct yourself prudently. The important point is that we have nothing to lose by pumping a few lead pills into you. I trust you'll be quite comfortable. Good-night."

Drew signaled his henchmen. Nate plodded from the room and Sam, who now looked to be in no need of sleep at all, took the chair in the corner. As Drew followed Nate out, Sam made himself comfortable for a period of sentry duty, his massive automatic ready in his hand. The bolt clicked into its socket as the newcomer gazed anxiously at Kerry.

"I was damned sure there was something crooked behind all this!" he exclaimed. "I've been trying to find Alicia. I managed to locate the Nordham place, but I couldn't get in. I watched it, and saw some men leaving. I followed them over here. Somehow they found out I was trailing them. They stuck those guns in my ribs and brought me up. God, they look like they're capable of killing without a moment's hesitation. Kerry, what the devil does all this mean?"

"Better make the best of it, Ballard," Kerry said quietly. "After all, it's not so bad here. In fact, it's getting to be quite clubby!"

CHAPTER SIX

RADIO PAY-OFF

AT INTERVALS, under Sam's alert gaze, Kerry moved about the room as if to limber his legs. During the small hours, his conversation with his companion captives had been of the most innocent variety, and his ambulations appeared to be as harmless. In reality, he was watching the windows on the top floor of the warehouse across the street.

It was not until dawn that he caught any inkling that his secret instructions to Eve were being carried out.

Quietly, one of the warehouse windows opened. Through it Kerry could see nothing, for the interior of the building was gloomy. He hoped, however, that the parabolic mike was being set up and that its invisible beam was being directed into the windows of this apartment.

In his hair-raising career as radio's ace flash-news reporter, Kerry had made use of various extraordinary devices developed by resourceful broadcasting engineers, but the parabolic microphone he had called for was by no means unusual. It was simply a sensitive pick-up affixed at the focal point of a sound reflector as big as an umbrella. It could be aimed like a searchlight and could collect, from a distance, sound impulses that would otherwise escape an ordinary microphone. It was in general use at football broadcasts, and had been utilized in broadcasting operas from the Metropolitan. It would be almost as good as a mike planted within the walls of this hide-away.

Concealing his jubilation, Kerry fixed Sam with a critical eye.

"Sam," he said in a normal tone of voice as he faced the window, "I've somehow gotten the idea that you're a bit hard of hearing."

"Can hear as good as you do," Sam answered in an offended manner, hefting his gun.

"Can you hear me without any trouble right now?" Kerry inquired.

"Sure I can," Sam said. "Only, you never mind about me hearin'. Just behave yourself."

Kerry appeared to comply, but when he glanced across at the warehouse, he saw one small object resting on the windowsill.

Eve was answering his question as to whether or not the parabolic mike was functioning with a mute *Yes.*

In another room, the radio was again playing, but Kerry's voice had not issued from it because the parabolic mike was not yet hooked into the network. Secretly elated, he waited for another opportunity. It came when Ballard was moving about near the windows, with Sam eyeing him menacingly.

"These mugs who've captured us—I wonder who they really are," he said. "I've been trying to identify them. Maybe you have too."

Ballard merely shrugged, but on the windowsill across the street, one small object again appeared. It meant that Eve, using a pair of binoculars, was watching the men in this apartment and endeavoring to discover who they were.

"Never mind wonderin'," Sam suggested, with a flick of his automatic. "Just you guys be quiet."

At another auspicious moment, Kerry faced the windows and remarked to Sam: "My regular program is due on the air tonight. I wonder what they're doing about it at the studio. I hope they're making the usual preparations. After all, I've never missed a program, and that record means a lot to me. I might make it this time even yet. Anything can happen, you know."

"Only it won't," Sam said. "Sit down and quit talkin', smart guy."

But again a single object appeared on the sill across the street—*O.K.*

AS THE day wore on, the radio remained tuned to WUBC, and frequent noises beyond the bolted door signified the coming and going of various members of the criminal combine. A growing tension in the air warned Kerry that the daring enterprise of the crooks were nearing a crisis. Smitty also sensed it. He gazed silently at Kerry, his plentiful freckles vivid against the apprehensive paleness of his face. Leonard Ballard moved about with increasing agitation.

"Great Scott, Kerry!" he blurted suddenly. "Do we have to stay caged up here like animals waiting to be slaughtered? Isn't there any way of getting help?"

"I'm afraid it's very doubtful, Ballard," Kerry answered, but, facing the window, he added: "If anyone happened to send help at a propitious moment, though, I wouldn't want it to be the cops who came. It would be much better if a bunch of strong-arm men from the studio barged in and—"

"Cut dat out!" Sam warned. "If you guys talk too much, you'll be goin' outa here feet first."

Once more, glancing across the street, Kerry saw the heartening signal. A single object on the sill, meaning again—*O.K.*

Ballard glared at Sam, then, defying the edict, he turned on Kerry. "This is driving me crazy. I don't know what it means. Where's Alicia? What's going on? Great Scott, Kerry, don't hold out on me."

Contemplating Sam's gun soberly, Kerry tugged at his ear. The signal assured him that Eve would listen with special attention to what he was about to say. He answered Ballard carefully.

"Our friend Sam may object, Ballard, but on the other hand he may be also interested in learning how much I know. He's itching to find a better excuse for using that cannon of his, but here goes. This little affair involves a considerable sum of extorted money, one murder and no less than six kidnapings."

"What!" Ballard blurted.

Kerry nodded soberly. "Melody Nordham was the victim of the first snatch. She was picked because her father's prominence promised a big ransom. The crooks who grabbed her were acting under the instructions of a mug who calls himself Murray Drew. Still, I have a feeling that Drew isn't the real brains behind this job. It was planned with a higher degree of criminal intelligence and ruthlessness than he possesses. I believe the man who engineered it is too smart to show himself under incriminating circumstances. I'd certainly like to learn who he is, because I believe he's the real murderer of Hugh Sheldon."

"Brother," Sam remarked, with evil satisfaction, "it certainly is interestin' to watch a guy diggin' his own grave with his tongue."

Kerry still eyeing Sam's formidable weapon, risked continuing. "Anyway, Melody Nordham was snatched. She was brought here. She's still a prisoner in this apartment. Her father was fearful that the kidnapers might kill her, as so often has happened when they've become afraid of being cornered with their victim. For that reason, he didn't notify the police. Yet, when the ransom demand was made, his funds were too low to meet it. Then the crooked genius behind this plan really went to work. He put into operation the most daring scheme I've ever encountered."

Sam toyed with his gun. "When you get yourself dug down six feet deep," he informed Kerry, "I'll let you know, buddy."

KERRY grimly went on. "The crooks moved in on Jan Nordham," he said. "After forcing Nordham to fire the servants, they took complete possession of his home, keeping him a prisoner. They took full advantage of the seclusion under which he lived. Their intention was to arrange some way for Nordham to collect a large sum of money, so they could seize it as ransom. Murray Drew actually began functioning as Nordham's business manager. He handled the contract for Nordham's series of radio recitals. Nordham won't collect a cent of the huge fee that U.B.C. is paying. The crooks will take away every cent he has—leave him destitute."

"But—Alicia?" Ballard asked quickly.

"Without her, Nordham couldn't have played a single program," Kerry answered. "The reason for that I must keep confidential. The important point is that the crooks needed her in order to collect from Nordham, so they pulled another snatch. Nordham must have begged her to cooperate. Having the greatest esteem and sympathy for him, she didn't resist the kidnapers' demands. But all these weeks, since she was made a prisoner in the Nordham home with Jan Nordham, she's been trying to help him escape. Her chance came when I invaded the Nordham house during Nordham's last recital."

Sam uttered a malevolent chuckle. "This is rich. This is the first time I ever seen a guy actually talkin' himself to death."

Kerry determinedly added another spike to his coffin. "When I saw your sister, Ballard," he continued, "she found a way of passing me a note. It told the whole story. It might have wrecked the game, if this had been a dumber bunch of crooks. But somebody with sharp eyes was watching. When I left the house, he sent some of his gorillas after me. They caught me reading the note, and about to put the flash on the air—and I became snatch victim Number Four. Smitty's the fifth, and you're the sixth. All told, we constitute a crime wave."

Ballard was peering hard at Kerry. "But if this man, this mastermind, killed Sheldon to protect himself, what's to prevent his killing every one of us?"

"Nothing," Kerry answered. "Sheldon smelled a whole nest of mice. He was on his way to headquarters when he was stopped. That situation called for swift and direct action on the part of the master crook. Our predicament is a bit different. Obviously, Jan Nordham and Alicia Ballard must live out the series of concerts, in order for the crooks to collect as much as possible. We four snatch victims in this apartment are likewise on the waiting list. It wouldn't do to clutter the place up with corpses prematurely. The neighbors might have keen noses. To avoid that danger, too many bodies would have to be disposed of, and it would be too risky. But the deadline is nearing, my friend. Within a very short time now, Jan Nordham will give the last in his series of recitals. Perhaps we'd better try to remember a few prayers. I hope Nordham concludes his last program with a requiem—it would be most fitting."

Kerry's long, dogged speech left Ballard silent. Smitty's eyes were round as chestnuts. Sam complacently fondled his automatic and looked upon Kerry with grimly pleased expectancy.

Kerry, fervently hoping that Eve had clearly heard his story, grew quiet—waiting.

Every tick of his strap-watch was bringing closer the deadline of his scheduled program. The watch was accurate and perfectly synchronized with the electric clocks in the U.B.C. studios by which the programs were timed. As the minutes spun away, Kerry's nervous tension sharpened. Activity audible beyond the bolted door told him that a period of vital importance was at hand.

"I have one satisfaction," Kerry observed wryly. "I'll have a fine funeral. Every city editor and newspaper reporter in town will attend, carrying torches and singing glad songs."

"That is," Sam remarked, "if there's enough of you left to make a funeral."

KERRY'S anxiety became sheer agony when he heard footfalls approach the door. As it opened, he glanced again at his watch. The *De-Luxe-Lax* Keyhole News program was due to hit the air within a few minutes. The radio in the apartment was reproducing the finish of the program which immediately preceded Kerry's. He heard it clearly through the open door as Murray Drew entered, followed by the phlegmatic Nate.

Drew was holding a metal can in his right hand. Kerry could clearly read its label—*Ether.*

As Drew paused, eyeing him with malicious triumph, Kerry raised his hand to his ear—the signal for Eve to be on her toes.

Drew asked slyly: "Feeling sleepy, Kerry?"

"I never felt wider awake in my life," Kerry snapped.

"We'll change that," Drew said. "You'll soon be sleeping soundly. You'll have this apartment all to yourself for a quiet snooze. As soon as we're sure you're resting comfortably, we're moving out. You see, we've just collected the final check for the Nordham series, and very soon we'll be off to tackle a new project—in a distant place."

Kerry tightened. "You mean to tell me you're going to use

that stuff on Melody Nordham, too? You don't know the proper amount to give. You might give her too much. She might never wake up."

"That's possible," Drew said gravely. "But I'm afraid your concern is a bit belated. Miss Nordham is already completely under the influence."

"Try to slap some of that stuff into my face, and you'll have one hell of a fight on your hands, Drew!" Kerry challenged.

"I'll say you will!" Smitty echoed belligerently.

Nate's guns, and Sam's, lifted in unison.

"I'm afraid we won't stand for any resistance, Kerry," Murray Drew said. "When we leave this apartment, you'll be in an inert condition, which may be due either to a dose of ether or a dose of lead. We won't insist upon killing you, unless you do. We don't happen to be worried about making a quick escape, you see. By the time anybody wakes up—if anybody wakes up at all—we'll be well away from here."

"What do you mean by 'anybody?'"

"The more you know, the less likely you are to wake up, Kerry, but I don't mind answering that question," Drew said. "Once you're peacefully sleeping, we're going from here to Nordham's studio. As soon as the program is off the air, both Nordham and Miss Ballard will also decide to take a nap. You see, no one will be able to sound an alarm until many hours later—if ever."

Drew twisted the cap off the can, took a towel from Nate, and began pouring ether generously from the one into the other.

"My God!" Kerry gasped. "That's enough already to kill a herd of elephants!"

And at that moment, while the pungent liquid saturated the towel, Sam plucked at Drew's sleeves and said quickly: "Listen!"

Kerry had already heard the radio lapse into silence. An announcer had made the usual station identification. Now, precisely at the moment when Kerry's own program was due to begin, Milton Raney's voice began extolling the merits of *De-Luxe-Lax.*

"I'm afraid, Kerry," Drew said, "the program won't be as interesting as usual tonight."

"I'm afraid, Drew," Kerry said grimly, "it's going to be a hell of a lot more interesting than usual. In fact, it's going to be the most sensational program—"

"Listen!" Sam hissed again, and Drew, the towel in his hands, his eyes fixed icily upon Kerry, stood motionless, listening.

THE radio was saying: "This is your announcer, Milton Raney, speaking, ladies and gentlemen. Since Keyhole Kerry is still among the missing, we cannot bring you his voice tonight in the usual manner. For the first time, shattering his perfect record, Kerry is absent from this studio. However, pinch-hitting for him, I am able to bring you certain startling revelations that will be of great aid to the legal agencies which are searching for your scoop specialist.

"One of the chief perpetrators of the Kerry kidnaping is a crook who is wanted both in the United States and Europe for having connived at a number of daring crimes. His real name is Mal Daly. His description, which is in all official files under that name, stresses the details of trim garb, a poised manner, and high cheekbones with the skin drawn tightly over them. In his present project he is working under the alias of Murray Drew."

Sam and Nate mouthed epithets. Mal Daly, or Murray Drew, stood ominously motionless, his eyes glinting with a murderous light. Smitty and Ballard, Kerry's companions, were staring at him. In spite of the danger of the guns, Kerry's face expressed wild elation.

"Murray Drew, Mr. and Mrs. United States," Raney hurried on, "is not, however, the real brains behind this daring crime. Official records show that Daly is the chief executive of a master crook who plans all the projects of the gang. This instance is no exception. The greatest degree of guilt for the kidnaping of Keyhole Kerry must be fastened upon a daring criminal known as Frank 'Doc' Coyle. Coyle has dark, sharp, deep-set eyes, football shoulders and a trim mustache."

Behind Kerry a rasping voice exploded. "Damn you! That tip came from you, Kerry! By God—"

QUICKLY, before he turned, Kerry raised his hand to his mouth. It was the signal he had been itching to give—the order to Eve to cut the parabolic mike into the coast-to-coast hook-up. The radio was silent as he brought himself around to face the man he had met as Alicia Ballard's brother—and to face the windows.

"So you're the big shot," Kerry said quietly. "All along, you've kept yourself in the background. When you came to the studio, you weren't worried about Alicia Ballard at all. Your real purpose was to find out how much I knew about her. For the same reason, you had yourself brought in here, pretending to be another prisoner, so you could pump me. I understand now—understand that what I've told you is enough reason for bumping me off pronto."

Coyle, or Ballard, snapped wrathfully: "Give it to him, Mal! Get that towel around his face!"

But Mal Daly did not respond. A strange expression had come over his face. He, as well as Nate and Sam, were listening through the door, to the radio. At the moment, it was silent, but its very silence seemed to fill Mal Daly with mounting consternation.

"Did you hear that?" Sam blurted. "It was Kerry's voice comin' out of that radio! Then it was Coyle's. Now—Geez!—now I can hear myself talkin'!"

Supremely, desperately happy, Kerry heard Sam's voice fade from the loudspeaker as soon as Sam ceased speaking—but the echoes of it lingered within the walls. The parabolic pick-up was functioning perfectly. The reproduction was so amazingly clear that Kerry could not resist the crazy impulse to project again his own voice into the ether.

"That's exactly right, my friends—and Mr. and Mrs. United States! This is Keyhole Kerry, your scoop specialist, actually broadcasting his regular program of sensational inside stuff—which he has never yet missed—directly from the room in which he is imprisoned, and in the presence of Frank Coyle and Mal Daly, his kidnapers!"

His twang resounded through the apartment, striking the crooks with paralyzing consternation.

"Don't attempt to look for the mike, you mugs!" Kerry warned swiftly, taking advantage of the second of suspension. "You can't reach it. No matter what you do about it, the entire nation will hear every word uttered in this room. You're powerless to stop this broadcast!"

A gasp broke from the throat of Frank Coyle, alias Leonard Ballard—a sound which, Kerry fervently hoped, was also issuing from millions of startled listeners' mouths.

Frank Coyle's fury suddenly broke his appalled amazement. "By God!" he snarled. "I'll stop it!" And even as his threat vibrated through the rooms, he jerked a gun from his pocket. "Nobody'll be able to hear *this!*"

In cold delight, Kerry peered at the weapon as it leveled at him.

"A twenty-two automatic pistol with a silencer attached!" he exclaimed. "I've been looking for that gun! You used it to kill Hugh Sheldon!"

Kerry's words, faithfully reproduced by the radio, turned Coyle's face white.

Sam and Nate, stunned as they were, were merely holding their automatics, but Mal Daly, alias Drew, swiftly snatched out his own weapon.

"Now you're getting it, Kerry!" he blurted. "I told you we've got nothing to lose!"

Kerry's twang followed swiftly into the echoes of Daly's reproduced voice.

"You stand to lose plenty, you idiots! You're smart enough to know that you still might beat the rap for the Sheldon murder. But you'll never get away with killing me—not with twenty million people listening in, as witnesses!"

"I'll take that chance!"

Daly's gun blasted. Kerry, seeing Daly's trigger finger squeezing, released the tension of his muscles at the same instant. He felt the tug of the bullet, ripping through his flying coat, as he leaped toward Coyle. Even at that desperate moment, Kerry prayed that the report was booming from coast to coast.

He flung himself against Coyle. Slamming the silenced gun down, he saw vapor puff from it twice. The bullets flew across the room and smashed through the window—making noise that grimly gratified Kerry. He struck out wildly. Spinning about, he saw Smitty tearing into Daly with the desperation of a cornered wildcat. While Coyle fell flat between the bed and the wall, Kerry turned to help Smitty with Daly.

Sam and Nate were crowding through the door. "Let's clear out o' here!" the radio howled back at them.

Kerry's knuckles connected with Daly's chin. Dragging Daly, he charged toward the living-room. He jounced the numbed Nate and Sam back. Smitty assisted. They slammed the door shut and pushed the bolt into its socket. Kerry made three desperate moves in swift succession: he gave Smitty a staggering push away from the door, slammed a terrific uppercut to Daly's chin, and jumped back.

Daly spilled down as thunder rocked in the closed room and bullets drilled through the panel.

Fists were pounding on the hallway door.

Kerry dived at the unconscious Daly, tore a chained ring of keys from a belt-loop of Daly's trousers, and swung them at Smitty.

"Let 'em in!"

HE SPUN to the window as Smitty dashed for the entrance. Guns were still barking in the next room and slugs were still splintering through the connecting door. Over his shoulder, Kerry saw four men rushing in from the hallway. He recognized them as members of the technical staff of U.B.C. Warning them back with a gesture, he stared across the street.

In the warehouse window, Eve was visible, staring across and making frantic gestures.

"Attention, Mr. and Mrs. United States!" Kerry rasped into the beam of the parabolic mike. "Your scoop specialist, is the first, as usual, to announce the break in this sensational case. The guilty men are now trapped.

"Attention, New York police! In a moment my assistant, Miss Eve Vane, will reveal to you the address of this apartment house, where you will find your prisoners in the custody of other members of my staff. In the meantime, Mr. and Mrs. United States, keep your radios tuned to this station. Your headline beater must be off to another location before the gendarmes arrive, but I'll be back in a very few minutes in order to give you the full story of the crime!"

Kerry made sure that Daly was pinioned down, that Coyle was still locked in the adjoining room, then raced for the entrance.

While he was speeding from the building in a taxi, he heard, from the car radio, the opening announcement of the program scheduled to follow his.

"As his first selection on his final program, ladies and gentlemen, Jan Nordham plays one of his own compositions, *Nocturne Macabre.*"

SOON after Jan Nordham's last concert number, Keyhole Kerry's abrasive voice again drilled into the ears of the nation. He opened his flash swiftly, kept firing words into the telephone at a breathless speed, and, having revealed the ramifications of the case completely, he rushed into a typical Kerry conclusion.

"I have been speaking to you and you and you from the library in the home of Jan Nordham. The police have arrived. Newspaper reporters are at the door, clamoring for admittance. Your radio oracle was, however, the first to arrive at this house. I found the place deserted, except for Jan Nordham and Alicia Ballard. The great musician was in his organ studio, broadcasting his concert, unaware that the rest of his house was deserted.

"The crooks who were on guard here had heard my previous flash, and had fled. They are known as members of the Coyle-Daly crime combine, however, and I am sure they will be apprehended soon. Likewise, the case against Coyle and Daly, as well as their chief lieutenants, is so overwhelmingly strong that their conviction is certain. I am confident that they will go to the chair for having murdered Hugh Sheldon."

Kerry looked over his phone. Jan Nordham, his fine face expressing vast relief, was smiling. Alicia Ballard's eyes were shining with profound gratitude. Yet an anxiety lingered in them, which Kerry quickly endeavored to assuage.

"I hope, ladies and gentlemen, that Jan Nordham's desire for privacy, which is so necessary to him, will be respected by the press. Considering the position of this great and sensitive man, I will henceforth refrain from disturbing his seclusion. Though some publicity in the papers will be unavoidable for him, I trust that he will be accorded the utmost consideration and—"

Glancing out the window, Kerry became galvanized.

"Flash!" he rasped. "An ambulance has just drawn up to the door of this house. Melody Nordham is being taken from it on a litter. She has been revived, ladies and gentlemen—I'm delighted to inform you that she seems unharmed. Now, having wound up his most sensational scoop, your newshawk of the kilocycles is signing off."

Kerry was signing off reluctantly, because of a loud hammering at the door. The imperative summons gave him no opportunity to receive the thanks of Jan Nordham and Alicia Ballard. Drawing the bolt, he sidled into the hall to confront a square-faced, officious man.

"You can't make a fool of me, Kerry!" Police Commissioner Endicott growled. "You're coming down to headquarters, and you're going to explain—"

"Explain that you carefully got the permission of the kidnapers before you interviewed Nordham?" Kerry shot back at him. "Explain that you came here looking for Alicia Ballard and didn't even know her when you saw her? Gladly, Commissioner! I'll be delighted to explain all that—over the air, if you don't keep your hands off me, you lug!"

"Not so loud!" Endicott blurted with a frantic gesture. Then his manner became expansive. "Well, of course, Kerry—at your convenience, whenever you get around to it."

Grinning, Kerry squeezed out of the entrance. The steps were crowded with newspaper reporters to whom Kerry was poison. Grinning at them, he found great pleasure in the fact that Endicott was steadfastly refusing them admittance. As he shouldered away, wilting at last in the heat, he saw Smitty and Eve scrambling out of a taxi.

"Guy!" Eve cried. She ran to him, flung her arms around him, sobbed several times—then enthusiastically kissed him. She paid no attention to his embarrassment. "Later tonight," she told him breathlessly, "I'm going to a sanitarium where I can quietly have a nervous breakdown, but right now you're coming with me, Guy Kerry. I've made an appointment for you with a blacksmith."

Kerry stared at her.

"A what!"

"In anticipation of the next time you grab onto a red-hot lead for dear old *De-Luxe-Lax*," Eve said grimly, "I'm going to have you measured for a suit of mail!"